Mark

The Lies

How far would you go to get what you want?

Wooded Hill Books Limited

www.woodedhillbooks.com

This is a work of fiction. Names, characters, businesses, places, events, locales, and incidents are either the products of the author's imagination or used in a fictitious manner. Any resemblance to actual persons' living or dead, or actual events is entirely coincidental.

There is more real pleasure to be gotten out of a malicious act, where your heart is in it, than out of thirty acts of a nobler sort.

- *Mark Twain in Eruption*

Dedication

I dedicate this book to our son, Daniel, for his belief that I could write my first book, for his enduring support, for his passion and his inspiration. One proud father. Thank you.

Prologue

We all have dreams. To succeed at work and get that promotion; to train hard in sport and hold up that winning trophy; to start a new business and reap wealth and reward well earned; to find love and hold on to that happiness.

We don't all make it, but we try. And at times, it isn't easy to let it go.

1

Samantha – Manchester

It has been a while since we had both been out separately with our respective friends on the same night, and we are both looking forward to it; we're ready for it.

As with all marriages, we need time away from each other, to be silly with friends, to forget the everyday bind of bills, home chores and hardworking careers.

David is going out with old mates from his rugby playing days, I'm meeting friends from my university days, and we both expect to have a great time catching up, swapping tales and reliving our younger lives of nearly a decade ago. It doesn't seem that long ago, but then it does; weird how time plays tricks with age and memories.

David has already left, looking to catch the second half of the match at the first pub, the men setting themselves up for the rest of the night, crawling from pub to pub. Chrissy is calling for me first, and we're sharing a taxi into Manchester, picking up Jess on the way in. This is going to be a great night, drinks planned on the rooftop at Valkyrie, dinner at Casa Bella and then cocktails and dancing in Montezuma's. I can already feel the hangover lurking in the shadows, but it'll be well worth it.

'Ding' from my phone, an incoming message from Chrissy. She's on her way and will be with me in 15 minutes; I'd better get a move on. I love the opportunity to dress up and spoil myself a bit, although there seems there has to be a reason first these days.

The taxi ride into town was great, a chance to catch up with Chrissy and then Jess, although Jess's talk was more centred around her kids and how well they're doing, to be expected and entirely forgivable. Chrissy is still single and a lover of parties, and I suspect she is looking for a different night than Jess.

As we walk into Valkyrie, the maître d' is almost knocked over when Jan and Mel come running over; I guess he took it for granted we already had a reservation. After we had finished hugging, I apologised and asked if he would kindly arrange for a bottle of house bubbly to be sent over to us, glasses for five. His smile and gentle nod said it all.

We are all excited but calm down after the bubbly is served; after all, it has been a couple of years since we were together on the same night. Odd nights out with different girlfriends is good, but they do seem a little more nuanced, but when we all get together, anything can happen.

We move on to Casa Bella a little later than expected, and I confirmed we were still coming for dinner when the restaurant called me to check, asking them to hold the reservation; we were on our way.

I've always loved this restaurant; the atmosphere, food, and cheeky Italian waiters all add together to make it a fun night out. I note Jess keeps looking at her phone, naturally a mother's instinct to keep checking in with the babysitter. Elliot, Jess's husband, is with David, and she kind of knows he won't be checking his phone. Chrissy is making eyes and flirting with one of the waiters; nothing new there then, although I suspect his accent probably puts him second generation here in England and not straight from Napoli as he suggests. That doesn't bother Chrissy.

Jan and Mel have always been closer to each other than the rest of us, coming from the same area in the Midlands, although we are a good tight-knit group with regular WhatsApp messages and Zoom calls. Mel's partner left her some weeks ago, and of course, Jan is being a great friend and offering the support needed, although her suggestion of cutting across Chrissy to catch the waiter was a bit bold and probably way too soon; I think it was the wine talking. Having the two of them fight over the waiter would have been awkward, although it could have been entertaining all the same.

A few bottles of white wine and three courses later, we're all recharged and ready for Montezuma's, and although Jess is fighting off some yawns now and again, she is intent on making it to the nightclub.

Settling the bill, we all leave happy, Chrissy swapping mobile numbers with guess who. The night is warm and dry with only a few minutes walk to

Montezuma's. As we get there, the queue is starting to stretch to the end of the building, but this is where Chrissy comes into her own, reserving a private booth area next to the dance floor in advance and, knowing the manager, we jump the queue like royalty. What a great feeling; being connected to the right people must be nice.

We're asked if we'd like to order drinks as soon as we sit down. This is the first time I've been waited on in a nightclub, Chrissy's influence no doubt. Without the need to look at the cocktail menu, it's Porn Star Martinis for Chrissy and me, a Cosmopolitan for Jan, a Woo Woo for Mel and a Pina Colada for Jess after some gentle persuasion.

Chrissy is straight up on the dance floor, dragging me along. 'Come on.' It feels great to lose myself in the music and the beating dancefloor, feeling uninhibited and free.

Jan joins us, welcoming a break from Mel's woes. Rob was a bit of a dick; she is better off without him but doesn't know this yet. We all suspected he was cheating on her for some time, but Mel either didn't want to hear it or believe it. This is one of the reasons to get us all together, to lift Mel, give Jan and Jess a break, for me to see everyone again and of course Chrissy to carry on with the party.

Our cocktails arrive, and we join Mel and Jess in the booth, 'Cheers! Best friends forever!' and Chrissy is trying to get a group photo of us all on her mobile.

The club's manager Freddie comes over and chats with Chrissy; it's clear there is or was something closer between them at some time, probably quite casual knowing Chrissy. The music is loud, and the next track is one of my favourites. As I make a move to leave the booth and head for the dance floor again, I see Jess looking at her phone again, 'It's Elliot calling; I'll be with you in a minute.' Jess tries to take the call where she's sat, but it's clear the music is too loud, and she shuffles along and walks towards the internal doors looking for some quiet.

Reaching the dance floor, I look around, and Chrissy, Mel, and Jan are right behind me, and we start to move with the rhythm. Looking over at the internal doors, I see Jess through the glass, and she raises a hand to her mouth, her expression a noticeable shock, and she turns to look at us, at me. I get a cold feeling something is wrong. One of the kids? Elliot?

Jess kills the call and looks directly at me. I freeze. Chrissy sees it too. Oh my god, what's wrong?

Jess's face is like I've never seen it. Chrissy grabs my arm, 'Come on, something's happened,' she shouts in my ear and moves through the dancers towards Jess. Mel and Jan are unaware that something is wrong and carry on dancing, the first time Mel has seemed happy tonight.

When we get to Jess outside the doors, she is pale, her eyes wide, and she struggles to find words. I look straight at Jess, 'What's wrong? Is it one of the kids? Is Elliot OK?'

Silence, but with her eyes locked on me, it feels like this is bad news, but my bad news. Even though we are in a night club, her silence is deafening; the look on her face is horrible. Chrissy shouts at Jess, 'What is it, Jess? Tell us?' And then Jess blurts it out.

2

David – Bolton

England have scored another try, 'Yes! Bloody brilliant!' We're all bouncing; everyone in the pub is cheering. Summer Internationals are the best in my book; they have great spirit and atmosphere, and if I'd not picked up my injury, I might have been there playing; no, I would have been there playing, I'm sure of it. I am proud to know a couple of the players on the field and can call them friends, mates.

Harry has his arm around my shoulder, pulling me in as he jumps, 'Get the conversion, and it's all over!'

Elliot loves rugby; that's why the husband of my wife's friend has become a real mate and fits in with my old crew. He knows the script, *what goes on on tour, stays on tour,* although it won't be one of those nights tonight.

Bob and Kieran are talking with another bunch of fans. What a great start to the night ahead.

Final whistle! South Africa 26 England 29. What a tournament this is. The cheer and roar are tremendous, beer getting everyone wet, singing as one. Brilliant.

We need some food, but nothing is planned as usual, so off to the local chippy for carb upload; this has all the hallmarks of it becoming a messy night. I've always loved the impromptu way we get together without planning the details other than where to meet and what time.

My local, The Tempest Arms, is the next stop, full of history, characters and excellent hand-pulled ales.

It is the one pub around here that still doesn't go in for big screens and game machines; that's why I love it. Harry heads straight to the bar, chancing his arm again with the barmaid, never giving in; he won't accept she prefers women over men; he won't admit that he has no chance. Our ale is pulled, and we all head towards the corner area and start talking the game through again. That pint didn't even touch the sides, and it's my shout, 'Same again?' like I needed to ask.

I lift the first three pints, walk back to the lads, and ask this chap for a bit of space so I can pass. He looks at me with a bit of a snarl; no foul mate, chill, I tell myself. I return to the bar for the last two drinks, pay, and as I return, the Snarler has stepped back a bit further, this time completely blocking my path. I ask him again, politely, and this time he tells me to sod off, go back to the playground and stop annoying him. I look at him and think, what an idiot, so I ask him again, politely, and this time one of his mates does a long low whistle followed by, 'He must be foreign, didn't understand you Gazza.'

Harry and the lads move closer, and the Snarler steps forward so I can pass.

'Cheers, mate,' I say ironically, to which he replies, 'No fucking mate of yours, am I.'

I know I'm eyeballing him now; I could knock this guy for six without blinking, and our collective mass is three times the stock of his group, and I know we're all fit lads and can look after ourselves if needed.

Harry leans into me, 'What's his beef?'

I reply, 'Must be worried about appearing for sentencing next week,' and we both burst out laughing.

Next round, and Kieran steps up. As he heads to the bar, Snarler looks over his shoulder at me, and I see his eyes are cold; he's up to no good tonight; he's looking for a fight, what a waster.

Kieran brings the drinks over without issue, and we all get into banter again, planning for the final now and talking about booking a couple of nights in a local hotel.

I down my beer, and the call of nature beckons; I let Elliot know where I'm heading. Walking across the room towards the Gents at the rear of the pub, I say hi to a couple of old boys sitting at the back corner, local heroes with their unofficial reserved seats, been in here for years, bet they've bought this place three times over with what they've put over the bar in that time. I continue heading towards the rear door out to the beer garden, the Gents just to the left of the back door and in I go.

I exit the toilets and turn right to go back into the main room, and Snarler is standing there in front of me, blocking my path. 'Alright, mate?' I say to him. He was quick, I'll give him that, but this narrow corridor is not the place to try a haymaker punch, I lean back, and his fist hits the wall. 'Twat!' he shouts, and as I know he won't stop there, I push him whilst he's off balance. He falls back through the open door into the bar area.

He gets up, swearing at me again and takes another swing. Again, I sidestep this quickly, but this time I'm straight in with a full right jab to the jaw.

Snarler flies backwards, stumbles again and falls, banging his head on the corner of one of the solid wooden benches. I think to myself, that's going to hurt.

His mates look at me, I look at my mates, and his backing singers soon back down. Harry and Elliot come over and ask, 'You OK?'

'Yeah, no problem, although I don't know his problem,' I nod towards Snarler.

Snarler gets up, holding the back of his head.

'You want some more, or are you calling it quits?' I say to him. Snarler shouts something to his mates, and they are obviously thinking better than he is; they look away from him, shuffling more towards the front door, the exit.

'Fuck you all then, and as for you, you'll get yours sure enough,' and he pushes past me towards the Gents and the rear door to the beer garden and car park beyond.

Bob and Kieran come over to see if I'm OK.

'Yeah, I don't know what that was about, but he sure wanted a fight.'

Harry is straight in with, 'Just your average loser; you come across them now and again. Come on my round,' and Bob cuts him up with, 'No, it's mine!'

We finish up our beers and say goodnight on the way out to the barmaid and one or two of the locals. Harry calls out as we open the door, 'Watch out for those losers; it wouldn't surprise me if they are out there with baseball bats.'

'More like folding umbrellas,' Elliot replies, and we all laugh, off up the road to the next pub, the Trafalgar, laughing and backslapping as we go.

It's now past 11.30, and I've lost count of the beers we've had. Out of nowhere, Harry bellows out those immortal words, 'Kebab! Feed me now!' and, as if like lemmings, we're all heading towards the Doner Palace on the High Street.

We're in, ordering food from photoshopped images. With training programmes like ours and the games we put in, these calories are nothing, although I know the after-effects in the morning will be a different story. *Why are kebabs so tasty after a few pints out with your mates?*

Laughing at silly remarks, we pay for our food with notes, put our hands up as no change is wanted in return, and I say good night to Raz, turn and aim for the door. I'm the first out onto the street.

3

Samantha – Manchester

'Oh my god Sam, David has been arrested! That was Elliot. He's being held at the police station for questioning as well; they all are!'

'What? What for? What have they done now?'

Jess is still looking shocked but not replying. 'Jess! Tell me! What's going on?'

'Elliot has just used his phone call to call me. I need to contact his dad to get a solicitor quickly. And I need to speak with the babysitter.'

'Jess, what about David? Is he OK? Why has he been arrested? For god's sake, say something!'

'I think they have all been arrested, Elliot, David, Harry, Kieran, Bob. Somebody is dead. The police think David is involved somehow, and they were all with him when it happened.'

'What? Absolute nonsense. David? No, it's got to be some mix-up.'

'Doesn't sound like it. Elliot didn't want to say too much as the police were there with him. All he said was that there was a bit of an incident in a pub that didn't look good, a man has died, and they all need to get a solicitor. He wants me to speak with his dad; he'll know a solicitor.'

'Jess! What else? What about David?'

'I don't know. That's all Elliot said. I need to phone Elliot's dad straight away.'

'Wait! How do I get hold of David? How do I get hold of David?' I shout out, grabbing her by the top of her arms.

'Elliot said they're all at Central Police Station on Morton Road. I don't know, phone the station, I suppose. I've got to call Elliot's dad now,' and with that, Jess pulled free, ran for the exit door at the front and shot out into the street.

I look at Chrissy, 'Bloody hell, what do I do?'

Chrissy replied, 'What do we do? I'm with you. Do you know a solicitor?'

'The only solicitors I know are our company solicitors, but I think they only do corporate law. Will they know who to call?'

Chrissy replied quite calmly, 'OK, give me their number, I'll contact them. Do you have a mobile number of one of the Partners? They'll not be in the office at this time of night.'

I pull out my mobile and start scrolling, find the mobile number of one of the partners at the law firm and pass my phone to Chrissy; she walks to the side of the room, looking for somewhere quieter.

What the hell have they been doing? Is someone dead? David involved? No way, it has to be a mix-up.

Chrissy returns and hands me my phone, 'Just woke him up. Someone will call you in the next few minutes, your lawyer knows someone, and he'll get them to phone you directly for some details. He said to stay calm. If any police come to us, say nothing and wait for the solicitor.'

When my mobile rings and I don't recognise the number, I answer it, 'Hello.'

4

David – Bolton

As we leave the kebab shop, I look back to laugh at a joke Harry has just cracked when BANG! My legs go from beneath me, and I fall to the floor, kebab going everywhere. There's lots of shouting, and I can't understand what is being said. I look up and see my mates being herded backwards towards the shop front by three or four police officers in what looks like riot gear. Just as my arms are pulled behind me with force, I shout out.

'What the hell's going on?' I shout towards a policeman's ankles. I hear a dog barking loud and someone shouting orders at it. Handcuffs are being forcibly locked on, and I'm picked up, firm grips under each arm lifting me, and another has my legs.

'David Alexander. You are under arrest on suspicion of murder. You do not have to say anything. But it may harm your defence if you do not mention when questioned something you later rely on in court. Anything you do say may be given in evidence.'

'What the fuck? Get off me? What are you talking about? Murder?'

A police van screeches to a halt at the kerb, and I'm bundled into the back, and a cage door is closed behind me. As the outer door closes, I hear one of the police officers say, 'That went a lot easier than I expected.'

The journey in the police van is rough, and I'm swaying all over the place, trying to prop myself up on the van wall and caged gate. When we arrive at the police station, I hear car doors closing and drunken shouting in the distance. The van's rear door opens, and before the cage gate is unlocked, one of the policemen speaks calmly to me.

'Now, don't give us any trouble, and we'll get along just fine. You're at Central Police Station, and we're going into the custody suite now. You'll be processed by the desk sergeant; we'll take some details, and then you'll be questioned about the events of this evening.'

'What for? What's going on?'

The reply hit me like a ton of bricks, 'You were in the Tempest Arms earlier tonight?'

'Yes,' I replied.

'And you got into a fight?'

'Well, I wouldn't call it a fight, more of a tussle. The guy was just being a bit of an idiot.'

'Well, sir, it seems like you killed the guy.'

'What? He was fine when we left. In fact, he left before us.'

'Come on, let's get you inside, and we can clear it all up.' He's joined by another officer, and I'm taken inside.

After answering some basic questions at the desk, all my pockets are emptied. I'm taken to a side room, the handcuffs are removed, and I'm told to stand and undress on a large sheet of paper. My clothes are bagged and sealed inside evidence bags. An officer is writing on each bag as they're sealed. This is looking very serious.

'Can I make a phone call?' I ask of no one in particular.

'Yes sir, shortly. We need to collect any evidence first, and then we'll arrange that call.'

Then I'm taken to a holding cell and told to sit down, remain calm, and someone will be along shortly. The door closes and the lock is turned; a window in the door is opened, and I see the officer watching me as I sit down, then I hear him walk away. Someone in another cell starts singing drunkenly, and the officer tells him to tone it down.

Sitting in this bare, cool cell on a thin plastic mattress, I turn events over in my head. There has to be a mistake here. He was OK when he left. His mates left via the front door not long after. No issue, if anything, we thought they might be waiting outside for us at one point, but they weren't. It's got to be a mistake; we'll soon sort it out. This is turning into a different night out with lads. Wonder what has happened to the lads?

About 30 minutes later, I hear the door unlock, and I look up, 'Do you want to make that call now sir?'

5

Samantha - Bolton

'So, Mr Wilson, what do we do now?' I ask our solicitor, 'How long will they keep him in here?'

'Malcolm is fine,' he replies. 'Well, it is a serious offence. Your husband is a man that looks after himself, not afraid of standing up to trouble when it presents itself. There is a chance he'll be released on police bail, although I have my doubts as there is a fatality involved, and David does have a bit of history which could go against him for bail. He may be held on remand until the court appearance if the CPS decide to prosecute.'

'What do you mean, a bit of a history?' He's never been in trouble with the police before.'

'Unfortunately, David has. I'm not sure what he has told you. I think it's best coming from him. David is my client and I need to consider his wishes and instructions.'

'Are you saying he won't let you tell me what's happening?'

'No, but I've seen this before, all too often, unfortunately. You don't really know someone until something happens, and the skeletons come out of the closet, so to speak. It's up to David to tell you what he wants; I cannot unless he instructs me to.'

'When can I see him?'

'I'm not sure, and you might not get to see him at all until the hearing on Monday. With a fair wind, we could get David out on bail. He's a reformed character, a respected local businessman, a reasonably well-known sportsman around here, and a supporter of several local charities. It should be OK, just a formality, but be prepared for a different outcome.'

'So, what happens next if he doesn't get bail?'

'Well. If David doesn't get bail, he will go on remand awaiting the full court appearance, a trial if the CPS decide to prosecute, which could be months away. Many months! You need to prepare yourself for that eventuality. He will need your support. Naturally, his whole world is upside down at the moment, and he is effectively powerless at this time. I'll see if I can pull in a couple of favours and get you a few minutes together. Wait here but don't speak to anyone without me present.'

As the solicitor stands, I touch his arm, 'Isn't this a big mistake? David has been confused with someone else, hasn't he?'

'It doesn't look like it. In fact, David has already admitted to being involved in an altercation in the Tempest Arms last night with the deceased, and it seems there are several witnesses. I'll be back in a few minutes, sit tight, let's see if I can get you two together.'

I'm left alone in this horrid room. I need more water and some paracetamol. An argument that's gone too far? A rival team thug? No, this isn't football; there's no tribal turf with rugby that I'm aware of. It's not a mistake, then; this is for real.

About five minutes later, our solicitor opens the door, and there's a policeman just behind him. 'Hurry, you can see David, but stay calm, no touching. This officer will be with us at all times.' I follow the two men out of the room, down a short corridor, turning left and immediately into another interview room.

'Wait a moment, he'll be here in a second,' and within seconds, I hear footfall and lowered voices, and as I look up, David walks into the room in handcuffs with a big burly sergeant just behind him.

'You have one minute. We shouldn't be doing this Malc. Gotta get him back to his cell quickly.'

Instinct takes over, and I stand, run up to David and throw my arms around him. 'Oi! Knock it off! Tell her Malcolm, no touching. You said she'd be OK.'

'It's fine, just calm down, cut a little slack here, let them have a couple of minutes peace,' our solicitor responds. And with that, the sergeant tutted loudly, deep sighed and turned his back to us to keep an eye on the corridors.

'David, what happened? What's going on?'

'I'm not sure; they said I've attacked this chap, fought him, and now he's dead. That's not what happened.'

Malcolm, our solicitor, chips in, 'Don't say anything, David,' as he beckons to the door, 'Manchester's finest are always listening.'

So, I just grab him and hug him tighter. David whispers in my ear, 'This will all get sorted out. I'll be home soon, you'll see. Have you heard anything about the others?'

'No, everything is quiet. They're here somewhere, I think. I'll try Jess when I get out of here and try to piece things together.'

'I didn't do this Sammy. You've got to believe me. I don't know what happened. I wasn't that drunk; it was just a misunderstanding, really.'

'So, you did have a fight?' I reply, 'And what's this about a past history?'

'No, well, not really, not a fight, he was just out looking to pick a fight, and he chose me. It was nothing, really. I just hit him once. Not hard, but he did go down; he stumbled.'

'Oh, David. Unbelievable. You had better sort this out. I'll see what I can find out, and if I can't get in to see you, I'll send a message back with Malcolm.'

'C'mon, let's be having ya,' the sergeant commands. I squeeze tighter, and then David quietly whispers, 'I'm sorry Sammy, you'll hear some stuff; it's all in the past. I'm not that person anymore,' and he kissed me.

I look up at him, 'What kind of stuff? What are you talking about?' but before David could answer, the sergeant pulled him away, and they were soon out of the room and down the corridor. As David looks over his shoulder at me, I just stand there looking back at him, lost.

Malcolm speaks, 'OK, Samantha, we need to get you home; there is nothing further you can do down here tonight. I'll be going back into the interview room with David in a minute. Go home, try to get some rest, and I'll call you in the morning with an update.'

And with that, Malcolm picks up his well-worn briefcase and rushes out of the room. A young police officer then escorts me through the station, using his pass to open secure doors, out into the front area, and as he opens the front door, he quietly asks, 'Do you need a taxi Miss, or ...?'

'No thanks, I'll walk. I need some air to clear my head and think.' And with that, I step out into the early sunrise and fresh morning air.

6

Samantha – Manchester Crown Court

The foreperson stood crisply and, when asked for the jury's verdict, her clear response, "Guilty". The silent courtroom erupted, people both cheering and rebelling at the same time.

I looked down at David, and he just dropped back into the chair in the dock. I can't believe it. Malcolm sitting behind our barrister, turned sharply to me expressionless, and I know I presented a stunned and shocked look back at him. David's dad just sat quietly with his arm around me, unlike others in the public gallery clapping and shouting, 'Yeah! Killer!'

The Judge was shouting with authority, 'Order! Order! Order!

I WILL HAVE QUIET IN MY COURTROOM! You will be removed if you cannot control yourselves in an orderly manner.'

After a few minutes, the room grew quieter. The Judge then spoke calmly and precisely, 'David Franklin Alexander, please stand. You have been judged by a jury of your peers and found guilty on the charge of involuntary manslaughter. I have received petitions from your counsel requesting that sentencing be deferred until such time as mitigation arguments have been heard. However, I am moved in this instance to decline this request and pass sentence now.'

Our barrister rose immediately, 'Your honour. We request this matter be postponed to a future sentencing hearing, allowing us time to prepare statements.'

'No Mr Rufford, I am aware that the family of the deceased have already waived their right to present a victim personal statement, and, during the course of this trial, the severe impact on the deceased's family has been quite observable.'

Looking at David, the Judge continued, 'David Alexander, you have shown little remorse in this court or at any time you have been held in custody. Throughout this ordeal, you have maintained that the death of Gary Stephen Roberts could not have been by your hand. In light of this and, given your physical prowess and your lack of control on the night in question, and that you of all people should have been able to regulate your manner, what with your experience in the higher echelons on the rugby field over many years, I hereby sentence you, David Franklin Alexander, to ten years in His Majesty's prison, serving a minimum sentence of six years before consideration for licenced parole. Time already served awaiting trial will not discount this sentence. Do you have anything further to say before you are taken from this court?'

David was just stunned. His head bowed whilst listening, he raised it slowly and having clearly lost all sense of the impact of what he had just heard, David simply replied, 'No, your honour.'

'Very well, take the prisoner away.'

The court officers took David down; he didn't look up for me.

After the courtroom cleared, I just sat there. Malcolm was below. He quietly shook hands with our barrister and, whilst collecting his papers, looked up and noticed me; he came up to the public gallery.

'Samantha, this is just the first hurdle. We can lodge an appeal. The Judge's approach to sentencing was disgraceful, and our barrister wants to take this further.'

'You didn't say that they got it wrong though, did you? You didn't say he was innocent. Even David had nothing to say for himself.'

'He was in shock, no doubt. Let me talk with our barrister, and we'll consider the options open to us.'

Sitting there, I quietly replied, 'How can this be? Roberts was clearly a thug. He started all the trouble that night.'

Malcolm sat beside me, speaking quietly, 'It was clear the crown prosecution wanted to make an example here, to push this case and send a message against fighting in public spaces, especially when alcohol induced. This wasn't a one-punch, king hit type killer punch scenario; Roberts got up, spoke, and walked out, he was fine, or so it appeared. The outcome was unintentional; it was simply an accident. However, the expert witnesses for the crown are well versed in this type of case, one having experience of seven such cases previously in the last few years, all with guilty verdicts. We need to find an expert to challenge his opinion if we get to appeal, I mean, when we get to appeal.'

I stand and slowly walk to leave the gallery and, without looking back, say, 'He did it though, didn't he? He is guilty.'

Leaving the building, I step out into the bright sunshine, the odd paparazzi shark still hanging around the feeding pool. I slip on a pair of oversized sunglasses and hope not to be recognised as I turn left and head towards the nearby taxi rank.

'Samantha!'

'Samantha!'

'Miss Alexander!'

I stop, turn, and as a camera clicks away, I say, 'It's Mrs Alexander, if you don't mind. It's been a horrid time, and I have nothing further to say,' with that, I climb into a taxi a few feet away and ask the driver to pull off quickly, which he does, seemingly used to such requests as it's a few minutes heading out of the city centre before he asks, 'Where to Miss?'

I sigh, 'Sorry, I'm just, erm ... confused at the moment. Please take me to Victoria Train Station.'

'No problem,' as the taxi driver crosses lanes and takes the next sharp turn right.

7

Samantha – HMP Witchull

Getting all the paperwork, permissions, governance etc, sorted was difficult when David was arrested and held on remand. Obtaining temporary control of all our accounts, business dealings, loans, mortgages, and contracts was a bit of a hurdle for David as he maintained his innocence and really was expecting to be released either on bail or ultimately found innocent after trial. But now David is spending at least the next six years in prison; I need the control to manage our lives, well, mine, that is, and that of our business.

Our company lawyers, Fothergill, Stanley & Leith LLP, have been great, very supportive and seemingly, at times, one foot ahead of where I think I need to be. They have prepared all the documents in hard copy, duplicate and triplicate where required, and Mr Stanley, Richard, will accompany me to HMP Witchull to meet David and work through everything, explain the need for the power of attorney, transfer of rights, sole control of the bank accounts and so. This is all needed as our investors need security, and as I'm the proprietary provider of the technology we're developing, with David running the business side of the company, our Investors want to make sure their already committed investment and forward-going investment is in safe hands with the copyrights, and IPR matters suitably clarified and controlled.

As we drive to the prison, I think to myself, I hate visiting this place. The formalities, the handing over of keys, mobile phones, and laptops, and the searches often taking up to an hour of pre-visiting time are just tedious and impersonal. I know it's all for a good reason, but still, I'm not the criminal here. There it is again; David is the criminal; it's hard to acknowledge this at times.

Richard asks if I'm alright, I seem quiet, 'Yes, sorry, just lost in my thoughts. Never thought I, we, would be in such a position.'

'I know, I've been through this a couple of times before and worse.'

'What can be worse?'

'Well, naturally, I cannot give any details, but one business partner had actually committed a serious fraud involving nearly a million pounds, and his business co-partner knew nothing about the fraud until the Serious Fraud Office came knocking with the police. First, we had to demonstrate that the co-partner was innocent and then work with the SFO to recover as much as possible. We had to take legal steps to remove the partner from the business, which was easier said than done, and then get the business back on its feet, showing a clean ongoing operation that was in capable hands.'

'I presume it all worked out in the end for the co-partner?'

'Yes, it did. He is now the sole owner of the business, which, after a year or so, started to grow again and is now quite successful. We remain retained by them and provide all their legal services exclusively.'

'That's good to hear.'

We eventually enter the visiting area, with its usual atmosphere of forlorn hope and resignation, for what seems to be only five minutes the closest a prisoner can get to any semblance of normality with their loved ones. I always feel sorry for the young children here and the noticeable absence of teenagers.

David enters the room in prison wear, and as he gets closer, I notice the cut lip and bruising to his face, his left arm tucked in as though he is holding something close to him. We stand, and I introduce Mr Stanley, and David just about acknowledges we're present.

I dread to ask what has happened as I can easily guess he's been beaten. 'What happened David? Are you OK?'

The only answer was, 'Yeah. Holiday camp in here.'

'I'm sorry, David, we are still awaiting a decision on the appeal, hopefully not long now. Soon have you out of here, Malcolm and our barrister are doing their best to get the courts to speed things up, but the whole system is backed up, and it's hard to get anything confirmed.'

'Yeah, I'm in contact with Malcolm, who keeps me up to speed. So, this is about the business papers then,' as he looks to Mr Stanley, giving him the once over, noticing the crisp navy suit, pin-striped shirt and red silk tie.

'Yes, Mr Stanley is here to formalise the documents we discussed, papers we need you to sign so we can process formally, allowing me to keep the business running and our investors on side. Are you

OK signing these today? You've had the drafts through, no changes except for formalising them ready for signing.'

At this point, Mr Stanley puts the collection of documents on the table along with a pen.

Richard Stanley speaks, 'Mr Alexander, I represent your company in these matters and for the company to continue to operate, pay salaries, invoices and so on, we need to amend the authorisation documents for the banks and investors, all as previously explained.'

'Yeah, yeah, let's get on with it. I'm not happy, but I know it needs to be done,' and with that, both David and I sign the respective documents with Mr Stanley acting as witness where required. I didn't expect there to be so much paperwork today, but when everything is either duplicate or triplicate, it takes most of the visiting time to conclude them all. Upon signing the last document, Mr Stanley collects the documents together, places them in a folder and puts his pen away.

'I would ordinarily say this has been a pleasure, but it would not be appropriate under the circumstances. Thank you for being so understanding, Mr Alexander,' and with that, Mr Stanley holds out his hand to shake.

David looks at the outstretched hand and replies, 'Yeah, whatever,' and briefly, they shake hands under the observation of a nearby prison officer. Mr Stanley stands, looks at me and quietly says, 'Samantha, I'll wait outside in my car for you if that's alright? Give you some time together.'

'Thank you, Richard. There's not much visiting time left. I'll be with you shortly.' And with that, Mr Stanley leaves the visiting suite.

'Well, the business is all now with you, Samantha, until I get out of course, don't screw it up, will you?'

'No, I won't, don't worry.

It has to be like this David. I didn't want to do it, and you know that. It's still our business, and once we get these matters cleared away, I can focus on the day job and make sure we have something for when you get out of here.'

'Out of here sooner rather than later, I hope.'

'Has Malcolm told you he doesn't expect to overturn the guilty verdict, that the appeal is only about your sentencing and the time you got, trying to reduce the term?'

'Yeah, he's told me that, but if we get a fair wind and a good hearing, this could be reduced down to time served. I could then walk out of court.'

'That's great. The sooner you're out of here and home, the better. We've never spoken about your *past* David,' I say, hoping this time he will let me into his secret, 'What do I need to know?' Did your past go against you at sentencing? Malcolm won't tell me anything, and I've asked you several times already. Whatever it was, I'm guessing it was before we met at university?'

'It's nothing, just young buck stuff. Most young lads get into a scrape or two, you know, being adventurous, finding your way. Honestly, it was nothing. The sentencing was just wrong, and Malcolm is sure we can demonstrate it was target motivated.'

'Are you going to tell me what happened then?'

And just then, a prison officer called out that visiting time was finished.

'David, tell me? Please.'

'I told you, it's nothing to worry about. It's all in the past.'

With only seconds left, I thought the better of it and said, 'OK David, it'll keep. I love you. Take care of yourself in there,' as I nod towards the back of the room. 'If you are being picked on in there, tell the prison officers; I'm sure they'll stop it.'

'It's not simple. It doesn't work like that in here, it's not primary school. Don't worry about me. I can take care of myself.'

'Isn't that the problem, David? Isn't that what got you in here in the first place?' I ask before letting out a small sigh.

'Oh, we're going to have a fight now, are we? Let's not. Sam, I love you. This wasn't meant to be, and I'll get it sorted soon. I'll be out of here in no time and prove it wasn't me.'

'I'm sorry. I love you too,' and with that, we stand, and I hug David and kiss him. The low wolf whistles around the room brought a reaction for the prison officers, so we separate.

I watch as David returns to the secure door at the rear of the room with his fellow inmates. He doesn't look back.

Richard was waiting for me in his car when I got outside the prison. We drive back in silence; I suppose neither of us has much to say that can't wait.

8

Samantha – Bolton

I can't sleep, I'm mulling things over and keep returning to the fact that we are where we are now, and I need to plan for the future.

We are so close to cracking that final obstacle with the bio interface that I must focus on what drives me forward. I need to decide what to do about David; he has his past and I have my future, and in truth, he doesn't fit into the latter anymore, of that, I'm sure.

Flicking on the bedside lamp, I look up at the ceiling. 'Now. Enough,' I say quietly to myself.

Reaching for and opening my laptop, I review the research notes from the lab over the last few weeks. We are close to a breakthrough, I'm sure. The theory is sound, but the reality is missing something. We are close though; I can feel it; I just can't see what's missing. What is it?

Going to the kitchen, I open the fridge, and the light comes on. Grabbing a chilled bottle of still water, I sip it slowly whilst closing the door. It's time to think of me.

Sitting at the breakfast bar, I open my laptop and email inbox. Flicking through a few more mundane items, I see an email from Malcolm, David's solicitor. On opening, it doesn't give me much more information than I already know, but it does spur me into action concerning legal matters.

I start to write an email to Richard Stanley, firstly thanking him again for his help earlier today in getting the various papers signed by David. I then suggest a meeting in the next week or so to discuss some other matters I need legal assistance with and leave it vague. I send the email, close down my laptop for the night and return to my bedroom. Feeling a little better and more empowered now I've decided what to do, I slip off to sleep quickly.

The following morning, I wake early, go for a short run, shower, breakfast and leave by 8.00 am.

Chrissy and Jess are meeting me for lunch today, I tried to take a rain check, but they were insistent, saying they had something important to tell me. I worked through office admin and business papers all morning, our senior accountant identifying which bills were crucial to pay, those that could wait and those that would be beneficial to pay. Another team member has served their notice to the HR manager, three in as many weeks. I need to ensure all the systems are watertight and no downloads of key documents and IPR are being taken. Our external IS security team are on this in minutes and running searches on who had accessed what information, made downloads of what etc. This is what David was good at; I'm not that interested in the business side of the operation. I need to remain focused on the technology side of the R&D we are into.

Lunch at 1.00 pm was a godsend. I needed to escape the office, and this gave me the perfect excuse. I walked into the restaurant and spotted Chrissy and Jess straight away, and as I walk over to them, it looks like Chrissy is trying to calm Jess down a little, and Jess does look flustered.

We all say hi and sit in the booth; cosy, I thought. After looking at the menu and selecting something light with house sparkling water, we are left alone and it was Chrissy that opened the conversation.

'Sam. We've come into some information which is quite ... er ... delicate and thought it best we let you know as soon as possible, but we're not sure how you'll take this news.'

'Oh, sounds ominous. Have you found out about my Mediterranean lover, Emmanuel?' as I chuckle.

'Actually, no, not *your* lover,' Chrissy says as she looks at Jess. Jess, ever so slightly, is shaking her head from side to side, and Chrissy says, encouraging Jess along, 'Come on Jess, it's for the best. We agreed.' But Jess remains quiet.

I look at Chrissy, 'What is it, Chrissy? Who's doing what with who?'

Chrissy takes a large swallow from her glass of pinot, and that's when I notice the half-empty bottle in the ice bucket standing beside her.

'Now, you've heard the expression, *don't kill the messenger*, right?'

'Come on Chrissy, out with it,' and she could tell my tone had just moved up a gear.

'David has been having an affair.'

'What?' Give over. Is this some kind of joke you two? It's not that funny unless you have a great punchline; I'm in no mood for this.'

Chrissy looks at Jess, still slowly moving her head from side to side. 'Jess, tell her, tell her what you told me.'

Jess just mumbled something about this being a bad idea.

'Chrissy, stop beating around the bush; if you have something to tell me, then tell me it all.'

Chrissy emptied her glass and reached for the bottle, now nearly empty when placed back in the ice bucket.

'David is, was having an affair. It seems it had been going on for some months; a woman called Monica he met whilst away on a business trip and then kept it going. We don't know her, but she contacted Jess about a week ago asking for some money to stay quiet; a bloody blackmailer, just after some cash, probably fleecing David for what she could get. We thought she would only return for more if we paid her off. Now with David locked up for a long time we ...'

'You,' said Jess looking at Chrissy with wide eyes, 'not *we*.'

'... we thought you were better knowing so you could decide what you wanted to do,' finished Chrissy.

I just sat there looking at Chrissy, then at a head-bowed Jess.

'Rubbish! Is this someone just trying it on? I can't believe you both fell for this kind of twaddle. It's laughable,' I said, but possibly not really as convincing as I thought.

Jess looked up, 'It's true, Sam, I've seen photos and videos of them together. I didn't believe her at first and wanted some proof. But it's true. She wouldn't leave the proof with me, but she wants money to stay quiet.'

I sit quietly for a minute, looking at the place setting in front of me, thinking.

Chrissy broke the silence, 'Would you like something to drink Sam? A bit of shock, I expect?'

'A shock? This? Try being married to a criminal in jail for manslaughter,' and I leave it hanging ...

Jess found some courage to speak up, 'I'm sorry Sam, Chrissy is right, you should know. I shouldn't have sat on this, I should have mentioned it to you straight away, but I needed to be sure; you've been through so much, and I didn't want to add to it.'

I stand, my hands visibly trembling as I clench my fists and then rub my hands together. I turn and walk for the door.

Chrissy calls out, and people in the restaurant turn to look. I just keep walking and leave the restaurant. As I get outside, Chrissy is right behind me, 'Sam. Sam. What are you going to do Sam?'

I turn and calmly say, 'Well, that's made my mind up. I'm in charge from now on,' and I walk to my car and drive off.

9

Samantha – Manchester

Sat at the conference table with Richard Stanley in his office, I pull out the Shareholder Agreement and Articles of Association and place them on the table. Happy that I've considered all angles; I can't wait to get this ball rolling, but I mustn't seem too hasty; I must remain professional.

'Richard, I have my reasons for this decision, and they are deeply personal, and for the time being, I want to keep them between us and these four walls. I found out last week that David had been having an affair for many months before that night of the fight. I had no idea, but like a fool, I supported him through the whole arrest, trial, and conviction and have been helping him with his appeal. I feel cheated and used now knowing what I know. David kept this from me even through all of this, and I simply can't trust him anymore.'

'Oh Samantha, I'm so sorry. Are you sure he was having an affair? Is this reliable?'

'Yes, I've looked into it and met the other woman. Nasty piece of work she is too, tried to blackmail me, well my friends actually, and they told me.'

'That's terrible. Have you been in touch with the police?'

'No. I've decided what I want to do; I want to get away from David altogether, no more links or ties. To be honest, I'm not bothered if these photos go public. Firstly, in the Articles of Association and Shareholder

Agreement, we have provisions to protect the company from bad public relations, criminal acts, misconduct, etc. They were part of our Investor's requirements, conditional on the investment we obtained.'

'Yes, I'm aware of them. Some of them are a little unusual, but when there is such a sizeable investment and the chance of a major public relations backlash, I could appreciate their intent in the end. Do you want to invoke these rights, force David to sell his shares back to the company and have him removed as a director?'

'Yes. And then I want a divorce. Don't try to talk me out of any of this, Richard. When I think of what a fool he has made of me, how I supported and stood by him through this and my darkest times, only to find out he was cheating on me behind my back before it all happened, it infuriates me. I bet he even used company funds for his "trips" away with her, passing it off as business expenses.'

'Well, there is enough to warrant those provisions being acted upon. We can conduct an audit of the accounts to see if David was using company money. Have you got the evidence of his infidelity in case he refuses to cooperate?'

'Yes, I have the evidence now. I paid for it, and it's now mine. I also have a statement from her, and if needs be, I will drag her into the limelight and have the police prosecute her for attempted blackmail. Believe me, she'll be uncooperative for sure. But my main objective is to protect the company.'

'OK, OK,' Richard says gently, nodding, 'Not my usual area of dealings, but we can set the ball rolling.

I'll have my associate draft the relevant papers, and we'll serve them on David at the earliest opportunity.'

'Thank you Richard, you are such a good comfort and friend. Does your practice handle divorce, or can you put me in contact with a robust lawyer to get what I'm entitled to?'

'No problem Samantha; probably best if you instruct another practice for the divorce-related matters to ensure no conflict of interest. Don't worry, I know just the person to help you.'

10

David – HMP Witchull

'The bitch! I can't believe she's doing this to me.'

'They're all the same, I tell ya! Out for em selves. Just cos you're doing a bit of time don't mean she can da this to ya. *Fight it*, I would!'

'Shut the fuck up! What do you know, crackhead? You've never had two pennies to rub together, and if you did, you buy some shit and try to sniff it or stick it in your arm!'

'Geez, sorry man, I know you're pissed, but not we me like. Not my fault she's taking the piss out of ya.'

There's a loud clunk outside the cell door as the lights go out; the cell goes dark save for some artificial light spilling in through the high window. I lie on my back, looking up at the ceiling, waiting for my eyes to adjust to the dark. Slowly I start to calm down.

I can't believe that bloody airhead tried blackmailing Samantha's friends. If I don't agree to sign all the papers, vulture Stanley will simply go to court, and it'll happen anyway. Agreeing on a decent purchase price for my shares plus the offer of a ten thousand pound sweetener when I get out is probably the best I can get; I'm surprised Samantha offered this in light of everything that has happened. I've nothing left now to pay for even more legal advice and court proceedings. I have my appeal to think about, and this income will help.

I put my arm over my eyes, not believing how everything has turned out. There's me thinking I'm on top of the world, with a great wife, brilliant mates, money, a growing business, cars, and holidays. And now I'm in here. *You've fucked it all up now Davey boy.* Eventually, I block out the world and fall asleep.

It's early morning, and life stirs in the corridors of penance. Doors are being unlocked, and familiar sounds of cocky despair echo around. I'm meeting Malcolm today; hopefully, he'll bring better news about my appeal.

As I enter the interview room, the prison officer remains standing at the back; usually, we're left alone on personal legal matters. It feels a bit odd as I look at him, and he tells me to sit down. Malcolm, already sitting waiting for me, says hello, and we get straight to it.

'David, it's not good news, I'm afraid. Your appeal decision has been delayed again. I know the whole court system has a massive backlog, and I'm pushing this as hard as I can; this is affecting people's rights, after all.'

My blood is starting to boil. 'When? When am I going to get my appeal? There had best be an appeal; I'm not doing ten bloody years in here! You said you'd get this reduced to time served and out at appeal. You're all the bloody same, you lawyers; it's all just about your fees, isn't it? Fuck the common man!' I stand quickly, causing the plastic chair to fall over.

The prison officer shouts out, 'Enough! Calm down Alexander, or this meeting is over!'

I turn, stupidly facing up to him, 'Or what?' when the door opens and two more officers rush in and grab me.

Malcolm jumps to the far wall holding his briefcase to his chest. 'David, minimum six years, six years, remember, if you don't create trouble and you don't get an appeal. Good behaviour and all that, you'll be out in no time,' as he looks at me and sees the anger in my eyes, and I think he can see for the first time that I could kill someone right now.

11

Samantha – Farmhouse, near Broadhurst Village

David eventually sold his shares back to the company, and I picked up most of them, with the rest being offered and bought by a couple of loyal senior employees. The Investors were happy with this as it demonstrated our commitment to further personal investment into making this business successful.

After eleven months, the divorce finalised this morning, decree absolute, and I became free of David ... totally. We split what we shared, and after selling the house, I bought a nice little apartment not too far from the laboratory for ease more than anything.

David has completed some 14 months of his sentence now, and all our contact has fizzled out; no need to be in touch anymore. In fact, the last time I saw him was when I confronted him about the affair and presented him with the divorce papers, not a good visit which I then vowed to be my last.

The request for an appeal has been turned down. David will serve his term as per the original sentencing passed down.

After settling all the finances, I bought a former farmhouse a few miles north of Bolton on the West Pennine Moors. It needed some love and attention, and I love escaping here for the peace, the air and the changing weather, the lovely sunny days, grey moody clouds, and rainy days. The road up to the farmhouse is about three-quarters of a mile of twisting stone track, giving me a real reason to have a four-wheel drive car whilst working in the city. I cross the cattle grid about 300 yards from the farmhouse, and the bars drum as I drive over them, giving me that sound of arrival I love. My space.

The sun is starting to go down as I pull up outside the farmhouse, and within minutes, I've carried in my food and wine reserves for the weekend. Within the hour, the fires and aga are lit, and the first bottle of Sancerre is open, and I'm taking a sip at the kitchen table. Never too far from my laptop, I'm flicking through the latest test results from the lab and making notes.

I return to the hot plate and place the cast iron pan on top, warming it ready to start cooking supper.

'Well then, I bet you thought this would never happen,' said a deep male voice behind me.

12

David – HMP Witchull

'Get up Alexander, you're moving rooms, free upgrade to first class.'

I look up at the Prison Officer standing in the doorway, 'What?'

'Come on, get a move on. You're moving down to the next landing. I'll be back in five minutes to take you over; make sure you have all your stuff ready,' and he turned and walked off along the landing.

That surprised me. I put my bookmark between my book's pages and get off the bed. I've not much to gather together really, some personal bits and my prison-provided stores. I'm done in less than three minutes and sit back down on the edge of the bottom bunk. I don't think I could get any worse than my current cellmate; well, I hope not.

Returning to the cell door, the officer peers in, 'OK, you ready?'

'Yes, I'm packed.'

'OK, follow me; you're in for a real treat.'

'Sorry? What does that mean?'

'Come on, get a move on. You'll see.'

I leave my cell behind and follow the officer along the landing, down one flight of the central staircase and turn left. He stands just past an open door and nods to his left slightly, 'Your new home and roommate, say hello to Mr Blaydon.'

I turn to look through the doorway and at my new cellmate standing, squarely looking back at me. Some six foot or more, well built, this guy exudes the *don't mess with me* look.

'Er, hello, Mr Blaydon, I'm David Alexander.'

'OK, pleasantries over, get in Alexander and put your stuff away. Food in fifteen minutes.'

And as I turn to register the prison officer's comment, he is already walking off.

'Come in lad, put your kit on the bottom bunk,' my new cellmate says, 'Cupboard and shelf there are yours,' as he points to the minimal furnishings His Majesty has to offer us.

'Cheers, ta,' I respond, placing my meagre belongings on the bed and starting to put some on the shelf.

'Nobody other than the guards in here calls me Mr Blaydon. Blade will do,' and he holds out his hand to shake.

That freaks me a little. I stand upright, and we shake hands, his grip slightly better and tighter than mine. 'Blade, it is then. I think I've heard your name mentioned about this place.'

'Probably have, aye, I don't suffer fools lightly, and this place is full of them. I hear you're in here for killing a chap?'

'Er, well, yes, I mean no. Not deliberately, that is. Disagreement in a pub, and he died later.'

'I see. You play rugby, almost made the Lions.'

'You're well-informed, Mr, er Blade.'

'Yep, you bet. Intel is important.'

Finding a little more confidence and registering what he just said to me, 'Can I ask, what are you in here for?'

'A disagreement with some officials that went a bit far, and I put some of them in hospital. Paying my dues now. All fair as I see it, I've no beef with my sentence.'

'You a fan of rugby then?'

'Yep, played some in my time. That's one of the reasons I asked for you to be moved here.'

'You asked?' probably showing a little surprise and disbelief.

'Why not? Got a good relationship with the guards; I help keep the peace in here for some small favours in return. Don't worry. I'm no nonce or fag or owt like that. I just want a cellmate with a bit of something about them; I fucking hate druggies and rapists. I want someone I can talk with that has something intelligent to say, something sensible that kills the boredom and broadens my knowledge so I can benefit from my time in here. You're intelligent, play rugby, you have something about you.'

'And you're ex-military, army or marines?'

'Army. See, I wasn't wrong about you. What gave me up?'

'Guards, kit, intel. Some of my former teammates were in the military, and it rubs off. And the nickname *Blade* from your mates in the army?'

'Yep. We all have or had a nickname. Now, come on, square your kit away before grub up.'

13

Samantha – Farmhouse, near Broadhurst Village

'Police! Police quick. I think he's dead. I think I've killed him.'

'Where are you?' was the calm voice at the other end.

'I'm at home. Nedwells Farmhouse, just off the Old Carters Lane near Broadhurst village.'

'Are you alone?'

'Yes. Yes, I am.'

'Take a breath if you can; slow down. What's your name?'

'Samantha Alexander.'

'Who is injured, Samantha?'

'I don't know who he is. He was just behind me in the kitchen. He must have broken in. Frightened me, and I hit him with the pan, and then he attacked me.'

'Is he on his own?'

'Yes, I think so. Oh my god, I don't know. There's blood everywhere. Send someone quickly.'

'Where is he bleeding from?'

'His head and chest.'

'Is he breathing?'

'I don't think so. No. He's not breathing anymore.'

'OK, Samantha, stay on the line; you're doing fine; keep talking to me. The police and ambulance are on their way. Are you injured?'

'No, but I'm getting really cold.'

'Samantha, keep talking to me. You are probably experiencing shock. It's important you keep talking to me, Samantha. Are you in a safe place, is the door locked?'

'Yes. I'm upstairs in my bedroom.'

'OK, good. Now get your duvet or a blanket and wrap it around you. Help is on its way. There is also a police helicopter on the way to you; it may get there quicker. Is there a field nearby where it can land?'

'Er, yes, at the front of the house, but it's dark.'

'Don't worry about that; they'll get to you quickly.'

I move towards the front bedroom window and look out. I can't see much. The phone handset beeps. 'Oh no, the battery is low,'

'I can see you are on a landline. Do you have a fixed phone you can pick up Samantha?'

'No, just this one cordless phone.'

'OK. Do you have a mobile I can call?'

'Yes. Er, no, mobile phones don't work up here. Oh my god.'

'Don't worry Samantha, they're on their way. Keep talking to me. Samantha? Are you there?'

'Yes, yes, I can see a blue flashing light across the valley.'

'Good, it's a police car that wasn't too far away; they'll be with you in a few minutes. Can the officers get in the house when they get there?'

'Yes. No. Well, yes, I suppose so; he got in, didn't he?'

'OK Samantha, when the officers arrive, go to them, they'll look after you. OK, Samantha, nearly over; you're doing great. How close are they now Samantha?'

'Just coming up the lane now. I'm going out to them.'

'Samantha, take the phone with you, keep talking to me.'

'OK,' and then I start to walk downstairs. The phone beeps more now. I reach the bottom of the stairs, the narrow hallway is filled with oscillating blue light, and as I open the front door, a police officer runs up to me. I stagger out, dropping the phone, and collapse into his arms.

Within half an hour, there are numerous police cars, a helicopter overhead and the ambulance I'm sitting in. A police officer is trying to talk with me, and I struggle to take in what is being asked. A paramedic is checking me over, I presume for wounds or injuries, whilst another is checking my pulse and shining a light into my eyes. It's at this point I give in, close my eyes, and pass out.

14

Samantha – Bolton General Hospital

I wake in a hospital bed in a quiet side room, all alone, the gentle beeping noise of the monitors beside me. The room light is low, and it seems quite peaceful as I lie here thinking about what had happened.

In a few minutes, a nurse opens the door, and as I turn to look at her, I notice a uniformed police officer sitting on a chair directly outside the door. The nurse walks in. 'Hi Samantha, how are you feeling? Any pain or discomfort?'

'No,' I reply, 'I ... I think I'm OK.'

'Good. Yes, we thought it best we keep you in for observation for a few hours. That cut on your forearm needed some stitches. Other than that, no other signs of any physical injuries.'

'What? How did I get that?'

'The police will fill you in, and I expect the detectives will be back shortly. They've been waiting for you to wake up. Do you feel ready to talk with them?' her manner is comforting, and her concern for my well-being is genuine.

'Well, erm, yes, I suppose so. Although I don't think there is much I can say.'

'OK, don't worry, let me just recheck your blood pressure, pop this oxygen meter on your finger ... there, and I'll just make a few notes, then let the officer outside know you are ready to see them.'

'Thank you.'

The nurse carried out her checks and left the room, saying, 'I'll send them in in a few minutes.'

I shuffled a bit in bed and tried sitting up a little. The door opened again, and in came two people wearing coats, one carrying a zip conference folder under her arm and both with cardboard coffee cups with lids.

'Good morning Mrs Alexander. How are you feeling? I'm Detective Chief Inspector Paul Silverton, and this is Detective Sergeant Jo Hansen. I am the Senior Investigating Officer assigned to this matter, and we have a few questions for you if that's OK? We just need to clear up some facts then we'll leave you alone for the time being. Do you mind if we sit?' as they draw up two chairs and sit, it seems to me they were going to sit and ask questions whether I liked it or not.

'It's Walsh, Samantha Walsh, Alexander was my married name, and I'm reverting back to my maiden name.'

'Ah, sorry, I wasn't aware of that,' DCI Silverton replied whilst DS Hansen unzipped her folder and made a note. 'We have the owner of the property down as ...' he checked his notebook 'Mrs Samantha Alexander, that is you, isn't it? That was the name you gave when you called the police'.

'Yes, I was waiting for my divorce to finalise then change everything back to my maiden name, just not got around to all of it yet.'

'Ah, OK, I see.' The DS was taking more notes. 'Who is ... sorry, was your former husband? Is that the man at the house?'

'No, my ex is in prison. I'm sure you'll find him familiar when you run a check. I have no idea who that was at my house. Is he dead?'

'Yes, unfortunately. You can see this is a serious matter; the sooner we sort out some details, the clearer things will become. So, do you know this man? Have you ever seen him before?'

'No, I've never seen him before.'

'You didn't invite him into the house?'

'No, as I've said, I have no idea who he is or how he got into the house.'

'OK. Can you run me through what happened earlier this evening, last night?'

I sigh and shuffle a little more against the pillow, 'Yes. I was in the kitchen catching up on some notes from work on my laptop, cooking supper, and having a glass of wine. I was at the Aga when I heard this man's voice behind me.'

'What did he say?'

'It was something like, *"bet you didn't expect this"* or *"I bet you didn't expect this tonight"* I can't really recall. I just screamed and turned, and he stood there about a metre or so away. I just panicked, I had the pan I was using in my right hand, and I just swung at him and hit him on the side of the head. It was all very quick. He staggered backwards and lost his footing for a second, and I went to run out of the room, but he grabbed me. I turned again, but this time as I swung the pan, he had a knife and lashed out at me,' touching my bandaged arm, it now made sense.

'And then what happened?' asked the DS as she scribbled away, taking notes.

'I can't quite remember, although I remember losing grip of the pan and dropping it.' I paused, thinking about what I did next. 'I think I pulled a knife out of the knife block, and as I turned, I just ... I just stabbed him, I think. I can see his face now. He was startled. He grabbed my hand with the knife as it was still in him, and I hit him with my other hand, and he staggered backwards and fell to the floor. He started mumbling something, and that's when I saw he was bleeding heavily. He started to get up again, and I just ran to the door to get out of the kitchen. I heard him swearing and then a loud crash, it sounded like pots or pans or something, but I didn't look back. I just ran upstairs to my bedroom. That's when I called 999.'

The DS looking at her pad, spoke again, 'OK. You asked for the police, not an ambulance, and said, "*I think he's dead. I think I've killed him*". Why did you think that?'

'I saw the amount of blood, and he was struggling to stand. I wasn't going to help him; he still had a knife.'

'He had a knife?' asked the DS Hansen.

'Yes, I think so.'

'Was he alone?' DCI Silverton then asked.

'I presume so. I didn't see anyone else.'

'After leaving the kitchen, did you go back into the kitchen?' he continued.

'No. I waited until the police car arrived and went outside straight to the officer.'

'OK.'

'Who is he, was he? Do you know?' I ask.

'We have an idea but just need to check first before we mention any names. You definitely don't know the man?'

'No. As I've said, I've never seen him before. At least, I don't think I have.'

The DS speaks up again, 'You don't seem certain about that. Have you seen him before or not?'

I close my eyes. I have an image of when I looked at him briefly. 'Now I think about it, there was something familiar about him, something I ...' and paused again, 'I'm not sure. No, I don't think so.'

The DCI chips in 'Samantha, do you know him? This is very important.'

I'm starting to feel suddenly tired and a little nauseous.

'No, I don't know him.'

The door opens, and the nurse re-enters the room, 'OK, officers, I think that's enough for now. Samantha has been through quite an incident and is suffering from shock. These questions can wait until later, I'm sure. Samantha needs to get some more rest now.'

The DCI stands while the DS closes her conference folder. 'OK, we have enough for now. If you recall anything further, let the officer outside your door know, and they will contact me. Is that OK, Mrs, er, Ms Walsh?'

'Yes, yes. I am tired. I'll sleep for a bit if that's OK?'

The nurse then took control, 'Not a problem. Thank you, officers, we'll see you later,' as she ushered them towards the door.

The DCI turned and looked back, 'You are sure you don't know this man? You've never seen him before?'

'Yes, I'm sure,' and with that, they leave the room.

As the nurse adjusts my pillows, she quietly leans into me, 'Don't worry about them; they do keep pestering until they're told to leave. I'll keep an eye out for them coming back; you rest now,' and the nurse dims the room lights slightly before leaving the room.

I close my eyes. Why did he ask if I was *sure* I didn't know this man? The way he emphasised the *sure* was curious, and his questioning manner was as if I should know this man.

15

Samantha – Bolton

I'm at the police station a day later to make a formal statement and to find out what more the police have uncovered.

DS Hansen meets me in the reception area, and we are buzzed through to the offices and rooms at the rear of the building.

After accepting a glass of water from DS Hansen, DCI Silverton walks into the interview room and sits at the solid wooden table. He places a portfolio on the tabletop and opens the interview, 'Thank you for coming in today to make a formal statement Ms Walsh.'

'No problem, please call me Samantha.'

'Thank you, Samantha. My DS will take some notes, and then we'll formalise this into your statement for you to sign as a record of your recollection of events that evening.'

'Sorry, I meant to ask, do I need my solicitor present for this?' I thought I'd better be clear on this, just in case.

'No, but if you want one to be present, we can re-arrange this statement meeting. This is just a formality; we are after a record of the events as you recall them. We're in the process of collecting together the events before and after, and this will help enormously.'

'Oh, OK. Can I ask, have you identified the man?'

'Yes, but we've not released his name to the general public yet as we are still collecting evidence and statements.'

DCI Silverton looked at me with a slightly assured expression. He had done this before and was guarding his information carefully.

'Who was he? What is his name?'

'Samantha, his name is Hugo Bonning-Wallace. Do you know him? Does his name sound familiar?'

'No, should it? I get the feeling you think I should know this man.'

'First things first, Samantha. Let's get your statement done, and then we'll bring you up to speed with the investigation and what we know so far. Is that OK?

'Yes, fine.'

And with that, I recounted the events as I recalled them, my day running up to travelling to the farmhouse, being in my kitchen, cooking supper, how he was just stood behind and spoke, startled me, we fought, and I hit him with the pan, he lashed out with a knife, and then I stabbed him with one of my kitchen knives. I fled to my bedroom, called 999; the rest is a matter of record.

'Thank you, Samantha. DS Hanson will get this transcribed whilst I bring you up to speed with the investigation, and then once you are happy with your statement, you can sign it.' Looking at the DS, 'Thank you, Jo. Please bring the statement back as soon as you have it ready.'

'Will do boss.' And with that, DS Hansen collected her notepad and papers together, stood and left the interview room.

'Right, Samantha. Firstly, can I ask that you keep this information to yourself for the time being? We have a number of officers working on this, and we don't want the press or others interfering with our investigation at the moment. The first twenty-four / forty-eight hours are crucial to us for collecting physical evidence.'

'Yes, absolutely. I don't want anything to get in the way of finding out what this is all about.'

'Thank you. Well, it seems that Bonning-Wallace had a bit of a past about him, and from what we have pieced together so far, it looks like he was stalking you, secretly following you for some time. That's why I asked if you had seen him before.'

'Oh my god, no, I didn't know he was following me. How do you know he was following me?'

'He had his mobile phone on him. We used his thumbprint to open the phone, and our tech guys have been going through its contents. It seems there are dozens of photos of you on his phone, taken clandestinely, you were not to know. Further, it seems that there are some diary records that apparently align with your diary on occasions.'

'Oh. How did you get my diary information?'

'We spoke with your secretary, Daryl, and he was happy to provide the information to us. As I said, these first few hours and days are key to the investigation, and any assistance is of great benefit. I trust this is not a problem?'

'No, no, it's fine; I just wasn't expecting this. I just thought he was a burglar or something, you know, a home intruder.'

'That was our first thought also, but as your farmhouse is quite remote, off the beaten track, it didn't seem to sit quite right with us. But the stalker approach does. So as far as you are aware, you don't know Bonning-Wallace; your paths never crossed knowingly?'

'No. Well, that was my first thought, but thinking more on this, I seem to have some vague recollection of his image, his face. Maybe I had just inadvertently looked at him in the crowd when he was following me; I don't know. Sorry.'

'Umm. OK. So, we will continue to download his photos, GPS history on his phone, his messages and so on. Look into his personal affairs, his home and social life, his car, work etc. and pull together a picture of what motivated him to this end.'

'Did you say he had a bit of a past, a police record, that he was already known to the police?'

'Yes, well, I can't say too much on that at this time, but he was certainly a person of concern and known to the police, although not around here in the Northwest. No doubt some paparazzi journalist will get to his identity and publish the information shortly.'

'I'd like to know; can you tell me anything?'

'Well, I can't say much at this time, but if you were to put his name into an internet search, I think the results would speak for themselves.'

'OK, thank you, I'll do that later.'

'Whilst we await my DS, can I get you a tea or a coffee Ms Walsh?'

'No, thank you, I'm good.'

'OK, if you don't mind waiting for my DS to return, I have a couple of calls to make if that's acceptable?

'Yes, that's fine; please don't let me keep you,' with that, DCI Silverton stood and left the interview room. This allowed me to pull out my phone, open the internet and type in Hugo Bonning-Wallace. There were several immediate hits, headlines from newspapers and online media.

"Hugo Bonning-Wallace – not guilty"

"Bonning-Wallace court case collapses."

"Bonning-Wallace Rape Charge"

"Allegations against Hugo Bonning-Wallace"

I read through a couple of these articles and can see what DCI Silverton was referring to now.

Some twenty minutes or so later, DCI Silverton and DS Hansen returned with my statement ready, and they both took a seat again. The DS handed the pages to me. I read through my statement in the quiet of the room, signed and dated it at the bottom. The DS then nodded to her DCI and left the room, taking my statement with her.

DCI Silverton then stood and held out his hand, 'Thank you for your time this morning, Samantha. We'll be in touch again shortly with an update.' We shook hands, and he led me out to the front reception area.

'If the press or reporters ask me anything, what should I say?'

'Simply say that the police are looking into the matter and the police expect to issue a statement shortly.'

'Thank you. I've never been through anything like this before and certainly don't want to jeopardise your inquiries.'

'We know. You take care, take a few days to process what has happened. Do you have family or friends to stay with? It'll help keep the press away if you can.'

'Yes, I have friends I can stay with. You can get me on my mobile phone if you need to speak with me. I presume I can't go back to the farmhouse just yet?'

'That's correct, it's a crime scene, and the forensic team are still up there working it. We'll be in touch to let you know when you can return.'

'Thank you, DCI Silverton.'

I leave the police station and walk to my car. I sit in the driver's seat, trying to take all this in, being followed by a stalker, and let out a deep sigh.

16

Samantha – Bolton

Following many weeks of investigation by the police, they concluded that Hugo Bonning-Wallace was a person with issues, a sexual predator with a history. He had selected me as his next victim and was planning his assault at the farmhouse. They were unsure why I was selected; however, he had recently moved to the northwest, possibly as he was too well known in the south of England, and I just happened to be his next victim.

The coroner's verdict stated that Bonning-Wallace's death was the result of self-defence and provided a narrative verdict.

The police demonstrated that Bonning-Wallace had been covertly stalking me, taking photos of me and the odd video. GPS records showed that he was following me now and again and was in the same restaurants and bars as me at the same time. It wasn't clear how he found out the location of my farmhouse, but then again, it probably wasn't that difficult for a determined person to find out, especially if he was adept at quietly stalking a person.

It came to light that Bonning-Wallace had been accused of rape two years earlier, and a criminal trial had eventually started in a London court. The trial collapsed due to the crown's witness refusing to testify and some of the key evidence being considered tainted. He was acquitted, distinctly different from not being found innocent in front of a jury, and the police were convinced there were other women he had assaulted, but none had come forward. This 'invincibility' belief then seemed to spur him on, and I was to be his next victim. Carrying a knife was considered an escalation, and the police thought he may have used it this time as a part of his insatiable growing power to dominate women. I was lucky if I could call it that.

Bonning-Wallace had driven up to the farmhouse but parked his car on the lane a hundred or so metres down from my farmhouse gate. He found the side door open and simply walked into my kitchen. I had forgotten to lock the door after carrying in my supplies, travel case and laptop bag for the weekend. Given its remoteness, I felt safe in the farmhouse and neglected to lock the door. I hadn't heard him enter the farmhouse or kitchen because of the music and sounds of cooking in the kitchen.

The police, CPS and coroner found sufficient evidence of his intentions, and with his previous background, the verdict clearly exonerated me on the grounds of lawful killing based on self-defence.

The press started to lose interest in me and this event after the coroner's verdict, and I began to get my life back together, working more and more, socialising less and less. I moved in temporarily with Chrissy whilst the media were hounding me. My time with Chrissy during the investigation was tense; Chrissy has a different lifestyle to me, and whilst in the first few days, Chrissy was supportive, she soon craved her own lifestyle back and the social scene she was used to. After a couple of weeks or so with Chrissy, I moved back into my apartment in town, running the gauntlet of the odd reporter harassing me for a comment.

I found comfort in working long hours in the research lab, focusing on what I was convinced would turn out to be a big step forward in cancer treatment. Three months later, we made the breakthrough we were looking for. Laboratory and then clinical trials followed, and after obtaining the necessary licences, Oxy-verrucotox moved into commercial production. The investors were ecstatic, their returns becoming many thousands of times greater than their investment. Oxy-verrucotox was a global success. The company shareholders, including me, became immensely wealthy on the back of this success, and international licences to manufacture and distribute OxyRuco© were in significant demand. As a course of treatment for many forms of cancer, the success in eradicating the cancerous cells was outstanding, and the speed of achieving this was unparalleled.

With my initial investors, the copyright, trademark and patent made us extremely wealthy. A year later, I was ranked just outside the Sunday Times Top 250 Rich List and was heading to be in the top 150 by the next count.

Our new corporate offices were established in London. New research facilities were built in Oxfordshire, and we maintained the original laboratories in Bolton, respecting the birthplace of our discovery.

My future was set. I had achieved what I set out to do: find a viable cancer treatment for the world. I am wealthy; I'm in demand for talk shows, technical seminars, medical journals, and Woman of the Year events. More and more interested investors seem to be coming out of the woodwork now with millions to invest in my next venture. I need to decide what that will be.

The events with Bonning-Wallace crop up now and again, usually during talk shows on TV, radio, and the internet, and I brush past them as quickly as possible. The one thing I say is that the event that night brought me to where I am today; it gave me the added focus and impetus to achieve my goal. You could say that something good did come out of it all.

17

David – HMP Witchull

Lying on the bottom bunk reading my monthly letter from Dad, I can't hold it in. 'Wow! She did it. You know, I never thought she would actually do it.'

'What's that?' Blade says from the top bunk, seemingly only half interested.

'My ex. She's only gone and found the cure for cancer.'

'Bollocks, you having a laugh?'

'No, I'm serious unless my Dad is taking the piss. Well, not all cancer but a lot of it. We had a research company together, she was the technical brain, and I was the business. She's worth a fortune now.'

This seemed to get Blade's interest, 'Like how much?'

'I don't know, but with this going global, it'll be millions, billions probably. Damn it.'

'Your ex, you say? What, ex-girlfriend, partner, wife?'

'All of the above. We met in our last year at university, married a few years later, set up the business, worked together and then I got landed with this, doing fucking time. The investors in the business wanted me off the scene; bad PR and all that; forced me to sell my shares back. I needed the cash anyway for my defence costs. Then Sammy found out about my affair when that bloody dimwit tried blackmailing her, divorce followed, and now I'm out in the cold whilst she's a major success.'

'Sammy, is it? Any chance of you two getting back together?'

'No, none whatsoever. I've burnt my bridges there, well and truly. But bloody hell, I could do with some of that when I get out.'

'Will she give you something? You know, to keep you quiet, off the scene, a settlement? Something for old times' sake?'

'I doubt it, Blade. I'm just a guy from the past that's long gone now and probably forgotten about. A very different life for the both of us now.'

'Fucking life. It's roses for some, dandelions for others.'

'Yeah, shit init.' I lie back and try to take all this in. Wow! I mean, Wow! She said she'd do it. I should have believed more in her, been faithful, not got into that stupid fight.

The following morning after breakfast, most inmates were either milling around the communal wing areas or in their cells with doors open. I came down the central staircase to the ground floor and looked around for Blade but couldn't spot him. There was a copy of the prison newspaper on an empty table, so I sat down, opened it and started to read, minding my own business.

'Who the fuck are you?' this gruff, deep voice with a heavy Scottish accent said behind me, and I turned to see this tattooed, muscle-bound skinhead of a beast flanked by two snarling terriers.

'Why? What's it to you?' I reply as I turn back to the newspaper.

'Cos I'm asking who the fuck is sitting at *my* table reading *my* fucking paper.'

'Sorry, I didn't see a reserved sign, and this ain't exactly your personal copy of Country Life, is it?'

I heard one of the terriers making a move, and muscles say, 'Nah, he'll keep. Word has it you're a killer. Don't look much like a fuckin killer to me, laddie, more like a washed-up crippled rugby player that likes long hair and group bathing wi younger boys.'

'You afraid you're not good enough for my bath, are you? Feel like you're missing out? Well, you don't pack what it takes to get an invite, so if you don't mind, I want to finish reading this paper in peace and quiet.'

'Oh, tough guy, aren't ya, confident little fucker, c'mon let's see how tough ye are?' and at that, I could hear the wing start to go quiet and see prisoners back away from the area. I go to stand, and as I half turn, I get a full punch down the left-hand side of my head, and I drop to the table like a sack of potatoes. I can hear some laughing behind me and someone say, 'Go on, boss, hit him again,' and a strong hand grabbed my shoulder to try to turn me.

'What the *fuck* is going on here?' I hear Blade say to my right.

'Er, Blade, er nothing, minor disagreement wi Killer here, sat at mi table without an invite like.'

'Last I looked McDuggan, this table and that newspaper belonged to HM Prisons, but then again, if you think it's yours, you'd better come here and prove it to me,' and as I look up, Blade is pointing his thumb to his chest, 'Well are you going to come and convince me then?'

'Er, no, you're right, Blade. I was kinda calling it mine, ya know, no harm done, eh?'

'I'm not so sure about that scumbag. Look at my mate here. Looks like someone thought it was OK to hit one of my mates and not think about the consequences.'

'Er, as I said, Blade, a misunderstanding.'

'Then it looks like you need to apologise to my mate for your misunderstanding, doesn't it.'

'What? Nah, he's alright, big lad like him, he can take a tap like that, no problem.'

'Well,' Blade said menacingly, 'it looks like me and you are going to have a problem then, is that how you want it to be McDuggan?'

'Er, no Blade, no problem between us. Sorry.'

'Not me dickhead, him, my mate, you owe him the apology, not me,' and Blade was pointing directly at me, and I could see three guys moving slowly up behind Blade, as wingmen, squaring up to McDuggan and his two terriers.

'Yeh, course, no problem, my mistake. Here mate, sorry.'

'Properly dickhead, or I'm not going to be happy.'

At this, I stand up and turn to McDuggan, face to face eyeballing each other.

'Look, erm, I'm sorry, it's not my table or paper, didn't mean any harm or anything. I'm sorry mate. We square?'

There are some low whistles from the back walls. 'Pussy', someone shouted, another shouted, 'You're as hard as fucking cotton dickhead,' and I could see McDuggan getting wound up. He was losing face, and Blade was making him look bad to a captive audience.

'Now fuck off and find a toy to play with,' Blade instructed. McDuggan and his two terriers turned to walk away. I heard him mumble something like, 'I'll show ya some fuckin toys,' and a few of the watching prisoners started to laugh. Holding the left side of my head and tipping my head backwards, two thoughts ran through my mind; thank heavens for Blade turning up when he did, and I knew this wouldn't end here.

'Thank you, Blade, but I had it covered.'

'You did, did you? Funny place to start down on the floor,' he replied with a wry smile. 'Come on, let's take a walk.'

We slowly paced the floor and loops of the perimeter, passing open cell doors. Some prisoners nodded to Blade whilst others slowly took a step away.

Blade spoke quietly but with authority and experience, 'Look, be careful. They'll pick their moment; they'll probably go for me first, then come looking for you. Just stay sharp in case they do surprise me one day.'

'This place is hell on earth, isn't it?'

'No, believe me, I've seen worse than this; *this* is a playground.'

'Where, in a maximum security prison?' I ask.

'No overseas, with the Army. I've seen living hell on this planet, seen some real nasty shit in my time.

It's hard to believe what one man can do to another in the name of religion, politics, land, the price of oil. Big money makes more off wars and famine. So long as they can scrape the barrel to find the bottom feeders to do dirty horrible things, the corporates will make more money selling weapons, security training, medical supplies, and re-building programmes. This place is heaven to what I've seen.'

'Bloody hell, Blade, I didn't know. I knew you weren't like the others in here but hadn't realised you had been involved in some of that shit.'

'Don't get me wrong, I could easily have been like this scum. My old man saw it, and he got me in the Army at 17, got me away from the gangs, got me in a place that had discipline, order, structure, and regular meals, and, if you respected this and bought into the system and the bull then it provided opportunities to advance further, and that's what I did.'

'What? You got onto an apprenticeship, learn a trade?'

'Of sorts, I learned how to be covert, stealthy, and kill at distance or close up. I learned how to control aggression and channel it. I was taught manners and conduct, to act like a gentleman when required, and I could see a future then. It helped me rise through the ranks. Put those skills together, and you have a unique offering.'

'What kind of unique offering?'

'A well-dressed professional killer you could invite around for dinner,' Blade replied and laughed.

'So how did you end up in here?'

'Just one firefight too far ... I snapped.'

'How do you mean, snapped?'

'Who are you, my shrink?'

'Oh no, sorry, I don't mean to pry; I am genuinely interested. I had a misspent youth and got into some trouble myself, but then I found rugby. It helped me focus, helped me channel my thoughts to more positive things.'

'Fuck, wish my old man was more into rugby than the Army. He served with the Green Howards and always said it made a man of him,' and Blade smirked slightly. It felt like he'd had a hard upbringing.

'So what happened?'

'I'd been in some pretty bad firefights, some close-up kill stuff in different countries around the world, a lot of it black ops stuff, you know, we weren't their kind of thing.'

'What, you mean special forces?'

'Wouldn't say special, but certainly, we were a force to reckon with. Then one day it just happened, I don't know how, I cracked. PTSD, they said, eventually. I was standing up in a serious firefight shooting at defended positions, fucking stupid, death wish, my colleagues said. They said it put them at increased risk, as they wouldn't leave me behind if I got hit. Ended up with a medical discharge.'

'That doesn't get you in a place like this, Blade.'

'No, it doesn't. So then I'm out. After nearly 15 years of service, I know nothing else, no trade to speak of unless you call mercenary work or door security a trade, and I wouldn't have lasted long at that, given where my head was at during that time. The Army were good to me, got me squared away in the end, got me sorted in civvie street. I had some seed money saved, some spoils tucked away, and an inheritance from my old man passing, so I went into business with a former army mate. Gyms and personal training, and it went well. We grew the business, recruited ex-forces types, you know, PT

Instructors and the like, opened up gyms in four local towns, and things were sweet. We looked for further investment and found it to expand.'

'Sounds great. So what happened?'

'Four years into this, my partner disappeared. Cleared out all the bank accounts and ran off. Found out he was having an affair with the accountant, and they'd hatched this plan which left me holding the can. They'd leased everything to the hilt, mortgaged properties, loaned against assets, the full works, then just left. One point eight five million sterling went missing. The company went bang, and my signature was on everything; I trusted him. I couldn't prove I wasn't involved. Things got heavy, and when a couple of bailiffs came round to evict me from my house, well ... the red mist descended, and I put them in hospital and ended up in here.'

'Jeez, Blade, that's bad. What happened to your business partner?'

'Nothing. Well, not yet.'

'You know where he is?'

'Yep. He's in Thailand, and he doesn't know that I know. I will call in on him when I get out of here, you know, reminisce a little about the old days.'

'Don't, Blade, it's not worth it. It eats at you if you let it. You've got to let it go. You'll end up back inside or worse.'

'Easier said than done, mate, although I will let it go after we've had our little reunion. When you're in the Army, you put your life in your mate's hands and his in yours; you have each other's back. You trust each other without question. You'll die for each other without a second thought. He broke that trust, and there's a day of reckoning to be had for that.'

'Just let the authorities sort it out, Blade. Tell them where he is. Really, it's the best thing to do.'

'You think so? You have more faith in the system than I do. Don't rely on PC Plod to sort anything out, or most of their superior officers come to that. Plod are just like regular squaddies; they do a mundane job, go out, watch football, get pissed, get laid, repeat. Whereas officers are ambitious, they protect their surroundings and themselves, but more, they're pole climbers. They want promotion, they want advancement, and when that clashes with doing the right thing, they play the game. They'll bury the scandal, keep it from the press, squash anything that could embarrass them or the regiment or, in our world now, the police force is no different. For me, it's about doing the right thing. You have to stay true to yourself and stay honourable. Being in prison is not that different to being in a foxhole or observation post; you have time, time to think, and often you think about the past and believe me, if you've done the right thing, you can sleep or die with a clear conscience. I've been put in situations that needed extreme measures, and I did them. I needed to do what needed to be done. I'm not proud of those times, and maybe this is all part of my penance, my atonement.'

'No, come on, Blade, you can't liken your military service to this?'

'I can, and I do. We're on one journey through life, we can change direction, but the trail behind us remains; we can't change what's done.'

'Those shrinks did a good job on you.'

'Nah, I have my journey map going forward, and the first port of call after getting out of here is to see my *old mate* in Thailand. We have some things to sort out; then I can sleep soundly again at night.'

18

Samantha – London

Well, I feel like a celebrity. Whatever I need or want is mine. Not sure I entirely like this lifestyle, but having serious money really does open doors. It is good though, to be chauffeur driven around London, not having to worry about getting from A to B, having clothes selected by a personal stylist, and having someone else organise my diary, make reservations, make payments, and pack for travelling.

My lawyer, Richard, has always been there for me, and his advice to consider personal security at first, I thought it was a little over the top, but having been to so many 'A' list events over the last few months and seeing how some fans and the public react with the mood changing quickly, it did start me re-thinking this. Look at David; look at where a night out with the lads got him. Some wannabe ended up derailing his life. I am now worth a lot of money, and there will be some out there that think they are either entitled to some of it or some that think I'm not entitled to any of it. Hence, the meeting I've just had with a recommended private security firm.

The meeting went well, and I will get to meet my private security team in the next day or so. They are hired, Richard will contact my accountant and together, they'll address all the paperwork and payments. The first part of this service is a review of my potential security risks, properties, offices, and even friends. I never really thought I'd become one of those people considered as a potential kidnap candidate. I suppose there is villainy everywhere.

I arrive at the hotel, and the car approaches the front door. The doorman gently opens my door, and as I step out, he touches his top hat with a white-gloved hand and welcomes me back. As I turn to thank him, I see my bags are already being removed and taken inside.

The concierge greets me as I enter the reception area and informs me my room is prepared. His assistant beckons for me to follow him, and we enter a waiting elevator, whisked up to the 15th floor, and I'm in my suite within 3 minutes of pulling up at the front of the hotel.

My PA, Daryl, is working away on a laptop in the adjoining study/office, and I walk in and catch up on messages. Daryl then runs through the itinerary for this evening's events. Another formal dinner, this time, I'm the guest speaker at the Royal Institution for Medicine and Surgery, which is to include me being awarded an Honorary Fellowship for my work and achievements.

As I soak in my bath, I wonder if life could get any better ... hard work, dedication, and focus through all the events of the last few years, and now I really have 'arrived.'

I lie there wondering about Chrissy and the others. I've been a lousy friend really. As soon as all this took off, I kind of neglected them all, not through snobbery or elitism, just sheer time commitments, work, meetings, dinners, and travelling. I do miss them all. I wonder how Jess is doing and the kids. I reach for my iPhone and click into our App space. I scroll through the chat messages and realise there are none from Chrissy or Jess in the last year or so ... and those that are, are from them without me replying. I've missed the kid's birthdays and those of my friends. 'Am I lonely?' I ask myself. I've been too busy to be lonely; it just never really dawned on me. Going daily at a hundred miles per hour makes the days merge into one long stream of work or commitment. I am somewhat pampered these days though, with spa treatments, a private masseur, a PA, anything I want arrives. Money is no object, Richard looks after all my business affairs now, and I get what it's like to be "truly comfortable".

My stylist will be here in a minute; I'd best get a move on. Focus on this dinner and my speech.

19

David – HMP Witchull

We are out in the exercise yard, generally milling around, when Blade wanders over and indicates we should have a quiet word.

We walk off to the side of the yard and lean against the solid stone wall. One of the Prison Officers shouts something, and Blade simply stares at him, and the Officer turns away, looking to busy himself with someone else's exercise time.

'Dave, you're in here for killing a guy in a pub fight, right?'

'No, not really. Well yeah, I suppose. He died, but it wasn't meant to be like that; I didn't mean to kill him. It was a stupid thing, really.'

'Was the guy that died called Gary Roberts?'

'Yes ... Why are you asking? Have you been checking up on me again?'

'No. Hear me out. There's a smackhead over in B Wing been gobbing off a bit about how his mate got paid by some guy to set up a fight with another bloke in a pub in Bolton a few years back, a stranger, he says, never met him before but by all accounts, this stranger had it coming to him, was screwing this bloke's missus or something. This guy wanted to teach him a lesson. Anyway, the guy that paid his mate pointed out this stranger, and later that night, a fight broke out, but this smackhead's mate came off worse, didn't he? He died. Now this stranger is found guilty and doing time for manslaughter whilst the guy that paid for this walked away. Does any of this ring a bell with you, Dave? Does any of this sound familiar?'

'Er, well, yeah, some of it. Are you saying this smackhead named the dead man as Roberts and says it was all tied in with some payment?'

'Yep, looks that way. Do you think there's something in this? Sounded a lot like your situation this.'

'Fuck me, yeah, it does. Who is this smackhead? What's he in for?'

'They call him Weasel, scrawny little sod, always on the make. In here for seven years, robbed a pensioner at a cash machine, didn't realise there was a camera on the machine, knob head. Cash for his next hit, probably. Anyway, what do you reckon? Could this be useful intel?'

'Fuck Blade, if this is right and I could show it was all staged, that somebody tricked me into that bloody fight, it might .... does he know who paid Roberts?'

'Don't know. It's just wing chatter at the mo, I like to know what's generally going on, and it sounded familiar, and it was in Bolton. You know what it's like in here; everyone has a story. This could just be bullshit.'

'I need to speak with him. How do I do that if he's on B Wing?'

'You work in the kitchens, right?'

'Yeh.'

'OK, I'll pull some strings, got some favours owing to me, get him transferred to the kitchens. Give you a chance to talk, see if there's anything in this. But Dave, some of these smackheads make it up, do it because they think there's something in it for them.

Lying thieving bastards, they are, all of them, you can't trust 'em.'

'I know, I've come across a few in here. But he doesn't know that the poor bastard stranger is in *this* prison, though, does he? So what's in it for him?'

Good point,' Blade says, 'He could just be telling a story to get some attention. You know, read about it in a newspaper, well if he could read that is?'

'But this story? With me in here? If he knows something about that night, I need to know it too. See what you can do, Blade.'

'Sure, no worries. It'll take some time, but I'll get it done.'

'I'm not going anywhere soon. Cheers, Blade, I owe you one.'

20

David – HMP Witchull

Well, he should be here this morning. Blade said he'd got it all arranged.

The door into the kitchen opens, and three prisoners walk in. I've to look out for the scrawny one with a rough skull tattoo on his neck. These three don't fit the bill, and they are put to work straight away by the Officer in charge.

The door opens again, and two more prisoners walk in, a big fat guy and an Asian lad. Then this little runt comes in, almost hidden behind the two prisoners, gobbing off a bit at the Officer behind him. Oh yeah, he's my man; *Elvis has entered the building.*

Weasel is sent to the sinks and told to get on with washing the pans. I'm getting the serving hatch sorted, ready to dish up the usual morning gruel.

Now I know what Weasel looks like, I need to bide my time before I get an opportunity to talk with him.

The five-star morning breakfast service is complete by 8.00 am, and the hatches are closed. The usual clean up and mop up starts after the dining room is cleared of satisfied customers. It's at this point, as we are sorting out mop buckets by the sinks, that I get my chance to speak with Weasel.

'Weasel, is it?'

'Fuck off. Who wants to know?'

'Me, you fucking idiot. I think you have something that I want. Are you interested?'

'Well yeah. What's in it for me?'

'A reduced sentence, out of here a lot quicker than seven years. Sound good?'

'Is the Pope catholic? Hell yeah, I'm interested. Hang on; this is not some scam you're pulling. I'm no grass, you know. Won't do that. No way. I'm no snitch.'

'No, no scam. You have some information which could be useful to me and my conviction. I heard you have a story to tell about a pub fight in Bolton a few years back; your mate died. That about right?'

'Yeh might be.'

'Well, the story goes, you say it was all some kind of a set-up. Your mate was paid by someone to hit a guy in the pub. Still, sound right?'

'Yeah, well, what of it?'

'Well, that guy hit your mate back, and he died, didn't he?'

'Yeah, Gazza was a bit of a dick though. Anyone could see that guy was fucking fit and could look after himself, and he had a bunch of meaty mates with him, too, fuck, they looked like paras on a piss-up.'

This guy was definitely there. 'Weasel, was your mate called Gary Stephen Roberts?'

'Yeh, I don't know about the Stephen bit, but yeh, Gary Roberts, Gazza.'

I've clearly got his interest now; he's stopped fidgeting and listening carefully.

'How do you know your mate got paid to start that fight?'

'He told me before it all kicked off. We never go in that shithole of a pub, lager's shite and too pricey.'

'OK then, if that's right, how much was Gazza paid?'

Weasel's fidgeting and sniffing returned. He was weaving slightly from one foot to the other, almost like he could smell opportunity here for a deal.

'Fuck you, no more. I'm not stupid, you know. Sounds like this is worth something to you.'

'It is, I was the guy that killed your mate, or so they say.'

At that, Weasel dropped the mop bucket he was holding, turned and looked at me, slowly moving his head side to side, moving forward and backwards as though trying to get me more into focus. 'Nah, you're not him.'

'Picture me without the beard and long hair.'

He continued to look at me, and then suddenly, like one of those legendary light bulb moments, he realised he was looking straight into the eyes of a killer, and he started to get nervous.

'Weasel, don't fuck with me, I am a different man after being in here for this long, and I've learned some new tricks. Look, if the information you have is good, we can use this to get you maybe a reduced sentence if you make a formal statement, you know, good behaviour, helping solve another crime and all that. It might even get you out altogether if it's used.'

'Look, OK, don't get mad, but no dickhead copper is going to believe a junkie like me anyway, so it's pointless.'

'Leave that to me. I'll get in touch with my solicitor, and we'll see what we can do. I've got some connections in here, and I'm sure a quiet word with them will keep you safe and maybe get you a few perks and extra privileges. I got you transferred to the kitchen, didn't I? You OK with that? You going to help me then?

'Yeh man, whatever. Look, there was more than me there that night, so there will be others that can back up my story, for the right price that is.'

'OK, I'll be square with you here. We can't talk about price and payments, we have to stop talking about money, or it'll just look like I just bought you and your mates to tell a story to get me out of here. Keep it buttoned up for now, don't tell anyone about this, and I'll be in touch soon.'

'Gazza's girlfriend was in on this too; she knew what was going down that night. They'd planned a big holiday or something with the money, go to an island somewhere like Spain, y'know,' he sniffed.

'So why didn't you all say something at the time when the police were investigating this?'

'Because you killed our mate, and we thought nowt would come of putting Gazza down as the bad guy. He didn't get paid in full anyway 'cos you killed him before he collected.'

'How do you know that?'

'Well, no wedge of cash was found on him was there unless the cops lifted it first,' he sniffed and grimaced.

'Right. Well, keep out of trouble. Don't say anything to anyone until we speak again. You got that?'

'Yeah'

'I mean it. I'll be in touch soon.'

I then picked up the mop and bucket and went back to cleaning the dining room floor. Life has to carry on as normal for the time being until I can get in touch with my solicitor and get things rolling.

21

Samantha – Queensland, New South Wales

As the AS365 Dauphin helicopter takes off from Cairns airport, I sit back and take in the view. Thank heavens the aircon is working. We fly out over the coastline away from the airport towards the ocean and then head north along the coast, and I think of my early days out this way. Nearly 25 years have passed since my parents packed up home, and we moved over to the UK. I always wondered why Dad took that job in the UK; I guess he had his reasons. This is paradise right here, in my opinion.

The pilot interrupts over the headphones, 'Pardon Ms Walsh. We will be landing at the villa in about twenty minutes. Would you like me to give you the scenic tour?'

'Yes, please, Ben, I would like that.'

As I look at Ben in the pilot's seat, I see the profile, rugged features of a man who looks after himself. His natural skin colour and aviator shades help portray that air of confidence and calmness. He banks the helicopter slightly, and we fly along the coastline a little further. The beaches, crystal waters, and remoteness all bring a feeling of peace and calm to me. Reefs pass by beneath us at speed and seem endless.

That's kind of how it all began. Down there is home to the Reef Stonefish, Synanceia Verrucosa, the most venomous fish in the world. As a child, we were warned to be aware of it, and it just created in me a fascination of how something in such a beautiful place can be so deadly. Then as you grow, you realise this is just normal for Australia.

After seeing Reef Fish in an aquarium in the UK brought back that fascination which led me to study toxicology and molecular medicine at university and specialise in venomous interactions with human biology. I believed such toxins, whilst debilitating or fatal, could also harness key proteins that could be manipulated for benefit. I became so focused on this I couldn't continue to work in a commercial laboratory after I graduated, and my routes to further research study became limited, so I broke away from more traditional routes to dedicate my time to this specific area of research and development. David had a successful career with an international bank in the city and could help fund and raise further funds for my work. A chance reading of a medical paper on the progression of cancerous cells made me align the two fields, and I became locked on this path like a missile to its target. The rest is history. I do owe a lot to David, the original David, that is, the one I fell in love with.

'We will arrive at the villa in a few minutes, Ms Walsh.'

'Thank you, Ben. Ben, do you have to rush back to Cairns?'

'No, Ms Walsh, no further bookings for today. Is there somewhere else you would like to go?'

'Yes, Ben, there is. I'll let you know when we land.'

We spent the afternoon together at the villa. Being naked on your own sun terrace, swimming in your private pool and making love wherever and whenever you like is a fabulous way to de-stress. In fairness, Ben was a little nervous at first, I don't suppose this happens too often to him, but I just craved some male company without any strings.

We spent the evening sipping chilled sparkling wine, eating local seafood and being close under the stars beside the pool. I slipped off to bed just short of midnight, and Ben followed shortly after. We didn't sleep for at least another hour.

Just before 7.00 am, I heard the Dauphin starting up out on the lawn. Ben was leaving early, kind of him not to wake me, but there is no quiet way of leaving by helicopter. I walk out onto the terrace, and he sees me wearing only a light cotton blouse, and he waves gently. As the helicopter lifts off, Ben turns it towards me and dips the front of the machine as though bowing before peeling away over the beach and off down the coast back towards Cairns.

As the noise of the helicopter fades to nothing, it's replaced by the gentle background of bird song and ocean; this is so peaceful.

I return to my bed, close my eyes, savouring the night before, and fall asleep. My private mobile ringing shatters the peace, and looking at the screen, it's Daryl. It must be important he knows it's early here, and I am trying to have some quality time for me.

'What is it, Daryl? I hope it's important.'

'Apologies Samantha. Richard Stanley wishes to speak with you urgently. He didn't say what it concerned, but he did say it was important and urgent that you speak with him.'

'Alright. I'll just grab a shower and phone him back. What time is it there in the UK?'

'It's just after eleven pm.'

'That's a bit late for Richard; it must be important; I'll phone him now. Thank you, Daryl,' and I hang up.

I scroll through favourites and hit the speed dial number, 'Richard, it's Sam. I'm at the villa in Queensland at the moment. Is there something wrong? Shouldn't you be asleep now?'

'Ah yes, Samantha, no, I'm fine, I've been out with colleagues this evening at a private dinner, and I picked up some news regarding your former husband, David Alexander. Apologies, yes, I know you are at the villa and figured it was daylight for you now, so I thought it best to let you know before you find out from others. It seems his lawyers have submitted papers requesting a review for appeal following new information coming to light relating to the incident that night when Gary Roberts died, new information that potentially may result in David's case being reviewed; it could even become a miscarriage of justice.'

'What? What new information? The police investigated everything thoroughly, and there were witnesses to David throwing the punch that floored Roberts, causing him to hit his head. There was clear CCTV in the pub that night which showed David hitting him and Roberts striking his head; even David himself admitted hitting him.'

'I know Samantha, I know. But apparently, this new information presents a different perspective on the event. David's solicitor is indicating that some legal steps are about to be taken, which may lead to revisiting David's conviction. I don't know what this information is yet, as we have no right to request it following your divorce, but it will undoubtedly become public record shortly. I thought you should know in case you wanted to get your PR team geared up.'

'Thank you, Richard. Please keep me informed as things develop. I'm at the villa trying to catch a few days in the sun and have some quiet time before flying to the Philippines to open the new laboratory and the second manufacturing plant. If you cannot get a hold of me, don't hesitate to get in touch with Daryl, my PA, he'll get a message to me.'

'Will do Samanatha. I'm not sure what could possibly cause David's conviction to be reviewed, but I will keep you abreast of developments. Safe journey, enjoy the opening ceremonies, goodbye for now,' and Richard kills the call.

What could this new information possibly be, especially after all this time? One thing is for sure, if David is released from prison early, my mind is clear, I don't want anything further to do with him.

It seems I'm never far from some controversy or an event trying to pull me down.

This latest development has caused my relaxation time to be lost; my brain is spinning with the news. I take a shower, and I decide to cut this break short while drying. I wander out onto the patio area, and the sun is already pleasantly warming me. I call Daryl back, and he answers in two rings.

'Daryl, a slight change of plans. Please arrange for my jet to be ready to leave Cairns at 4.00 pm today, flight plan to Manila. Can you also speak with the helicopter charter company at Cairns and ask them to send their pilot back for me at three o'clock this afternoon?'

'Yes, Samantha, no problem. Shall I also bring your reservation at the Grand Hyatt forward to this evening?'

'Yes, please, Daryl, thank you.'

'Any other arrangements you wish me to take care of?'

'No, that's all, Daryl, thank you,' I close the call. Then, I remembered what time it is back in the UK and forgot to respect this for Daryl. He is good at his job though, and I make a mental note to arrange a nice bonus for him.

I dress in light clothes, pick up sunglasses and wander back out onto the patio. Fiona has set breakfast for me at the table, and to the side are several of today's newspapers to flick through. Leaving the papers untouched, I take in the view, the air, the calmness.

After breakfast, I start to feel a little at a loose end; it's the calm; nothing is happening. I am so used to the fast life and jumping between meetings, calls, and travelling that I'm feeling a little anxious about this void. It's like I've forgotten how to unwind, how to relax. Last night was great, but I'm alone now. I pick up one of the newspapers and begin flicking through the pages, but after a few minutes, I realise this isn't salving my agitation, and I take a walk around the gardens. This only has me thinking about what this new information could be. How could it possibly change David's sentence or even conviction? On returning to the house, I give in, go to my bedroom and start to pack a few things ready for this afternoon, open my laptop, and catch up with emails.

Damn you, David, just when I thought this was all behind me.

22

David – HMP Witchull

Over the following weeks and exchanges with my solicitor, we arranged this meeting in one of the prison interview rooms. I have been left alone with my solicitor so we can discuss the legal steps we'll need to take.

'Good morning, David, how are you? Bearing up well?'

'Morning Malcolm, so, what do you think? I've been banged up now for the best part of four years for possibly something that was set up by others. I want to know what happened and who was behind this whole thing. Has Weasel given you a written statement yet?'

'Weasel, er... Mr ... Johnson, no, not yet, but he's prepared to make a formal statement, naturally for some assurances, and he would be prepared to identify other persons who may testify to the events that led up to the fight that night. Whether or not these others will make a statement is another matter. As it is, given the time involved, and that you've already had an appeal turned down, we contacted the Criminal Cases Review Commission and submitted an application. After an initial review, the CCRC have decided to look further into this and assigned a Case Review Manager as they need to investigate further, collect records and further statements. Naturally, the police will be contacted as they'll need to review the interview and records to see if the Police considered any of this during their investigation or if they discarded any material that could have opened up this line of enquiry.'

'How long is all this likely to take?'

'It won't be quick. Your case isn't presented to the Court of Appeal yet; the CCRC process is required to see if you have new grounds for a further appeal. It could take many weeks, a couple, or three months maybe, possibly longer.'

I lower my head and quietly shake it from side to side. After a minute or so, I look up at Malcolm, 'Is anything quick in the legal world? No, don't bother to answer that. We need to get Weasel's statement quickly as this isn't a holiday park in here, and if he says the wrong thing to the wrong person, he could easily find himself at the foot of some stairs with a couple of stab wounds. You risk getting shanked in here for just looking at someone the wrong way.'

'I know, I'm sorry. As I mentioned, we have been in touch with Mr Johnson, and he will make a statement. The CCRC need it as a part of the investigation process. But you do have to consider that Gary Roberts died as a result of that altercation, and you did hit him, causing the head injury leading to his death. So, whilst there may be some mitigating argument relating to the sentencing, it may not relieve you of the conviction, and that is assuming the CCRC decision committee decide to send your case for an appeal.'

'Yeh, I get that all that, slowly, slowly. But even if the sentence can be reduced, then maybe I can get out of here sooner rather than later, maybe time served, you know? After all, I wasn't out looking for a fight, and it's clear to me now that someone else had reason to arrange all of this. If it weren't for Roberts provoking me that night in the way he did, I wouldn't have hit him, I know that.'

'Yes, well, we must obtain the right to be heard at appeal first, and then we take it from there. Have you found out anything further that may help?'

'Nothing more than the names of the others with Weasel and Roberts that night; I've not much more to go on. But one thing is for sure, if this was all staged, it must have something to do with the woman I was seeing at the time, you know, the affair? It may have been her partner that organised all of this, Weasel kind of suggested there was a reason for me to get a kicking that night. Any luck finding out who her partner is?'

'No, not yet, but we do have someone looking into this. We are struggling to find her at the moment.

Since that blackmail attempt, she seems to have gone to ground. Do you have any idea where she might be?'

'No. I've already given you the list of places we met up, all hotels, and I know it's pointless checking out the hotels we met in; they were just pay-on-arrival kind of places or the hotels I stayed at when *away on business*. I don't recall her talking about friends or family; really it was just about the sex for me.'

'Erm, ok, well, er, we'll keep looking. Did she mention her partner's name or a nickname? Anything?'

'No, not that I can recall. I know she was a little wary of him; he was a bit of an enforcer or something, not a good guy for sure; that's why we met up in different hotels. He paid for her apartment, so we never met there; too risky, she said.'

'It does all help to paint the picture that this chap could have been behind paying Roberts to teach you a lesson, and he wouldn't want the fight to connect back to him.'

'And there's my concern, he could get to the other witnesses or even Weasel in here if he is that inclined and has contacts. If I remember anything more, I'll let you know. So, we're now in the hands of the great British legal system again, are we?'

'Best legal system in the world, David, believe me. I know it may not seem like that to you, but the legal system will address any miscarriage openly and fully; that is the safety net we all must believe in and rely upon.'

'Yeah, but it still got me locked up, and I feel powerless to get to the bottom of all this from in here.'

'Be patient, David; let the process run its course. Being in here did actually get you this lead, so there is a bittersweet twist to all of this.'

'That is a free man's way of looking at it, I suppose. What more can you tell me about Samantha, my ex? Any update?'

'Yes, she is quite the role model now, famous naturally, successful, a very well-connected influential lady by all accounts. She is currently in New Zealand, attending a global medical conference. Her discovery ... er,' flicking through some papers, 'yes, ... OxyRuco, is so successful that it's generating all kinds of potential offshoots and investment. I suspect Ms Walsh will be on the New Year Honours list this year or next and probably in line for a Nobel Prize in medicine or something. Remarkable, really.'

'I know how differently our destinies turned out to be. Still, she did it, and she said she would. I always thought it was just one of those discoveries that would take a lifetime to find, if ever. I just wanted to live the high life while the money was there. Being locked up in here, twenty-four-seven, does give you plenty of time to think.'

23

David – HMP Witchull

After standing in line for my turn to make a call, I lift the receiver and connect with my solicitor.

'David, good news. Leave to appeal has been granted. The new evidence and investigation by the CCRC have been reviewed by the Appeal Court and there are grounds to re-consider your conviction. It may have the potential to overturn your conviction if pre-planned malicious intent by others can be demonstrated. The CCRC believe there is sufficient substantive evidence to support this position and they have supporting opinion of an eminent expert witness regarding the injuries Roberts sustained.'

'That's great, Malcolm. Any idea when this will go to court?'

'We're not sure. The Court of Appeal aims to address matters like these without undue delay, especially if there is potential of a miscarriage of justice. We await confirmation of a date and venue.'

'Do I need to appoint another barrister now?'

'As I mentioned some time ago, it would be preferable to appoint a barrister. If we did, you would be responsible for their costs. As you indicated earlier that you may consider this, we have had preliminary discussions with clerks at several chambers specialising in this type of case. However, to reiterate my earlier advice, the matter of cost needs to be considered if you want this further legal representation.'

'That'll only be a problem if I lose, right?'

'Well, yes and no. There are no costs for you with regards the CCRC, however appointing personal legal support will remain a personal cost for you regardless of the outcome subject to what costs could be recoverable if you had a favourable result. If you do appoint a barrister, they do like to know they will be paid regardless of the outcome, and regularly paid as time passes. If I recall, you do have some funds available from your divorce settlement?'

'Yes, I do, and I'm sure my father will help if needed. Pick the best barrister available; I'm not worried about costs anymore. Anyway, I'm confident I'll get a favourable result.'

'If you have your conviction quashed, there may also be entitlement to compensation due to you, but we'll cross that bridge at that time.'

'OK, appoint a barrister, please. How is the search going for Monica and her partner? Any luck finding them?'

'No. Unless we find her, we won't find him; we don't know who he is until we do. There are still no leads to either of them. To be honest, it's like she has disappeared. The police are also looking into this now.'

'Do you honestly think the police will push this as a priority? After all, they got a conviction and now won't want to look bad?'

'I'm sure they'll do their best. They will have to testify in front of the Appeal Court and will not want to feel the wrath of the Appeal judges. This can certainly be career-limiting these days.'

'Thank you, Malcolm', and I hang up the phone. The general drone of the wing reminds me of where I am and where I do not want to be.

As I turn, Blade is standing looking at me, 'Someone got to Weasel. He's in a bad way. Cut him up this morning in the showers; he's on his way to the hospital. Touch and go, they say.'

'Fuck me! What next?' I shout out, and everything goes quiet.

Blade, remaining controlled, quietly says, 'He's made his statement right; it's with the lawyers. It should still stand.'

'If he doesn't pull through, he can't testify, he won't be heard and challenged. He'll just be some other smackhead telling a tale.'

'You have the other statements as well, you know, from his mates. Anyway, it's not over yet; you're still in the fight.' Blade puts his arm around my shoulder and pulls me in tight.

'Fuck it, Blade. I really must have pissed off my guardian angel. I just want a decent break so I can try to get my life back together, you know.'

'I know, mate, I know,' and he pulled me in again.

'Do you think Weasel getting shanked has anything to do with my Appeal?'

Blade removed his vice-like grip on me and we walk away from the phones. 'I don't think so. It would be a stupid move to do this so late on, his statement is made, and the others have made their statements. Any change now would indicate that there is a conspiracy against you and reinforce your argument.'

'I suppose so, and I get that, but apparently, Monica's boyfriend is well connected; it just makes me think that's all.'

'Well, if he could get to Weasel, then why not just get to you?' Blade reasons sensibly.

'I don't know, having you watch my back in here possibly?'

'Nah, I'm good, but I'm not that good,' as Blade put his arm around my shoulders again, 'C'mon, let's see what we can find out about Weasel.'

24

David – Court of Appeal, London

The wait was beginning to become unbearable, worse than counting down to the end of the prison sentence itself. As the prison van pulled up to the vehicle gates of the court, I could see through the slot window that a small crowd had gathered, a couple of banners with the crudely painted word "Guilty" on them, the holders shouting something I couldn't pick up; I guess they are from Roberts' family. There are a couple of TV cameras and reporters talking into fluffy microphones and a number of the usual paparazzi jackals with cameras trying to get a shot of me for the evening papers or net news.

I could see a couple of police officers between the van and the crowd, not very convincing crowd control if needed.

The barrier raised, and the driver took us inside to the rear yard and stopped the engine. The officer in the van opened the internal cell door and checked my handcuffs, and then told me to stand and walk towards the rear door of the van. As I got to the van doorway, I could see over the officers at the foot of the small steps to the jeering crowd by the barrier.

'C'mon, Alexander, let's be having you. Big day today.'

'Yep, I hope so. Hope I'm on the evening news for the right reason tonight.'

'We'll see, c'mon.'

We walk into the court building by a security door at the rear of the court, and straight away, it looks like I'm back in Witchull, the same old depressing paint job, scuffed walls, even the aroma is the same. I'd better get a result today; not sure how much more of this I can take.

I'm shown into a secure waiting room where my solicitor and barrister await me.

'Morning, David. Ready for your big day?' asks my barrister as we shake hands, wearing his black gown and wig on the tabletop next to a bundle of papers.

'Yes. Good morning. I am. Any idea how things are looking?'

'Looking quite good, actually. The police submitted their full investigation findings to the CCRC and the Crown Prosecution Service. We've seen these findings, and they do seem to corroborate the facts as we describe in the pleadings. All the witnesses are present here today to give their version of events, including Mr Johnson, who miraculously has made a remarkable recovery following the attempt on his life. It appears that Mr Roberts' girlfriend has confirmed he received £250 cash as an initial down payment and Roberts was expecting to collect a further £750 after he had attacked you up in the pub.'

'That's even better for me then, isn't it?' I ask, trying to keep my excitement checked so I don't give any wrong impression.

My solicitor took the opportunity to answer, 'Yes, it is. The CCRC position, which is ours, is that this was all orchestrated by a third party, and you were unwittingly pulled into the altercation by provocation initiated by Roberts. If nothing else, this should have your sentence revisited and reduced as mitigating circumstances that had not previously been available to the court. As we've mentioned previously, there is the potential to have your conviction overturned.'

'That's great, but I'm not counting my chickens just yet; I've been through the legal system before and that didn't turn out well for me.'

'You have to remain confident, David,' my barrister instilled, 'look confident, and when asked questions, answer clearly and precisely as possible, try not to wander off with your responses.'

Easier said than done, but I know I have to play to the legal system to increase my chances of a good outcome. 'But all this information and evidence was available before; it's just that no one bothered looking for it. All the Roberts family wanted was for me to be behind bars, the police simply thought they had their man, and the Crown were on a mission to make examples of loutish behaviour fuelled by alcohol. I was in the crosshairs to be made an example of, and I really didn't stand a chance.'

'Well, you'll need to park that, David; remember, you must stay calm in court. We don't anticipate there being a reason for you to speak much today other than recount the events and possibly indicate how you came across this new information. If asked any questions, it'll be on things you are already comfortable with, as this is a review of the evidence and chance for the appeal court to examine the witnesses in person,' my barrister says as he lifts his wig and papers. 'We need to go through now David, you will be called shortly, and the court officers will escort you in.'

'Um, OK. Thank you. Really, I mean it; thank you for taking this up and fighting for me.'

As my solicitor headed for the door, he looked back over his shoulder and simply said, 'It's what we do David. See you in there.'

My barrister turned back and looked at me, portraying an air of calmness and confidence, 'We have a good argument, David. The pleadings, the statements, the CRC investigation, and the latest police reports are all encouraging and align in our favour. The court is obliged to consider this new evidence that wasn't available at the time of your trial. There is also the suggestion the original Judge, Mr Justice Golley, may have been influenced or distracted by the Crown Prosecution Service and their agenda, and a drive to make an example of you.'

'Will the original Judge be here today?'

'No. This is the Court of Appeal; he won't be present. Now let us speak on your behalf and get the outcome we believe you are entitled to,' as he walked through the door held open by Malcolm, he nodded to Malcolm and said quietly to Malcolm that I could just hear, *"fiat Justitia ruat caelum"*.

And instinctively, I reply, 'I agree with you.'

My barrister stopped, looked again at me, smiled, nodded in acknowledgement, and then continued on his way.

25

David – Court of Appeal, London

'It is the unanimous finding of this Court of Appeal that the conviction is found to be on unsafe grounds. The new evidence indicates the appellant, Mr Alexander, had been coerced into a reaction that was planned by others to elicit a reaction from him and that the appellant's actions were those of a person defending themselves using reasonable force. It is regrettable that Mr Roberts died as a result of the actions that he now clearly had instigated, and we find there was no malice aforethought on the appellant's part. We have the authority to reduce the sentence imposed, and we have considered this at length. We also have the authority to overturn the verdict decided by the jury. In this instance, we consider that had the jury known these extenuating circumstances; we believe they would have found the appellant not guilty of the charge against him. With that, it is the unanimous finding of this court that the appellant's conviction be overturned, that the appellant be released from His Majesty's prison and that Mr Alexander be a free man.'

And with that, I dropped back into my chair. I can't believe it; I'm free. I put my hands up to my face and started to cry; the relief was overpowering.

'Mr Alexander, your record will show that this court finds that a miscarriage of justice has occurred and that you are to be exonerated of all charges. The Crown extends their sincerest apologies to you, Mr

Alexander. Congratulations, Mr Alexander, you are free to leave this court.'

My solicitor reached over to me and grabbed my hand, 'Well done David, well done.' My barrister looked up from his table and gently nodded to me with a content look, then turned to the CPS barrister, and they shook hands. It felt like they were acknowledging a good round of golf or something. My solicitor noticed this, 'Don't worry about that, David, it's merely a professional courtesy. Let's get you out of here; I'm sure you'll want a celebratory drink.'

26

Samantha – Los Angeles, California

My driver cuts through traffic on the 110 freeway as we leave downtown Los Angeles. The meeting was good, and constructive, although a little lawyer heavy. We are on the brink of the biggest pharma licencing deal ever, and if all goes well, the income from this deal alone will easily fund all the work I want to do in the developing world; I have so many plans to help others.

I open the drinks cabinet, pull out a chilled still water, and take a sip. I open my bag and reach for my phone, flick it off airplane mode, and it's not long before the messages start to ping in, along with missed calls from Daryl and Chrissy. Chrissy, why would she call me? Of course, I'd forgotten it was David's appeal outcome today. I'd asked Richard to have one of his team attend so that I could prepare for the PR frenzy that would follow; regardless of the outcome, I'm prime-time news stock these days. Richard was still back at the downtown offices going through the finer details of the licencing agreement with their lawyers and probably hadn't phoned the office himself.

I speed-dial Daryl. 'What is it, Daryl, the appeal court result?'

'Yes, Samantha. Mr Alexander's conviction has been overturned; he is a free man. It's all over the evening news here in the UK. Has it hit there yet?'

'Not that I'm aware, I'll just check the internet,' and sure enough, it was picking up speed here too.

'Thank you for letting me know Daryl. Please call Beverley at West & Samson; she will need to get in front of the spin on this and organise some press releases.'

'Already on that, Samantha. I'm unsure if Richard knows yet, is he with you?'

'No, I left Richard downtown going through the contracts. Have any of the board members been in touch?'

'A couple, the usual suspects. I told them you were tied up in a confidential meeting in LA and could not be interrupted. They will be looking for a statement from you.'

'To be honest, Daryl, it has nothing to do with them, the board, or the shareholders. It all happened way back before we, I, discovered the protein matrix and created OxyRuco, long before it concerned any of them. I had already cleaned up the mess beforehand, and David is no longer part of the company; the divorce solidified our personal position. Sorry Daryl, you don't need to hear me sounding off. Please get a hold of Richard and ask him to phone me. I suspect my ex will be in contact soon looking for a slice of the cake.'

I cancelled the call and threw my head back. David will be on a mission now, I know it. He will try whatever he can to get a slice of the company or a decent payday, he was always competitive, and that trait will have him try for something, I'm sure. He only has himself to blame; that affair was the last straw for me; I couldn't trust him again after that. I'm sure Richard and his team will have my back here; I must stay focused on these deals. I look down at the drink cabinet and say to myself, 'What the heck, champagne it is', and with that, I select a bottle of Armand de Brignac from the collection of four champagnes available and open the bottle.

I had just released the cork from the bottle when my phone rang. 'Richard, thank you for calling so quickly. You've heard I take it?'

'Yes, Samantha, Daryl mentioned the news, and I've just spoken with my associate in the UK. The Court of Appeal overturned David's conviction, and he has already been released. Do you want me to reach out to him first or wait for him to contact you?'

'We'll wait. I don't want to be seen as eager to do a deal just yet.'

'You mean *you are* considering something?'

'I'm not sure. Honestly, I didn't think he would be released from prison on a shorter sentence, let alone have his conviction overturned. But one thing is for sure, he will be in touch at some point; I know him; he will.'

'I will obtain the Court of Appeal decision; see what brought this about.'

'Thank you, Richard. How is it going back there, is all the paperwork completed?'

'Yes, more or less. A late tax query came up, and we're working it through now. Nothing for you to worry about.'

'I don't know what I'd do without you, Richard. Thank you.'

I fill my glass, and as I sip the champagne, my mind wanders back to those University days. We were all great friends, no real worries, studying hard and partying even harder. I do miss those days; they were simple, easy, fun. David was the boy of the moment, full of life, charming, and attentive; you really did feel like the only girl in the room when he was with you. I know Chrissy showed quite a bit of interest in David too, but as soon as she realised I was smitten, Chrissy made sure the path was cleared of all competition. I miss Chrissy, wild and vivacious Chrissy. And Jess, so supportive and caring, polar opposites in some ways ... I ought to take some time to get back in touch with them both.

27

David – Court of Appeal London

Along with about three or four TV crews, my Dad was waiting outside the court building. He has always stood by me, never doubted my innocence, and had a faith only a father can have in their son that all will come good in the end. We embrace to the sounds of camera clicks and reporters baying for a comment or statement.

'Good to see you, Davey Boy. Let's get you away from all this,' he said, nodding his head to his right in the general direction of the news crews and photographers.

'Thanks, Dad, thanks for being here and for being there for me when others weren't.' We hug to the sound of clicking cameras.

'It's their loss; you never did this; I've always known that. It's times like these when true friends show their colours. Come on, let's get in a cab and leave these hyenas.'

I pull back from my dad slightly and look at him squarely, 'I just want to say something first, Dad, give me a minute; that, OK?'

'Are you sure, Davey, whatever you say will be all over the TV and internet in no time?'

'Yes, I have a stage and I want to be heard now,' and I turn towards the pack, who step up a level when they realise I want to say something.

'David. David. You're a free man. What have you got to say?'

'What's the first thing you're going to do, David?'

'David. Are you suing for compensation?'

'Ladies and gentlemen, I have a few words; please bear with me. Firstly, I want to thank my legal team for this outcome,' and I turn to Malcolm and my barrister, and we shake hands. I turn back to the cameras, 'The English legal system has its faults and its strengths; however, I was told not long ago that it is the best legal system in the world. Nearly five years ago, I would not have thought that,' to a little chuckle from the pack, 'but today, you can see it does correct the mistakes it makes. I will consider my position regarding wrongful conviction and discuss that with my lawyers. In the meantime, I would ask for a little space and privacy so that I can spend some time with my father, family and friends; we have much to catch up on. Thank you.'

As I turn to look at Dad, another question was thrown at me.

'Will you be looking to reconcile with your former wife and share in the success story of OxyRuco?'

That threw me a little. I look at my dad; he is ever so slowly shaking his head from side to side. Probably good advice, Dad, but ...

I turn back to the pack, 'That is a good question. If the events of that night hadn't occurred, I certainly wouldn't be on this pavement with you good people this morning for sure. Samantha Walsh has achieved her goals and done great things for medical advancement; I am immensely proud of her. I wish her all the very best, but as time and tide wait for no man, we are in different places now, and we have different paths to follow now. Thank you.'

'David, so you're happy to let things go. You're not interested in the success that you've been robbed of?'

'I had my faults back then, which everyone knows about now. Samantha did what Samantha thought was right at the time, and that's that. I will not hold that against her. Thank you.'

'David. David.'

'No, thank you. I have nothing further to say.'

Dad tries to hail a black cab as we walk away from the Court, trailed by a couple of the more carrion types.

'Ignore them, Davey; it's not worth it. They're just baiting you to get the next headline.'

'I know, but sometimes these people just really piss me off. Sorry, Dad.'

'What are you sorry for? Carrying the frustration or the swearing?'

'Both, I think, definitely the latter. His Majesty's Prison does bring out the best and worst in people.'

'No bother, come on. We'll lose this lot. I have a decent lunch planned up north, and a couple of people want to say hello.'

'Erm, not today, Dad, if you don't mind. Lunch with you will be fine, but I'm not in the mood for small talk and belated reunions just yet with others. I just want a nice pint of real ale, some good food and to sit quietly with you if that's alright?'

'Sure. Not a problem. But something tells me I might need to arrange a taxi later.'

'Yep, I know what you're like when you get a taste for the ale Dad,' and chuckle.

'I've missed this Davey. Although I bet, I'm paying again though?' Dad sighs.

'Yep, my earnings for the last three years have not exactly been in the higher tax bracket,' and we both laugh.

Dad manages to attract the attention of a black cab, and in no time, we are at Euston Train Station.

We board the 11.10 at Euston and pull into Manchester Piccadilly two hours and fourteen minutes later. In the open carriage, our talk on travelling back north was of rugby, old friends, family events, the Appeal and some of prison, but not the real scary stuff; nothing that would upset Dad.

Dad blew the expense and had parked his car at the train station's multi-storey car park, and we were soon on our way back towards Bolton.

We stop for fuel on the A6, which I think is Dad's way of slipping away to make a call to let others know not to turn up. When Dad gets back behind the wheel and pulls away from the forecourt, it feels like the right time to ask him.

'Have you heard from Samantha? Has she been in touch with anyone?'

'No, not that I'm aware of,' he replies, remaining focused on the road ahead.

'Umm, I thought you had a pretty good relationship with each other, Dad.'

'We did, but when all this happened, it became strained, and then when your affairs came to light, she just broke all contact. I did try to keep in touch with Samantha because I thought she would welcome the support; after all, you're not me, you know *that cool calming influence* I bring and all that, but she never returned my calls. Just cut loose and that was that. I was amazed at how quickly things changed between us.'

'I kind of know that feeling, although mine was self-imposed; it's not right she cut you off like that.'

'Well, I'm a realist; it would have just petered out anyway, you know, after the divorce and all. It is what it is, I suppose.'

'Yep,' I say with a deep sigh, looking out the passenger window over the fields and hedgerows.

Turning off the A6, Dad continued to drive along the country lane, and I could sense he was holding something back. After a few minutes, I ask, 'Were you really that close?'

'I thought so. Loved her to bits. I could see she was besotted with you even though you couldn't.'

'No, I could, it was just that .. er .. well .. you know, I thought I could still be ... *me*.'

'That was the problem. You needed to grow up and see what was right in front of you. But no, your trousers got the better of your cap, and you didn't think twice.'

'I know, Dad, the biggest mistake of my life, as it turns out. Runs a close second to knocking down Roberts.'

'Where are the police at finding out who paid Roberts? Have they turned up anything new?'

'No, they keep saying the trail is cold. It was a few years ago now, cash was involved and the only person who knew the payer is still dead,' I reply with a tinge of irony in my voice.

'There must be something; something in Roberts' past or digital trail, you know, text messages, emails or something.'

It is beginning to sound like Dad has been spending his time reading crime novels or watching CSI on TV. 'Police say not, nothing there. To be honest, I'm surprised I was let out, and my conviction squashed based on the statements of his former colleagues.'

'Yeah. Anyhow, the Appeal Court believed them, the sentencing was poor, and the police didn't investigate wider; the rest is now history. So, what do you want to do next?'

'After lunch, you mean or life in general?'

'Both, but yeah, life in general. Single man, some compensation to come your way possibly, new start and all at that.'

'I've not really given it a great deal of thought.' And we sit silently for a few miles as I look out of the passenger window again.

Then I thought I'd better ask, 'How's mum?'

'To be honest, I'm not really sure. She's healthy and all that but with you getting arrested, the trial, the conviction etc., it seemed like it was all too much for her. I could never understand her not believing in your innocence; it was like it was all about public image and social standing with your mum. It certainly strained our marriage and was the catalyst to our separation a couple of years ago. We'd end up arguing about my letter writing to you and my visits to Witchull to see you. It was like you were a pariah, *a stain on the family name*. I kept telling her it was my name, not her precious lineage that was in the public eye, but she wouldn't have it. Anyway, it looks like it's time for humble pie for her now, but you know what she's like; she'll never back down or apologise.

Anyway, I'm past all that; we were strained for some time before, us actually separating just needed a catalyst.'

'And that was me. I'm sorry, Dad, if that fight had never happened, you'd still be together, as would Samantha and I.'

Dad shrugged a little, 'No, from my perspective, it's fine. As I said, we were strained anyway, and I think the separation and then divorce has been the best thing for us both in the long run.'

We turned off the lane into the car park of the White Hart. Good old Dad, he remembered. I love this place.

As Dad turned off the engine, he reached for the door handle, 'Come on, let's get inside and have some lunch.'

'And a couple of beers, eh, Dad?'

'Yep. I'd best have a chat with the landlord to see if I can leave my car here overnight,' and he winked at me with a smile, 'Neither of us has anything to rush back to, do we?'

The following morning I woke up at Dad's place, a nice apartment by the river. My mouth was parched, and my head felt like it was in a vice in a blacksmith's shop. I've not taken in alcohol in over four years, and definitely not to that extent. I can hear Dad singing in the bathroom; I don't know where he gets his energy from at times or his ability to avoid a hangover.

I stand, walk over to the kitchen area, fill a glass with tap water and take it all down in one go. I fill another and do the same. Slapping my bare feet on the polished wooden floor, I walk across the room to the bi-fold doors and look out to the river. The sun is up, and it's a bright day; squinting my eyes makes my headache pound even more. I open one of the doors and step out onto the terrace and take in a deep breath. The contrast between this morning and yesterday morning is surreal, no locked doors, no bars, no officers giving instructions, no prisoners to watch out for.

Dropping onto one of the padded terrace chairs, I rub my palms across my cheeks and chin over the twenty-four-hour stubble that was trying to restart a beard. The light breeze was refreshing and welcoming, and the gentle bird song was peaceful.

Dad appeared at the open door, 'Good morning, Prisoner 236745. The usual porridge today, sir, excellent choice.'

'Haha. And not so loud, please, officer, wounded man here. I think I drank a little too much last night.'

'I'd say. It took some convincing and an extra £20 for the taxi driver to let you get in the car. Thank heavens you didn't throw up. You hungry champ? The best cure for a hangover is a full English breakfast, the works.'

'Sounds good, although a shave and shower first, I think, Dad.'

'No problem, you'll find what you need in the bathroom. I'll get started on breakfast, well, brunch I suppose. I'll get the coffee going; you fancy one?'

'Cheers, Dad, yes, probably more than one.'

28

Samantha – LAX Executive Lounge, Los Angeles

'So Richard, what can you tell me about the Appeal and how the hell he managed to wheedle his way out of that?'

'My associate informs me that several witnesses who hadn't been interviewed properly by the police at the time of the incident have provided new statements that indicate that Mr Roberts, the deceased, had taken a cash payment from another party to assault your former husband as some form of retribution or punishment for what, we don't rightly know, but as things turned out Roberts came out the worse for his actions.'

'Really? So, what ... David was defending himself then?'

'It seems so. I think with that information coming to light, the narrow investigation conducted by the Police at the time, coupled with the sentencing issues Mr Alexander's legal team raised when they applied to appeal the original sentencing, all played with the Court of Appeal.'

'Has he been in touch yet, Richard?' I ask, unsure what to say if I get an affirmative answer.

'No, nothing yet. You're still convinced he will make contact Samantha?'

'Yes, I have too much money now for him not to try. I presume the Police will re-open an investigation into who was behind hiring Roberts to attack David?'

'Yes, the Appeal Court has instructed it, although it had apparently started before the Appeal decision was declared. I suspect the police complaints commission was already aware of a potential public relations backlash and wanted to get in front of the media and political storm that could result from the conviction being overturned.'

'And what do your sources say, Richard, any idea who hired Roberts?'

'That's just it, as the trail is cold, it's lost energy; what with the time and expense and the Police having limited resources available, they are focusing on other matters. There is nothing further to report as yet.'

'We have contacts with private investigation companies, don't we? Should we hire a private detective to see what they can uncover?'

'We could, but I have to ask why you would bother Samantha; I thought David was ancient history?'

'No, you're right. Nothing to be gained, I suppose. If or when he gets in touch, please let me know immediately, Richard. David's affair wasn't the only issue I was hearing about at the time; it seems he was playing around quite a bit.'

'I'm sorry, Samantha; of course, I will let you know. Now, shall we talk about this new venture in India? There are a few pressing matters we need to address.'

'Yes, of course, what's first?' and we enter into discussions lasting the next hour or so.

29

DS Jo Hansen – Bolton

Detective Sergeant Jo Hansen was quietly reading through the case files and records of the incident in The Tempest Arms public house of nearly five years ago. The re-investigation hadn't uncovered anything of substance, and interest in it was sliding. The re-investigation team assigned to it had been re-assigned to another current serious crime with crucial evidence to collect, so everyday priorities took over.

As the case had been given a lower priority, DS Hansen had asked if she could investigate it, given that she had been involved with the incident involving Alexander's ex-wife some months later. Her curiosity was getting the better of her. She had always carried a dislike for coincidences. To her, David Alexander's fight resulting in the death of Gary Roberts followed some months later by another incident involving another death, but this time concerning the ex-Mrs Alexander, all felt a little *too coincidental* to her. Her boss, DCI Silverton, had told her if she wanted to look into it, it would have to be on her own time as, with the backlog of work, there were no regular work hours available to commit to it. That was fine with DS Hansen; she had a lot of spare time on her hands these days with her partner taking that new job in the US and them not really keeping in touch, no doubt soon to be her ex-partner.

DS Jo Hansen had reviewed everything available. There was nothing new save for the fresh statements provided by the witnesses used in the Appeal, and having reviewed these, no new leads seemed evident. Jo would have been the first to admit she didn't know what she was looking for, but there was now someone else involved, and the mistress had still not been located.

30

David – Bolton

Dad and I are walking along the river near his apartment, and this seems like a good enough time as any to let him into what I'm thinking, although I'm not expecting an easy ride here from Dad.

'I don't know why Dad, and I know you think I shouldn't do it, but I just want to see Samantha one last time, to talk to her and explain what I was like back then, why I was like that, and that I recognise and acknowledge that I was completely in the wrong and she was absolutely right to divorce me for the affairs I was having.'

He looks at me outwardly demonstrating frustration, 'I wouldn't if I were you, I'd let sleeping dogs lie. You are both in different worlds now and have no ties whatsoever. I just can't see any good coming from this. Trust me, your mother and I had our problems, and when we eventually blew up, things were said that could never be unsaid or forgotten. We don't speak at all these days, and I honestly feel better for that. I don't see your situation as really that different.'

'Yes, but we've never really had the chance to talk about it, what with me being banged up and us only communicating in the end through solicitors. I want her to know I thought we were good together until I screwed it all up.'

'Is that the real reason, or are you thinking of some kind of handout from her?'

'Dad! No! It's not that at all. Why is that everyone's first reaction?'

'That's how it will look. Assuming you could actually get to speak with her, what real benefit is there to it?'

'I don't know, but I want to try.'

'I wouldn't do it Davey if I were you, but you're old enough and dumb enough not to listen to me. You always did want to do things your way; isn't that what got you into this state in the first place?'

Eminently sensible sage again, my dad. 'Yeah, probably, but we were good together once, and it ended abruptly and by detachment. I feel we owe it to each other to at least clear the air. I'm not after any of her wealth or a share in anything; I just want to start afresh after properly closing some doors behind me. I was really angry the first year I was locked up, feeling impotent, my marriage and business taking turns I couldn't control; I know, my own fault to some extent, but over the next couple of years, I calmed down, there is nothing worse than a frustrated prisoner penned in with four hundred nutters and wanting to let off some steam believe me. You know, we had plans for kids together, get a nice place outside of town, tour the world a little, you know, dreams, but ... anyway, all that changed, and I feel like we need proper closure. I don't know; maybe I have self-destruct complex or something.'

'You could say that again. Look, try if you must, but Samantha is a wealthy, influential woman with assistants and managers, an entourage of people that look after her and filter all approaches, etcetera. You can try but don't pester her, or it could look like you are baiting or even stalking her.'

'Geez, Dad, after what happened to her at the farmhouse, that's the last thing I want her to feel. I'm no stalker.'

'I know that, that's not what I meant, just be careful; Samantha has private security now, that's all I'm saying. She is wealthy, talented and in demand. Ironically, I bet there are any number of twisted people out there annoyed that she found a cure for cancer as it robbed them of their incomes and livelihoods. You'll be surprised what some individuals or misguided groups believe in. Social media is the new wild west, lawless really. I bet there are hate groups and trolls having a go at Samantha whenever she speaks publicly or online. Even you'll have fans and trolls out there somewhere.'

'I doubt that, but I suppose there is a price to success or infamy in this modern world. I'll be careful, I promise.'

'I know you will. Actually, I'm quite pleased you're thinking like this. I can appreciate what you're trying to do; I don't see others appreciating it the same.'

My dad lightly punched my shoulder as we walked. I got a feeling that he was quietly proud of me. Maybe I have grown up some over the last few years.

31

David – Bolton

I returned to HMP Witchull some days later to collect the balance of my personal things. Leaving the prison, the governor and officers congratulated me on my newfound freedom. To the prisoners, I'd beaten the system; to the officers, a realisation I shouldn't have been inside in the first place. It's ironic, really; some in here can't leave today, some will leave today but return tomorrow, and then there's me, leaving today and absolutely no intention of returning tomorrow or ever.

I wasn't allowed to meet Blade, but I'd asked one of the officers to give him a message from me, *"Stay strong. I'll be waiting outside when you come out. Find me. Dave."*

Dad's gone off to play golf with his buddies again. He left me the run of his pad to chill and recover. After sitting out on the terrace for a couple of hours sunbathing, the heat is getting to me a bit, and I wander back inside for some shade and refreshment. Dad left his laptop for me to use with the access PIN code on a little yellow sticky note beside it on the worktop.

Flipping the laptop open, the screen springs to life and asks for the PIN, not a difficult one, my birth date, bless him. Does he not know how easily a hacker can get that? Tapping into the internet search engine, I type "Samantha Alexander", and the hits are pretty old, mainly more around the time of my arrest and the court case, a small note in a chat room blog about the divorce, nothing new there. Stupidly I'm not thinking of today; I then type in "Samantha Walsh + cancer + news", and the hits roll in.

"Samantha Walsh ... talented medical researcher discovers cure for cancers."

"Samantha Walsh ... OxyRuco© passes clinical trials and approved for ..."

"Samantha Walsh ... meeting Royalty at the annual award ...."

"Samantha Walsh ... attacked in remote farmhouse ... attacker died in struggle ..."

"Samantha Walsh ... police not investigating further ..."

"Samantha Walsh ... opens new OxyRuco© manufacturing facility in Manila ..."

"Samantha Walsh ... agrees global licencing agreement with giant pharma ..."

"Samantha Walsh ... Sunday Times Rich List ..."

"Samantha Walsh ... hosts charity gala event in London ..."

Samantha has been busy over the last four years. Cutting me free and focusing on her research provided her with drive and clarity.

And the web search hits roll on and on. I click on the farmhouse links and read the articles. That must have been terrifying for Samantha. Hugo Bonning-Wallace. I click to enlarge his photo; he looks like a well-groomed, public-school type, not the image of some of my former inmates at Witchull that I'm used to seeing for this type of crime.

Samantha was lucky that night. His past, following the police investigation, showed a pattern of offences of increasing severity against women. Ironically, Samantha now knows what it's like to kill a man, a complete stranger, at an unplanned, random time. However, her involvement with the police and CPS had a completely different outcome than mine. I keep scrolling ...

"Samantha Walsh ... honoured by the Royal Institution for Medicine and Surgery..."

"Samantha Walsh ... presenting at the International Medical Treatment Conference in Vancouver in September ..."

A very busy lady, I think to myself. I click on a couple of photos of Samantha, reminding myself of what I saw in her and the good times we had together.

Clicking back to the search engine, I type "OxyRuco" and press enter. The first few hits are sponsored links and advertisements, and then I scroll through press releases, news reports, and articles and then into some scientific papers and journals. What a success story, there are some fantastic quotes from patients and family members, how fast the medication works, the diagnosis was awful until we tried this new wonder treatment, and numerous stories of patient recovery, remission and reversal. Brilliant really.

I wander over to the fridge and pull out a bottle of Italian beer; Dad won't mind, pull off the cap, take a good swallow and then return to the laptop. Eventually, I started reading investment news and commentary. This is equally astounding. Our original company "Reef Medical Research Limited" had morphed into parent company Reef Medical Research IBC, operating out of the Bahamas, sprouting offshoot subsidiary businesses and companies all around the world, including further R&D businesses, manufacturing facilities in the Philippines and soon India, with revenue from global licencing agreements for further manufacturing, distribution and sales. On-screen, these have pushed the ultimate parent company share price to over 13,856 GBP per share and rising. 'Bloody hell!' I say out loud to myself, 'Thirteen thousand eight hundred and fifty-six pounds per share! Unbelievable.' I sold my shares, all four thousand of them, back to the company at thirty-one pounds per share, returning one hundred and twenty grand, which all went on my legal bills; those shares would now be worth over *fifty-five million pounds*. I lean back in the breakfast chair and down the remainder of the beer bottle in one go.

This is unbelievable; I had no idea of the size of this. I know OxyRuco is successful, but I never thought it was *this* successful. The ultimate parent company has a value of over thirteen billion US dollars! I can now see why my dad said what he did; this is too big not to think I'll be after something. But I'm genuinely not. The one thing I learned in prison is the value of friendship, family and trust. Money doesn't come into these values.

But wow, with so much money washing around, it does make you think a little.

I wander onto the terrace and watch a couple of row boats slip by going upstream. Couples and small groups sit on the grass bank opposite, families out walking along the riverbank, and all looks peaceful.

"*Thirteen billion dollars*," I say quietly to myself.

The landline telephone rings, and I wonder whether or not to pick it up, then think, why not? I can take a message for Dad. I pick up the handset, 'Good afternoon, David speaking.'

'Oh, sorry, Mr Alexander?' asks the male voice.

'Yes, the younger, not the older; I'm Henry's son.'

'Ah, oh, sorry, erm, yes. It was Henry I wanted to speak with.'

'Would you like to leave a message, and I can pass it on later when he returns?'

'Erm, no, no problem, sir, I'll call back later.'

'Is everything OK?'

'Yes, everything is fine, not to worry. Sorry for disturbing you,' and the caller hangs up.

No message, no name, and I think no more of it.

32

Samantha – London

The deal has gone through, funds will be transferred in the next twenty-four hours, and the new construction work in India can commence. This also gives me the green light to officially open the charitable trust in Mumbai to support women in need following sexual assault. This is a cause close to my heart and the third such charitable trust I've opened in the last year or so.

I use my newfound influence, business and fund-raising events to promote these trusts, help publicise issues, and bring in further charitable donations from corporations and celebrities alike. These trusts have given me a new purpose for the personal work I do; to help women oppressed by male predators, women injured both physically and psychologically. My own personal experiences give me the drive to want to help other women who find they cannot help themselves. My access to funds and influential people helps me enormously now.

Picking up my mobile, I scroll through my favourites and dial Prisha's mobile to give her the good news.

'Hi Prisha, it's Samantha. I have great news. The funding is in place for the trust. We can move ahead now with the building plans for the new sanctuary.'

'Hello Miss Walsh, it is so good of you to call me personally with this great news; thank you. We are finding we are more and more in need of your beautiful help and charity. Bless you Miss Walsh, bless you.'

'Prisha, it is my pleasure to assist and support you with your work. If you encounter any issues or obstacles, please do not hesitate to contact Mr Richard Stanley, Richard is my new Chief Legal Officer, and we'll make sure any problems are resolved.'

'I will Miss Walsh. Thank you for all your support and thank you again for calling me. When you return to Mumbai, please be a guest at my home *"Athithi Devo Bhava"*.'

'Thank you Prisha, that will be an honour and delightful. I will be travelling again to Australia soon and will be sure to include a stopover in Mumbai; goodbye for now,' and I cancel the call.

Richard looked across the table to me, 'A good cause Samantha, and I presume Prisha is excited to get things moving now.'

'Yes, she is. I'll need to arrange a visit again soon.'

Richard then looked a little more serious than usual, 'Your former husband has reached out and tried to make contact through our London office yesterday. Clearly, he does not have direct contact details for you and tried firstly to be put directly through to you, which didn't fly, then asked if you had a PA. Daryl spoke with David briefly and advised that he would take a message, and if you wished to speak with David, then Daryl would be back in touch to arrange a diary opening.'

'And so it begins. I knew he would make contact; I knew he couldn't resist. What do you think Richard? Should I speak with him?'

'I can't see any real benefit of doing so Samantha. If he is desperate for money, it could be some kind of trap, with one of the daily red tops or gossip magazines in tow or just a simple shakedown for some cash so he won't feel the 'need' to go to the newspapers. Do you have anything to hide Samantha from before OxyRuco and your time with David?'

'No, nothing at all, well, nothing I can recall anyway.'

'Personally, I think it's best left to fade away. He'll get tired of trying to make contact.'

'I suppose so. You always give the best advice.'

'And now for something a little different, you have received a letter from Buckingham Palace asking if you would care to be an Officer of the Most Excellent Order of the British Empire. Assuming this is a yes, we need to reply confirming your acceptance, and this will be announced in The Gazette with the next New Year's Honour List. Congratulations Samantha, very well deserved.'

'Wow, thank you Richard, I wasn't expecting that. Of course, it will be an honour to accept. Would you mind drafting a gracious reply of acceptance for me to consider? I've never really been one with such royal formalities.'

'Not a problem, Dame Samantha, it'll be my pleasure,' and we both smile at each other. 'One of the rules is that this be kept confidential until it is formally announced by the Palace, so if you don't mind, the easiest thing is to keep this between the two of us for the time being.'

'Absolutely, mum's the word.'

To which Richard replied, 'No, I think it's pronounced *ma'am's* the word,' and we both laugh.

'This will help enormously with my charitable work; it is surprising how a title or an honour can help open doors or remove hurdles.'

Richard looked at his watch, 'Sorry Samantha, I have a conference call with New York in about half an hour and need to sort one or two bits beforehand. Can we meet later?'

'Yes, no problem, I've plenty to do this afternoon. We can meet for drinks at Malone's at six if you are free?'

'Six at Malone's is good, and it will give me a chance to brief you on the New York negotiations following this conference call.'

'Thanks Richard; if we don't speak this afternoon, I'll see you at six.'

After Richard leaves my office, I return to my laptop and key in the eight-digit pin. My itinerary is open for tomorrow, and I can see it will be another day of bouncing from one call to the next meeting back to another call. I'd better speak with Daryl, David will try to get a hold of me again, and I don't like leaving things hanging.

I hold the page button on the desk phone, 'Daryl, can you come in for a minute, please?' and within 10 seconds, the door opens and Daryl walks in.

'Yes, Samantha.'

'Daryl, my former husband David Alexander called this office yesterday, and I believe you spoke with him?'

'Ah yes, Samantha, I did. I referred to Richard first as you were engaged with the British Consulate call.

Richard had notified me that your former husband might try to get in touch, and if he did, I was to take a message and let Richard know. I'm sorry, was this wrong?'

'No, no, that's fine. I've been thinking that I should speak with David. After all, we were once married, we started out on this venture together, and he is innocent of the crime he was sentenced for. He's had a terrible time over the last five years, and I should recognise that. Did he leave any contact details?'

'Yes, he did. I'll put his details in our personal chat room if you like?'

'Thank you, Daryl. Can you keep this between us for the time being?'

'Yes, if you like. I shouldn't mention it to Richard?'

'No, just between us for the time being, thank you. Richard has my best interests at heart, but this is something from my past that David and I never concluded properly, and I would like the opportunity to close out this matter quietly.'

'No problem, Samantha. I'll forward the details immediately.'

'Thank you, Daryl. Oh, and one other matter, I'm meeting Richard for drinks at six tonight at Malone's. Can you make us a reservation and inform my seven o'clock, I may be a little late?'

'Not a problem, will do it straight away,' and with that, Daryl left my office.

Thirty seconds later, a little ping notified me I had a chat message, and David's details popped up in the bottom right-hand corner of my screen. I clicked on the message and entered David's mobile phone number into my personal mobile phone. I haven't quite decided what to do just yet, but I know I have to meet him. Things didn't work out like they should have done, and I want to conclude this completely so I can move on without giving this another thought.

With a long afternoon of business matters behind me, I hadn't realised the time. I quickly pack away my papers and laptop and head over to Malone's to meet Richard.

Daryl had arranged a private booth for drinks at Malone's for Richard and me, not a booth out of sight but one just private enough to talk but where one can still be seen. Richard was already seated and had two drinks prepared, and waiting.

As I walk up to the booth, Richard stands, ever the gentleman, and I sit opposite him.

'I hope you don't mind; I took the liberty of ordering two dry martinis. Daryl mentioned you were meeting the Secretary of State for Health for dinner at seven this evening.'

'Thank you, Richard. I may squeeze another in before dinner. I will need a little fortitude to get through the evening, no doubt,' and we both raise our glasses and toast my news from earlier in the day.

On placing my glass on the table, I look straight at Richard, 'I have thought a little more about David making contact, and I have decided to meet him quietly somewhere private, away from the glaring eyes of the fourth estate. You may be right about there being some angle or play here from David, but we did separate due to circumstances that are now known to have been fabricated, which does put a slightly different light on the matter.'

'Samantha, I respect your opinion, and naturally, this is your choice, but the reality is your marriage probably would have ended in separation, given what we now know David was doing behind your back, breaking that essential trust that a marriage needs to succeed. I don't want to see you hurt again.'

'I see that Richard and I know you only have my well-being in mind, but we did share a lot of good times together, formed this business from nothing, and our separation, inevitable or not, was the result of another person's premature intervention.'

'Would you like me to arrange the meeting with David?'

'No thank you, Richard. I have David's contact details and will arrange to meet him when my diary frees up a slot allowing me to escape for a few hours.'

'You will be taking some security with you, won't you Samantha? I mean, he is a very different person now than the one you last spent time with.'

'I will discuss this with my personal security team. I will need to include them anyway; otherwise, if I go off the grid for any length of time, it could start an issue if the media get a hold of this or our Board hear of it. We both know one or two of the shareholding Directors would like to see me 'retire' so they can squeeze every penny out of the company sooner rather than later. I have got to a place where I can do real good for many less fortunate than us, and I want to stay in this place.'

'OK, if you promise the security angle is addressed, let me know how I can help.'

'I promise, and I will.

Now shall we get that second Martini? I did say I may be a few minutes late,' with a slightly cheeky smile, I raise my hand to the approaching waiter, 'Same again, please.'

33

David – Bolton

My new mobile rang in my pocket and I fished it out, number withheld showing on screen. Not many have this number so I swipe to answer the call 'Hello, David here.'

'Is this David Alexander?'

'Yes, and you are?'

'Hi I'm Daryl, Ms Walsh's executive personnel assistant, we spoke a few days ago. Ms Walsh would like to meet with you and has confirmed Thursday the 15th, 8.00pm at the Royal Observatory at Greenwich. Please confirm this is acceptable.'

'Well, er yes, it is but I'm pretty sure the Royal Observatory will be closed at that time of night.'

'It is closed to the public, however Ms Walsh has special access for private meetings.'

'I see, in that case yes, I will be there on Thursday evening, I presume I use the public entrance?'

'No sir, I will send you the relevant details in a text shortly. I will arrange for a car to pick you up from a designated location. Thank you, have a good day sir.' Daryl hung up the call.

Well, that was efficient. So, Sam wants to meet after all. Not a bad venue, private at that time of night. I'd better book some train tickets and get myself down to London, wouldn't want to miss this meeting. 'Ping' and the details land on my mobile.

Now I've just got to let my dad know what I'm doing, he's not going to be happy but he knows it is something I, we, need to do.

As I've got a couple of days in hand, I can try to sort a few things out here first before I travel south. I need to see where my compensation claim is up to with my legal team, I need to visit mum and have a difficult conversation with her, and I need to visit Blade in Witchull, I said I would stay in touch, he was there for me when it mattered.

Taking the longest to arrange first, I open the laptop and make an application to visit Blade at Witchull and I indicate three potential dates as required. Just need to await the reply. Next for the hardest one, dad gave me mum's mobile number, she changed it when the court case was going through. I prepare a short text message indicating we should meet up, there are things we need to say to each other, please indicate a preferred time/date. The next is the easiest and I select my solicitor's number from phone contacts and press call. It's answered in three rings "Good morning, Dunrow and Wilson, how may I help?'

'Good morning, please could I speak with Mr Wilson regarding my case? Sorry, it's David Alexander here.'

'Ah yes Mr Alexander, I'm sorry, Mr Wilson is currently busy with a client at the moment, could I pass you to a colleague or if you care to leave a message, I'll make sure to pass it to Mr Wilson?'

'Not a problem, I'll leave a message. Please ask him to call me on my mobile, I'm just after an update on my compensation claim. Not urgent but want to stay up to speed with how things are progressing.'

'Certainly sir, I'll pass that along to Mr Wilson. Can I help you with anything else?'

'No, that's all thank you. Goodbye,' and I cancel the call.

My laptop is open in front of me and I open the search engine typing in my mother's name to see if there are any hits. I'm surprised at the list generated and the photos, although that said, mother was always a bit of a socialite, moving in society circles of connected people, her reason for putting image and status over her son's predicament. She is so different to Dad, he's stuck by me throughout this and it's easy to see why their opposing positions would create differences between them. I do believe Dad is better off now, away from all that falseness and thin veneer of family and friendship from my mother.

I scroll through some of the articles and notice one of Mum and Samantha at a charity event, obviously I was an embarrassment but now Samantha has 'arrived' following her success and that her businesses are funding good for people all around the world, it's a good image for Mum to be associated with.

I'm now regretting sending the text message to Mum, I can't imagine much will come from it.

My mobile rings and the screen indicates Mum is calling, I answer with a simple, 'Hello.'

'Hello darling, I'm glad you reached out, we do need to meet. Are you free tomorrow for lunch, I'm thinking of Cortinas in Manchester, say 1pm?'

'Hi Mum, yes I'm fine, dad is too. How are you?'

'Oh you know, busy, lots to do, we can catch up tomorrow. Must dash, 1pm tomorrow, oh and darling, wear a nice shirt and tie, bye,' and the call ends.

I shouldn't have bothered, but there are some things I want to say, things to people who were key in my life before prison, so that I can then move on with my life.

Later in the afternoon Malcolm Wilson returns my call and brings me up to speed,

'We are going through the related submissions, red tape and preparation of the appropriate agreements but rest assured there is clear intent to address a compensation settlement with you David.'

'Thank you. When do you think this will be concluded?'

'I expect some time in the next few weeks, the wheels of administration turn slowly but they do turn. Are you OK for funds currently, do you need any financial support?'

'Yes, no, I'm fine. I'm currently staying at my father's place and I have access to cash if I need it. My father is very supportive.'

'Good. If you do need anything in the meantime, please let me know and we'll see what we can do, after all, this is a matter that wasn't of your making David and you shouldn't continue to suffer from it. I hope to be in touch soon with an outline agreement for you to consider.'

'Thank you. What's another few weeks now compared to the years accused and then my time in prison. Hopefully we'll speak soon, good afternoon.'

'Good afternoon David.'

Now I'd better see about picking up some smart clothes for tomorrow's lunch, wouldn't want mother to be embarrassed by me. So, I take a train into the city and wander through a few stores. The styles have changed a little and my physique slightly. I'm not really in the mood for this. However, I feel like I need a full overhaul so first port of call is to a salon for a haircut and trim of my light beard and then off back around the stores to pick up some clothes, new shoes, and a jacket, I'm certainly not going to wear a tie, I'm not conforming anymore, had enough of that.

I call my dad and suggest if he's free we have dinner out this evening and we arrange to meet at 7.00pm at a Greek restaurant I'd heard about, seems like the best way to mention lunch with mum tomorrow.

Dad is already there when I arrive and we are taken through to a table on the terrace, we order a couple of Greek beers and start to scan the menu. I suppose now is a good a time as any.

'Dad, I'm seeing Mum for lunch tomorrow,' I just say out loud without raising my gaze from the menu.

Dad lays his menu down on the table and looks at it with lowered head for a few seconds then looking up I can see his disappointment.

'It's your call, you know what I think but you're big enough to make your own decisions, just don't go getting your hopes up, you know what she's like.'

'I know, I'm sorry, I know you don't want me to open up old wounds with mum, Pandora's box and all that, but it's another piece of unfinished business for me. I'm not expecting anything really, just want to speak my mind, get things off my chest then move on. What mum does with that is up to her.'

'Your mother has her own agenda all the time, you facing a criminal charge upset her agenda, what with all the news and public airing, she couldn't cope with the *shame* as she called it, it had nothing to do with you being innocent or guilty. It took me a long time to see her for what she had become and I'm glad I have no more dealings with her. Did she contact you?'

'Er, no, it was me, I contacted her. I'll get through tomorrow and then we'll see. I'm not expecting this to become the return of the prodigal son or anything, it's just that, she is my mum.'

'OK, enough said on the matter. Now I'm more interested in fried haloumi followed by mixed souvlaki, olives and dips alongside. You?'

And that's how dad is, a straight forward plain speaking man, he knows it's my choice and he won't change my decision, so we move on. 'Spinach and feta parcels then lamb koftas, let's get extra olives to share,' and we raise our beer glasses and chink with a "Yamas".

34

David – Manchester

The following morning, I take the train back into the city and a leisurely walk to Cortinas, I have time in hand and the weather is good. Not sure how this is going to pan out with Mum, but she certainly won't want to make a scene in Cortinas. It'll be all around the golf club before afternoon tea is served.

I walk into the restaurant and receive a warm greeting at reception. Mother hasn't arrived yet, but she has left instructions that I be shown to the table. Still, in control, I see. Nice table, centre of the large bay window overlooking the gardens. The waitress waits whilst I sit and asks if I would care for a drink. 'Yes, I'll have a glass of chilled still water, please no ice.'

I'd finished my water and noted the time at 1.26 pm when I heard Mum enter the restaurant saying hello to other patrons as she glided across the room to our table.

It took some time for pleasantries to be satisfied before Mum arrived at our table. I pushed my chair backwards and stood. Mum embraced and kissed me on the cheek as though this was a normal outing and took the withdrawn chair at the table and sat down, thanking the waiter. 'Hello darling, so good to meet you again.'

'Mother. You look well.'

'Thank you, darling one tries. I see you chose not to wear a tie?'

'Really, you're second sentence is commenting on how I didn't fulfil your brief?'

'Now, David, let's stay civil. It was just an observation.'

The waiter returned and asked if we would like drinks. Mum asked for a Spritz, and I felt like I needed something with a bit more substance, 'I'll take a Dirty Martini, please. In fact, I'll have two.'

'Darling, your time away has taught you some bad manners.'

'It wasn't a trip to the Alps, Mother; it was prison, and I think this conversation is heading in the direction of at least two Martinis.'

'David! Please don't mention that place.'

'Why not, Mother? It exists, I was wrongly sent there, and now I have been cleared of all convictions and allegations concerning events that night. You can be such a snob, mother.' I'm already wound up and can feel that this isn't going to get any better.

'David, please. I thought we could have a nice lunch, discuss your plans for the future, and how you and Samantha are getting along.'

'There is no me and Samantha. We've been divorced now for years. Or did you not like that either?

More shame on the family name?'

'Now, that's not what I meant. You two were perfect together, the two of you and now that Samantha's business is blossoming and you have been declared innocent, I thought you two young things might get back together and try again. That's all, darling.'

'Unbelievable. Now it makes sense, a prominent table, grand entrance opportunity, my innocent son looking to rekindle his relationship with the very successful and eminent Samantha Walsh, my former daughter-in-law, soon-to-be daughter-in-law again. It's all like something from the Edwardian era with you mum. I brought some stain to your image, some distraction that didn't fit your narrative or expectations. You couldn't wait to drop me when I was arrested. There was no doubt in your mind that I did this thing, and the shame would be unbearable. Dad was always there. He believed in me. Where were you, Mother? Where?'

'It wasn't like that, David. I was very busy and distracted with many things at the time.'

'Have you actually heard yourself? Your only child is accused of a serious crime, and you are nowhere to be seen. You didn't attend the court hearings or sentencing, never contemplated a visit to the prison, and now that I'm considered *clean* again, you want me to hook up with Samantha, for what, so you can rub shoulders with other prominent figures in social circles? For god's sake, mother. I knew this wasn't going to be easy, and Dad said it was a mistake.'

The waiter appeared with our drinks. I took the first Martini from the silver tray and downed it in one, placing the empty glass on the tray and lifting the second before Mother had even sipped her Spritz. The waiter was a little surprised, and Mother just looked at the waiter and quietly said, 'He's had some problems, but we're working through them. Thank you.'

'What?' I yelled as the second Martini touched my lips, 'He's had some problems?' Now I've heard enough. I stand, look at Mum and say, 'Thank you for the drinks, Mother, enjoy your lunch,' and turn slightly, raise my glass to the restaurant and say loudly, 'Cheers and congratulations to being found innocent. *Arrivederla mamma!*' I down the second Martini, place the glass on the table, slightly nod my head towards Mum, and as I turn to leave, raise my right arm, and with a single backward wave, I don't look back.

I step outside and look up at the blue sky and quietly say, 'Well, that went well,' and as I walk away, I think to myself, I tried but can now move on with the closure of that part of my life ... onward to the next part.

35

Samantha – Greenwich

As the day progresses, I focus less and less on work-related matters and give more thought to meeting David later this evening. Being a generous benefactor to a number of charities has given me connections with key people and, in this instance, allowed me to gain out-of-hours access to the Observatory, which has proven invaluable as a setting for some private discussions and meetings. I've found most people are interested in a meeting when I suggest the Royal Observatory; the history and global tie to Greenwich, coupled with the 'Royal' prefix and unique out-of-hours private access, brings an air of importance and influence; it's never failed me yet.

This meeting I certainly want to keep sub rosa; I don't want the press or Board hearing anything about my meeting with David.

My private security team have arranged the access, checked the premises and organised transport logistics for us both. David will be picked up from Greenwich Pier and brought to the Observatory.

I arrive 15 mins before our meeting time and enter the Observatory through the side security entrance, make my way to the Octagon Room and wait for David to arrive. I love this place at this time of the evening, the peace, the views, the history. I'm not too sure where we will be this evening in terms of outcomes and expectations and how we'll conclude, but we do owe it to each other to have an open conversation following the events of that night.

I hear the car approach and the gentle murmurings of one of the security team outside the door; they will be checking David, a frisk, removing his mobile phone to make sure he is not recording our discussion. After a minute or so, the door opens, and David walks in. The door closes behind him, and we are on our own. We look at each other, not quite sure what to do next; the stillness of just looking at each other was mesmerising.

David breaks the ice, 'The last time we met, I was in Witchull starting my sentence, and I wasn't in a good place. You took control of the business, and the divorce papers landed soon after. We didn't really discuss much; it was all one-sided, as my hands were tied. I needed cash to fund my appeal, and you needed to operate the company without ties to a partner locked up in prison. The investors wanted me out and had the pre-agreed documents to facilitate that; after all, you were the real brains behind the company, as has been proven over the years since.' He pauses slightly, 'Congratulations Samantha, you did it.'

That was a well-rehearsed opening. 'Did what, David?'

'Your breakthrough. OxyRuco. What did you think I meant?'

'No, sorry, I'm just a little nervous. I wasn't sure how you would be this evening, hence the security and privacy. I'm really sorry about what happened to you regarding prison and all. Yes, the breakthrough was fantastic, everything I'd dreamed of and more.'

'Everything and more? What about us, Samantha? You were very quick to drop me at my lowest point.'

'Well, come on, David, put yourself in my shoes. I am married to the man of my dreams, and things are wonderful; we had a fledgling but promising business together, and I was so happy. Then one night, you are accused of killing a stranger. I then find out you have a past that you'd never mentioned to me before. You're found guilty and sentenced to five years in prison. Then, some woman tries to blackmail my friends over her long-running affair with you, and she'll keep silent for cash; I saw the videos and photos. Chrissy and Jess told me all about it. At that point, I couldn't give a toss about image or privacy; it could all come out, so the blackmail attempt collapsed, and I filed for divorce. Do you blame me for taking control of my life?'

'Actually, Samantha, I don't. I've had a lot of time to think about who I was, what I was doing, how I was unfaithful and only thinking about what I wanted, not what you wanted or needed or deserved. Being locked in a small prison cell in a completely different environment gave me a lot of time to calm down and think. You needed me to be trustworthy, to be supportive, and dependable. We were a couple, a happy couple, but I couldn't see it. It was all me; I was the fool. My Dad has helped me over the years to see this; he's been my rock and mentor.'

'How is Henry? I always liked your father.'

'He's good. He was surprised you didn't contact him when he reached out to you years ago. Mum and Dad are divorced now because of what happened to me; well, when I say me, it put them on diverging paths shall we say. Dad said I shouldn't meet with you as nothing good will come from this. He said you'll think I'm after some payout, and like I told him, far from it, I wanted to meet with you for closure, nothing else.'

'I must admit I thought you would be after a payout of some kind; OxyRuco is the hottest thing since the microchip. You're not after money then or claiming a stake of OxyRuco?'

Shaking his head, 'No. I should have some decent compensation coming to me soon due to the miscarriage of justice and being robbed of years of my life, my reputation, and my marriage, and I suppose I could say losing out on the success of OxyRuco, but that's all for me to address. I don't want anything from you, quite the opposite, I only wanted to apologise to you, face to face. Besides, I bet even if I try, the legal waivers and settlement agreements will be watertight, and all that I will do is burn a shed load of money making even more lawyers richer.'

I wasn't expecting this; it seems prison has actually reformed David. He sounds like a different person.

'We were good together though, David; you have to admit that we actually made a good team. But why the other women? Was I not enough for you?'

'It was me, all me. I just thought I could have it all, and for that, I am really sorry and regret all the hurt and upset I have caused you.'

'Wow, thank you. I must admit it did take some getting over, but now I've moved on and presume you have too? What are your plans?' I ask now, trying to take control of the direction of the conversation.

'I'm not fully sure yet. Naturally, I need to sort out this compensation, and then depending on the value, I'll plot a course. I wanted to clear the air between us as the last time we spoke, we didn't say the right things, and then the divorce came along. I wasn't saying nice things about you, I was an angry man locked up in a place where I had no real control or say in matters; the prison regulated everything, the prison officers and my fellow inmates. And now I see what you've achieved without me, and I am seriously impressed. It's truly magnificent.'

'Thank you, David. I always knew there was something of benefit in my research.'

'I was shocked to hear about the stalker at your farmhouse. That must have been really traumatic?'

'Yes', as I turn slightly to look out the window, 'I was terrified, but I think that my in-built survival gene, you know, fight or flight, kicked in, and I fought back so I could get away from him.'

David moved a little closer to me, 'He died, though. What did that feel like for you? This is something we now both have in common.'

'I never really thought of it that way before; of course, now everyone can see your action was a self-defence reaction also. It was scary, and I certainly don't want to go through anything like that again, hence the private security team now that I can afford it.'

'It is interesting how one seemingly innocuous event that night in a local pub significantly altered the course of our lives. I'm glad you came out of the whole stalker thing unharmed.'

'Well, I wouldn't say unharmed. I had a bad cut on my arm, and I struggled at times when I was alone. It did take some time before I felt comfortable staying on my own again. Chrissy was a big help at that time.'

'How is she? And Jess, are they well?'

'Yes, both seem to be. I'm swamped down here now with work and jetting around the world, with little time to catch up with them, but I keep promising myself I will do it someday.'

'Do it; life is too short. One minute you have everything, the next, it's gone, and that's when you find out who you can really rely upon. Have you got a special somebody now?'

I turn back towards David and look directly at him, 'No, I find it hard to hold down a relationship with all my travelling and work commitments I have. That said, I don't feel like I need a special someone anymore; I had one of them, and look what he did to me?'

'I know. I'm sorry, Samantha.'

David lowers his head, and I can feel the remorse; he really does look apologetic and sincere. I wasn't sure what to say next, and an awkward silence screamed out. David started to pace the room slowly.

'You must have some pretty decent contacts and influence now to arrange a venue like this?'

'Er, yes, I suppose so. Being in the spotlight pretty much all the time is an issue, and it's a struggle to find a private meeting place, and I do enjoy this space. The gate security and long driveway approach is useful for stopping unwanted followers. Just think, if we could stop time and turn the clock back, what better place could there be to do it?'

'Is that what you're suggesting? We turn the clock back and try again?'

No, that's not what I meant; I should have kept that to myself, 'No, not at all, David, I plan to remain single for the foreseeable, and you need to put your life back together again.'

Now we really do have an awkward silence.

David broke it again, 'Well, I've said what I wanted to, so I won't keep you. I think it's best I leave now. Will your chap drop me off at the Pier so I can get the water taxi back to the city?'

That's a relief, 'Sure, tell the driver where you want to go and he'll take you there, David, anywhere. As we are going our separate ways, can we, er, part with a hug, for old time's sake?' as I say it, I can't believe what I've just asked.

'Of course,' and we move towards each other and embrace quite tightly. I must admit he looks good, and he has kept himself fit. I pull my head back slightly and kiss his cheek, 'Go well, David. I hope you find what you're looking for.'

'I will, you too, Samantha,' he said as he released me without a return kiss, turned and walked to the door. David looked back and nodded as he spoke, 'Keep up the good work,' and then he was gone.

A few seconds later, I heard one of the Range Rovers start up and doors closing, and I heard it turn on the gravel to leave. I certainly didn't have that jotted down in my playbook; I would never have imagined he would be so sincere. To think my personal security outside the door were armed and had instructions to come in hard if I shouted out.

As I walked down the stairs and out into the clear evening, the air felt cleaner and fresher somehow. The journey back into the city was quiet, uninterrupted for once, and I used the opportunity to sit quietly and think. Just before arriving at my apartment in Kensington, I turned on my mobile phone.

36

DS Jo Hansen – Bolton

Every now and again, I turn back to the Bonning-Wallace case when time permits. David Alexander has been out of prison for some time now, and the heat on finding the person that paid Roberts has died away; the trail is cold.

Having just finished my shower after my daily five-mile run and whilst my laptop is booting up, I pull the prepared smoothie from my fridge and pop a croissant on the toasting rack above my toaster. Sitting at my small breakfast bar, I look around at my new apartment, not much, but clean and tidy and it suits my new solitary needs now after my ex decided to work in the US. I didn't think we'd last long together with the Atlantic between us, and unfortunately, I was right. It was fun while it lasted.

I know I shouldn't have the archive box of evidence, trial records and notes for the Roberts case here at home, but as I'm using my personal time to look into this, I'm not spending my Sunday driving across town to have it to hand. It is noticeable that there is less and less paperwork these days, more CDs, pen drives and plug-in hard drives, coupled with secure online cloud storage. I suppose the one archive box is far better than lugging four or five boxes around like we used to, and it's far easier to search through content quickly now.

Given the number of times I've been through this material and still, nothing new comes to light, I'm beginning to think it's bordering on the obsessive, something I've been told is an excellent quality and destructive trait in equal measure, as a person looking at the same information expecting it to change can often miss the bigger picture, miss the obvious that's right in front of them.

The small bundle of CDs is held together with rubber bands. I put them to one side and look at the records index folder; again, I don't know why; I can almost recite this verbatim. The photo log list is attached, and as I read through it again, nothing new has mysteriously been added since I last looked at it; why would I think it had?

It's just coincidences; I don't like them, never have. I get that there can be everyday coincidences like two people wearing the same outfit to the same wedding, but that's more probability and easily explainable. But two violent deaths with a link to the same couple ...?

My mobile rings; I should think of changing that ringtone, '*You don't own me*' doesn't sit well with some of the guys at the station who are not keen on independent women. I press the green button, 'Hi Boss, what's up?'

'Sorry to call you on a Sunday morning Jo, but we've had two suspicious deaths in the early hours, and we're a bit stretched; any chance you could be SIO on one of them?'

'Wow, me? Senior Investigative Officer, er sure Boss. You think I'm ready?'

'Yes, Jo, I've already told the Commissioner you're ready to step up for this and she's OK'd it. I'll see about getting Acting DI status; that OK with you?'

'Cheers Boss, I won't let you down.'

'I know you won't. Now you need to get over to the old Carrington Lane Brickworks at Greenmount, the scene is cordoned off and the CSI team are on their way as we speak.'

'Sure thing, Boss,' and the line goes dead. I toss the bundle of CDs and paperwork back into the archive box and push it back under the breakfast bar; it'll keep for another day. Priorities change, I suppose.

Quick change, pick up my croissant and drink and leave. This is what I love about this job, the variety, the unknown, the challenges. I suppose it is a good job; I'm not tied down to anything or anyone at home. I can see why so many on the job end up with relationship problems. The Alexanders will have to go on the backburner for the time being, the first 48 hours are crucial in any serious crime, and I need to use this opportunity to show I can deliver as SIO.

Yes, I am ready for this. I know I am.

37

David – London to Manchester

The following morning I'm at Euston Station just after 9.00 am waiting for my train back to Manchester. The concourse is busy with a mix of commuters carrying laptop bags, day trippers arriving with day sacks, students, backpackers carrying their life possessions in overstuffed rucksacks and overseas tourists milling around with one or two suitcases each, upsetting the direct path of the commuters on their mobile phones making a line across the concourse to the exit and Underground. Workers in orange safety gear wander through with casual confidence whilst I note a couple of cleaning personnel quietly and slowly clearing away the early morning detritus left behind by the masses. All these different stories and lives right here under one roof.

My train north is on time, and I make my way to platform 8, pass through ticket control and find my reserved seat in coach H. The journey back is thankfully uneventful, and I listen to music with my head tilted back most of the journey. At Macclesfield, I kill the music and think about the last 72 hours or so while sipping my soft drink. If I'm honest with myself, the meeting with Mum went as expected; I shouldn't have bothered, and again, Dad was right. The meeting with Samantha was completely different. Samantha didn't have an agenda as such, which I suspect is not her newfound style. She looked terrific, slightly tanned and perfectly toned; her clothes style exuded business but casually comfortable, a confident woman. To see her with professional personal security in such a public yet private place added to that air of confidence and control, everything planned and organised.

No point in dwelling over what is already lost; I need to think of my future now and decide what I want to do. Not many people get an opportunity to restart their lives other than those that decide to take a risk and start something completely new in their thirties. Most thirty-somethings are either married, in a relationship or starting families, considering house purchases and mortgages or are focused workaholics like Samantha seems to have become, with no apparent relationship, driven by a will to succeed at what they do. 'Succeed,' I say quietly to myself. Ha, one of Dad's favourite fall-back jokes, "*What does a toothless budgie do? It succeeds.*" I'd forgotten that, and I laugh out loud. The chap opposite me looks up from his laptop, and I smile back at him.

After seeing it at its best and worst, I'm not sure where I want to 'fit in' with society. I might travel overseas, but then I argue with myself about where and what it will achieve. By the time I arrive at Manchester Piccadilly, I am still at a loss and feel like I need a sign of divine intervention or something.

As I step outside the station, the sky is practically overcast, with little sun, and I decide to gamble and walk to Dad's place. Dad left yesterday, away with his golfing buddies, to play chase the little white ball around Turkey, back in just over a week's time. It's good to see him enjoying what he wants to do when he wants to do it.

Near Dad's apartment, I call into a small corner shop, pick up some basic foodstuffs and continue on to the apartment. As I open the door, a couple of letters are pushed backwards by the door, sliding on the wooden floor. On picking them up, I assume they are all for Dad and toss them on the side table with my key and head for the kitchen area to pack away the shopping. All squared away, I open my laptop to check out any emails … nothing, save for a few junk messages.

I open the outside doors to let in some air; dropping into Dad's reclining chair, I flick up the footrest, close my eyes and listen. The world is going on out there without me, but my inner self is telling me I need to re-engage somehow and get back into it. Before prison, I didn't have an empty time like this, Samantha and I were busy, or I was either playing or watching rugby with my mates. I think of Harry; we were great mates once, inseparable. His visits to Witchull soon started dropping off when the original appeal was rejected. He had recently become engaged to his long-standing partner, life, planning their future and losing half a day at weekends for visiting time at Witchull was creating friction that wasn't healthy for them. The other guys didn't even visit me; they just sent their best with Harry. On hearing about my early release, Harry did get in touch with my Dad and Dad passed me the message, but somehow, I didn't feel like our relationship could be what it was, and I've still not been in touch; in fairness, neither has Harry. Again, for different reasons, both Samantha and I have something else in common, we've both lost touch with close friends and people we cared for. We have more in common than we think.

After a few hours in the local gym during the afternoon, I return to the apartment, shower and decide to chill. I open a bottle of my favourite whisky, pour a glass, and swallow deeply. The warmth and calming effect are almost instantaneous. I take another sip and savour it this time; I have missed this nectar over the years.

Having nothing to do and nowhere to go, I just continued with my chill time, flicked on the TV and searched the movie channel for something interesting. I settle on a movie involving a private investigator, a former New York police detective, plagued by a crime he couldn't solve and couldn't get any decent leads to find out who had killed a teenager in Central Park. I carry on sipping my whisky as the film gets deeper, and the PI comes across some minor detail that everyone, including himself, had overlooked, and the domino effect kicks in that lets him solve the case. As the credits roll up, I say out loud to the TV, 'Bullshit, if only real life were like that.' I turn off the TV with the remote and go to stand; that's when I realise the whisky had crept up on me whilst I sat there. Looking at the bottle, it's three-quarters empty, 'Bloody hell,' as I stagger towards the bathroom to relieve the pressure on my bladder. As I stand there, weaving a little but aiming with a purpose, I remember the appeal documents and all the evidence that was used against me. *Somebody did this to me.* Somebody set me up, and I paid a price. An unfair price. Samantha was being blackmailed, the Police still haven't found

Monica or her boyfriend who may have been behind this, and I've lost my mates.

'Bastard,' I call out, 'I'll find you.' I flush the toilet, wash my hands, throw cold water over my face and look up at the mirror; you can do this. I have the time, and there's only me with a genuine vested interest in finding this bastard. So why not?

I cautiously walk back into the living area and wonder where Dad has stored all my appeal documents and archive boxes. He had them for safekeeping, and knowing Dad, he never throws anything away. I look in cupboards in the living area, in the kitchen cupboards, not being very methodical at all. I then go into Dad's bedroom and look through his wardrobes, drawers, and cabinets, searching for anything that relates to my appeal. Nothing. Nothing anywhere. Stupidly, I then pick up my mobile and phone Dad; it's only 7.47 pm here, and he'll be up and about still. The ringtone for Turkey runs, long ring, gap, long ring .... just as I'm about to hang up, Dad picks up.

'Davey, you OK, everything alright?' and I can hear the sleep in his voice.

'Hi, Dad. Yep, all good. You sssleep already?'

'Not anymore. We're teeing off at 6.30 in the morning, a bit cooler that time of day. It's nearly eleven o'clock at night here, you know, right?'

'Oh, er, bloody' ell Dad, sorry, never thought.'

'Have you been drinking?'

'Yep, 'ad a couple or three.'

Dad sighs a little, 'What is it, Davey? I'm awake now.'

'My defence and appeal papers Dad, you kept them all, right?'

'Yes, of course, they're all in boxes in my storage lock up in the undercroft; why?'

'I need t'check summat.'

'Surely it can wait until tomorrow, son?'

'Nah, now Dad, strike while iron's hot and all that. Where's the undercroft?'

'OK, OK. Look, the key to my storage unit is in the kitchen drawer, top right, fastened to an orange key fob, unit 5B. Take the rear service stairs to the basement and follow the signs for the Resident's Storage Area. But leave it until morning; you'll need a torch as the light is pretty poor down there all the time, and you'll struggle to find what you want in there in that state.'

'Ta. OK, will do. Break a leg at golf tomoz Dad.'

'Not really what we say in golfing circles, but I catch your drift. I'll phone you tomorrow at 4.00 pm your time. We can talk through then.'

'K Dad. Soz fa phonin sa late. Av a gud un.'

'Night Davey. And Davey, drink some water, or you'll be in a bad state tomorrow if you don't.'

'Wilco, night Dad. Luv ya,' and I hang up on the call. Well, that's me in trouble again. 'Oops.'

Dad has a point though, I'm pissed, and if there are stairs involved with basements and torches, it's best left until morning. After all, my Dad has never let me down. I best get some water, and I'm gone as soon as my head hits the pillow.

38

David – Bolton

I wake just before nine, and yep, my head is aching again, my mouth is dry and eyes still tired. Order of play, more water, a quick cold shower and some coffee.

Having come around to a state of being semi-alive, I pick up the key with the orange fob and lock the apartment door behind me. The service stairs at the end of the corridor are quite basic and functional, concrete steps with tubular steel handrails. I follow it down to the basement, and as I open the door, an automatic ceiling light flickers on. I see the signs Dad mentioned and follow them to the Resident's Storage Area. Easy enough to find Unit 5B and the door unlocks with a noisy click; it opens easily but it is dark in there. I switch on the torch and illuminate the room; looking around, I locate the light switch and twin fluorescent light tubes chatter into action. Wow, I knew Dad kept stuff but I didn't expect him to hoard this much. Not exactly a search for lost treasure in an Amazonian temple, more like wading through the roadside wreck of a house removals van, the search begins.

After about half an hour of wading through old banker boxes full of household stuff and papers, moving aside golf equipment that doesn't look that old or worn, training equipment, three bicycles, an old television, and other items of life's luggage, I find three cardboard boxes, with lids all sealed up with tape, on a low shelf stacking system at the rear of the room. I bend down to shine the torch on them and see numbered boxes 1 to 3, each labelled "Davey's Appeal", and say out loud, 'Eureka! The man with the hangover has found the gold,' only to get a reply of 'No, hands off. That's my gold!' come straight back at me.

'What the fuck?' I say aloud as I stand and spin a little too fast, losing my balance and falling against the shelving system, some of life's hoard crashing to the floor. I look up and see a burly man standing in the doorway wearing what looks like a side holster.

He speaks, 'Sorry mate; I didn't mean to startle you. I'm the block caretaker, Mike, Mikey to friends.

And who might you be?'

'Jeez,' catching my breath, 'I'm David Alexander, Henry's son. Apartment 214?'

'Is that a question, or are you telling me? Haha, just kidding. Henry told me about you, but we've not actually met yet,' he says as he steps into the room, holding out his right hand for acceptance.

'Scared the shit out of me then, Mike,' as we shake hands.

'Yes, sorry, saw the light on down the corridor and thought I'd better investigate. Everything alright?'

'Yep, just looking for something, well, found it now. I don't suppose you have one of those stacking trolley trucks or something do you? I have three boxes here I need to take up to the apartment.'

'No worries David, I'll get a trolley and we'll take them upstairs; we can use the service elevator; I am the magic keyholder after all,' he chuckles.

'Cheers Mike.'

'Mikey is fine.'

We spend the next 15 minutes or so getting the boxes out of the storage room and up to the apartment. Mikey leaves me after I thank him.

I clear Dad's dining table and rustle up some more coffee before setting to. Where better to start than box 1? The box contains a couple of lever arch folders full of documents, several bound reports from expert witnesses, the CPS case and disclosure documents, and a small blue PVC case when opened containing six DVDs and two pen drives. Starting with the CPS allegations, I sit at the table and read through the prosecution's case and how they managed to piece together my movements on the night. Surprisingly, there is not a great deal about Roberts' movements before the event, just some short statements from a couple of his mates out with him that night, where they went, how much they had drunk, and statements from various pub personnel corroborating these statements.

After a couple of hours of reading through the paper material, I learn nothing new. Having read through this information years ago for the first time, nothing new has been added that I can see, and there are no obvious nuggets of information that might lead to the person behind paying Roberts, which I'm beginning to appreciate is the same conclusion that the police arrived at following their recent case review.

I open the laptop, insert the first pen drive and start to work through the contents comprising a selection of scanned copies of written police reports and forms, autopsy information, arrest and custody documents, and transcripts of interviews with different people. Again, after another hour or so, nothing new is gleaned.

Inserting the second pen drive, it contains more of the same and I work through them diligently, making notes for cross reference should these help lead to the mysterious payer.

As I stretch and yawn, I decide it's time for a break and I start to think this might not be as useful as I first thought. Rustling up a sandwich and pulling a beer from the fridge, I sit outside on the balcony and watch the river silently glide by. The sun makes an appearance, and not long after, I must have dozed off; the reading, the beer and last night's drinking session all conspired to put me into sleep mode.

I wake with a start, a boat crew rowing by with the cox shouting out the stroke. Unsure of how long I've been asleep, I rise, stretch and wander back into the living area, back to the table and my work. A quick look at the laptop clock and I realise I've been away for just over two hours.

Back to it, I reach for one of the DVDs and look to insert it into the laptop, only to realise there is no CD / DVD built-in drive capability on this machine. A quick search of the internet and I find there are portable plug-in CD/DVD drives I can purchase. 'OK, off to the shops I go then,' I say to no one but me.

There is a computer and accessories shop on the high street and the young assistant is very helpful, describing what I need, how to install it and use it. Purchased, I make my way back to the apartment but stop to buy further food supplies and another bottle of whisky to replace the one I attacked last night.

Back in the apartment, I follow the installation process for the plug-in player. I unbundle the DVDs and note they are all numbered 1 through 12, and the contents list that wrapped the disks indicates DVD No.1 is the very first police interview I attended with my solicitor. I insert No.1 and sit back to watch my premiere performance in the latest serial of *The Accused*. It starts coming back to me now; my first interview was a bit of a haze, still in shock, I suppose, after being detained and questioned under caution in a murder case. The initial talk was of the rugby match and my mates, my playing days, no doubt to get me settled a bit, to lower my guard unwittingly; thank heavens my solicitor was there with me, and I had someone to rely upon and guide me.

While working through the interview recordings, I don't expect any of this will add new information, but I do want to be thorough. From a police perspective, I can see how it looked and why they genuinely thought they had got their man when they had me. Looking back at the interviews now, the technique and style of interviewing were quite good; it was crafted in such a way to elicit information from me or, if I remained silent, how my silence indicated a kind of guilt, something to hide.

After watching interview DVD No.3, I stopped; I couldn't see how my questioning and responses would help me find the guy that paid Roberts to attack me. The questioning was focused on the incident that night, with not much preamble leading up to the incident save for my mates and the rugby.

I take out the bound pack of DVDs marked "CCTV". Again, there is a contents list and the disks are numbered, with disk No.1 being *"CCTV from The Tempest Arms Public House, 17 June 2016"*. Marked on the disk in black ink is a note, *"Fast forward to 20:23Hrs"*. I insert the disk into the player, and just as I press "Play", my mobile rings out, and I see it's Dad; it must be four o'clock already. I stand and walk towards the window, stretching and curving my back, 'Hi Dad, how are you doing?'

'Good Davey, all good. Great golf today despite having little sleep last night.'

'Oh yeh, I'm sorry about that Dad, I never thought, but if you played well, you can thank me for the intervention later.'

'Hah, will do, you cheeky sod. It's great out here, I should have done this sooner. It can be a bit hot around mid-day but fabulous courses.'

'Mad dogs and Englishmen, Dad.'

'Yep, that's why we go earlier and have a cool beer or two at lunchtime. Anyway, did you go down to the storage room and find the boxes you were after?'

'Yes, I took your advice and went down this morning. Bumped into Mikey, scared the crap out of me he did. We found three boxes, and they're here in your apartment now. I'm slowly working through the files and DVDs.'

'Why do you want them? Something gone wrong with your compensation?'

'No, no, that's all going ahead, hopefully without a hiccup. No, I wanted the info as I thought I'd use some of my free time to try and identify who paid Roberts to hit me; the police seem to be taking their time about it.'

'Ah, OK, it'll keep you busy no doubt, keep you out of trouble. If the police are struggling to find out who paid Roberts, then you'll do well to solve the puzzle with your limited resources. So, how's it going?'

'You know, so so. Just running through the information to see if anything pops up that could be of interest.'

'We've all been through that information Davey, a couple of times at least. I'm sure there is nothing in there that will help, or we would have picked up on it before the court hearing and afterwards when we were awaiting the appeal request.'

'But back then Dad, we didn't know that a third person had paid Roberts to have a go at me, so I'm looking at this from a different perspective now,' saying as I look back at the laptop screen and notice the DVD was already playing, skipping along at four times speed. I walk back towards the laptop to put it on hold.

'Good point, good point. Anyway, who is Mikey?"

It was when Dad spoke I noticed something on the screen; something in one of the cameras caught my eye, looking a little familiar. I reached for the mouse to stop the video from playing and noted the time at 11.46 am.

'Dad ... just a sec, I just noticed something on the CCTV film I'm watching.'

'What is it?'

'Not sure, wait one. I just need to replay this again.'

'Davey? What is it?'

'I'm not sure; I thought I recognised someone in the Tempest Arms CCTV recording.'

'Well, that wouldn't surprise me Davey, it was one of your favourite haunts, after all. You'll have known most people in there; you knew all the regulars.'

'No, someone else, Dad. Let me re-run this again slowly and I'll let you know what I find.'

'OK, OK. Phone me later if it's anything of use.'

'Will do Dad.'

'See you later son.'

'See you later Dad,' I said whilst already in the process of hanging up the call.

39

David – Bolton

I press the playback function, stop the recording, and then press play to run back through the video at normal speed. The screen is split into four shots from four different cameras. Top left is a view at the front of the pub covering the pavement area from up high, the second view is of the bar area looking towards the front door, the third view is of the bar area covering both customer and bar staff, and the final camera view is the rear entrance/exit area to the beer garden.

It's then that I see what has caught my attention. There is a man entering the pub through the front door with head bowed, wearing a flat cap and large overcoat, at least one size too big for him, but there is a glimpse of something familiar about him which I can't quite put my finger on. I watch him as he orders a drink at the bar, camera 3 still not catching his face. He then sits quietly to one side, just in the edge of frame view, and it looks like he's reading a newspaper, but the more I watch this man, the more it becomes apparent he is not reading the paper at all; no pages are turning. After about 20 minutes or so, he finishes his drink and cuts across the bar area, heading towards the gents toilet. On his way past the bar, he orders another drink and points towards the table he's just left. There is a period of some fifteen minutes when he is off camera when suddenly camera 4 dies; it just shows a dark grey fuzzy picture, and the clock stops working. But within a few minutes, the man returns, pays for his beer, sits at his table again, picks up the newspaper, and continues reading. At four times the speed, it looked like the man went out, camera 4 died, and the man returned. I can't make out what he looks like, but there is something familiar about him. I rewind and watch it again, then again. What is it? Who is this man?

The one thing I do note, though, was that at lunchtime, all four cameras were working, but after this man went to the toilet, but before he returned, camera 4 was no longer functioning. I hadn't noticed any of this before as the annotated note says, "Fast forward to 20:23 hrs", a useful note for any viewer wanting to avoid watching hours of mundane pre-viewing, allowing the viewer to just cut to the chase and watch the fight event that night. Is there something in this? Had the police viewed this video recording from the beginning or only from the advised jump to point?

Nah, it seems too obvious. Someone in the police investigation team would have watched all these recordings from the beginning, wouldn't they? They would have gone backwards to see when camera 4 failed, surely?

I play it back again and again. Where is this man for those 15 or so minutes? He is not on camera anywhere; he never left the back entrance/exit to the beer garden. Camera 4 breaks, and within a few minutes, he's back at his table, sipping his beer and reading his newspaper. That's a bit of a coincidence in my book. Has this chap got something to do with Roberts and the fight?

This is something I need to discuss with the police, not that I trust them or we're like old buddies now, but they still have the task of finding out who this mysterious payer is and why they did what they did to me.

Stopping the DVD, I eject it from the player and put it into its protective sleeve. I grab my keys, wallet and phone and, armed with the DVD, I leave the apartment, heading for the Morton Road police station across town.

At the station, I wait my turn in the reception area, and when beckoned forward, I provide my name and ask to see a senior detective. The civilian assistant behind the desk replies, 'Anyone in particular, sir?'

'Yes, but I'm not sure who it will be. It'll be the detective in charge of the re-investigation into the Roberts death. The accused was David Alexander,' and with that, the assistant looked up at me.

'Yes, one and the same, I am him. I was found innocent, released from prison, and there is an investigation in hand to look back into the incident.'

The assistant shrugs slightly and starts to tap away at a hidden keyboard. 'I'm sorry sir, you'll need to speak with DCI Silverton, but he is on leave this week. Can anyone else assist?'

'I hope so. I have uncovered some information, and I need to discuss this with the investigation team.'

'Ah yes, one moment .... you'll need to speak with DS Jones, but DS Jones is out of the station at the moment.'

'There must be someone I can talk to?'

'If you want to leave a message, I will make sure it gets to DS Jones.'

I let out a deep sigh. My displeasure was obvious, 'Yes, please, ask DS Jones to contact me urgently. There is potentially some new evidence to consider which could be useful to the investigation. You have my mobile number there.'

'Yes sir, I'll pass that along. Thank you.'

I leave the police station, thinking that that was a wasted journey. I should have phoned ahead first. I start the walk back and keep mulling over in my mind *what it is that seems so familiar*. Is it someone I know, a local at the bar, or just me with some wishful thinking? The police would have gone through all this previously. Let's see what they came up with, assuming I get a callback.

I'm almost nearly back at the apartment when my mobile rings, number withheld. I tap the screen to answer it, 'Hello.'

'Mr Alexander, DS Jones from Morton Road station CID. You called into the station earlier this afternoon?'

'Ah yes, thank you for calling back so quickly.'

'No problems. I understand from the message you have something urgent to discuss?'

'Yes, I do, but I'd rather show it to you if possible, explain the context for the information I have'.

'No problem sir. I'm just about to log off shift for today. Is there any chance you can call back into the station tomorrow morning, say 9.00 a.m.?'

'Yep, I'll be there.'

'Great, see you in the morning, Mr Alexander,' and the call closes.

We'll hopefully get somewhere tomorrow; I feel things are starting to happen.

Walking through the park near the apartment, I hear laughing and jollity from patrons at the Eagle & Child at the far entrance/exit gate and think, "*Why not, let's have a beer*". Within ten minutes, I'm talking to the barmaid, Nicole, and given most customers are outside in the warm afternoon sun, we chat away unhindered, save for the odd round of drinks being ordered by customers.

One drink leads to another, and before long, I'm thinking of some food and ask if Nicole would like to join me, 'I'm sorry, work first. But I do get off at ten tonight; maybe we can have a drink then if you like?'

'Sure, that'll be great. As I'm starving, can I order a club sandwich with small fries?'

'Yep, no problem.'

A few more drinks later and chats with random customers, ten o'clock is getting closer when a pair of hands come around from behind me and cover my eyes, and a sultry voice whispers, 'Guess who?'

I take hold of both wrists and reply, 'It sounds like it could be the love of my life,' and I turn slowly to look straight at Chrissy.

'Wow, I wasn't expecting that reply,' Chrissy said as she tipped her head to one side and smiled.

'Oh, no, sorry, I was expecting someone else.'

'Am I not good enough to be the love of your life then, David?'

Chrissy was playing with me; she always was an exceptional tease. I look over at the bar to see Nicole with hands on hips, pursed lips and an enquiring look straight at me, 'Just an old friend,' I said in a louder voice to hopefully carry down the bar to her.

'Oh, just an old friend, am I? I thought we were more than that once?'

'Hi Chrissy, long time no see. What are you doing around these parts?'

'With some friends, just dropped in for a quick drink and loo stop before heading into the city. Want to tag along? It'll be good to catch up.'

'Er, no thanks, well I'm kind of waiting for someone,' as I look across the bar again and see Nicole serving a couple of lads.

'Umm, pretty, a little young maybe. Umm, but then again, I suppose you have lost some of your years and have some catching up to do.' Chrissy opened her small clutch bag, pulled out a simple white card and handed it to me, 'My contact details, call me and let's catch up; we have a lot to talk about,' and with that, Chrissy planted a firm kiss on my lips and squeezed my hand, 'Make sure you call me David.'

Chrissy pulled back, smiled and walked past me to join her friends at the end of the bar.

As I look at Chrissy, my thoughts remember times gone. What a surprise that was, after all this time, a really pleasant surprise.

Just then, Nicole tapped me on the shoulder, 'Remember me?'

I turned and felt I needed to apologise, 'Sorry Nicole, that was an old friend of my ex-wife; I've not seen her in years.'

'She looked a bit more than an old friend to me, not the cause of your wife becoming your ex, was she?' raising her eyebrows with an inquisitive look.

'No, nothing like that, although back in our University days, things were a little more, er, liberal, shall we say.'

'Oh my, not only is he single, he's educated, and he likes to play with a little fire at times, my lucky night.'

'Well, it may just be. Shall we skip this place and find another?'

'We could go one better. Have you got any booze at your place? We could, you know, sit and chat over a nightcap,' Nicole said with a sultry tone and a look that would tempt any man.

'I may just have the tipple to please you.'

Grabbing my hand, Nicole turned for the door and looked back, 'Well, come on then, take me there, professor.'

I wake in the morning with a bit of a headache; the daylight is bright, and I can hear the shower running. That was a seriously passionate night with Nicole. I roll over and reach for my watch, 'Bloody hell!' I shout as I jump out of bed; 9.13 a.m., I've missed my slot at the police station. As I enter the bathroom to use the toilet, I see Nicole in the shower, and she notices me and starts a little slow dance, taunting me whilst I pee. I don't have to be asked and decide to step into the shower with her. Nicole turns away from me at first, and I embrace her from behind, my hands caressing as Nicole reaches backwards to clasp me. Nicole slowly turns, and we kiss passionately; our hands start to find each other all over again, and I lift Nicole as she throws her legs around me, and we make love under the warm water, not a further thought for the police station.

We partially dry each other with towels and re-enter the bedroom, and it's clear Nicole, seductively swinging her naked hips and buttocks, that we are away yet again, falling on to the bed to complete our lovemaking, although this is more heated sex now.

It's nearly 11 o'clock before Nicole leaves the apartment. I'm shattered but well-sated; I'd forgotten how much passion a couple can have in less than twelve hours, and now I'm starving. Another quick shower, dress and I leave the apartment to grab a late breakfast or early lunch whilst I make my way back to the police station across town.

Arriving at the station, I wait my turn again in the reception area, and when called forward, I ask for Detective Sergeant Jones to find out he had left the station on other matters. The desk assistant then advised that a Detective Constable would be with me shortly to discuss my matters further.

After about fifteen to twenty minutes of waiting, a young officer looking tired and overworked came through the side door and called my name. As I walk up to her, she introduces herself as Detective Constable Bovary and indicates to follow her to one of the interview rooms. After sitting opposite each other DC Bovary speaks first.

'I'm sorry my boss isn't available, but he mentioned you may call in at some point today. He says you have some new lead or new evidence or something for us to consider further; is that correct?'

'Yes, although I was hoping to speak with someone a little more, er, more senior?'

'No, that's fine; I get that all the time. Sarge said he was expecting you at nine this morning?'

'Yes, sorry, I was tied up with something else that was unexpected; I got here as quick as I could.'

'OK, no worries, I can listen to what you have; put it to my Sarge later, and we can take it from there. Is that OK with you?'

'Yes, yes, that's OK. Well, er, are you familiar with my situation?'

'I know the basics; Sarge is the one running your case. I know you were released from prison following a wrongful conviction, and there is another party involved that is the focus of our current investigation.'

'Yes, how's that going? Any nearer to finding the person?'

'Sarge has some leads, I think. But this kind of thing is quite slow. We have to run down all avenues to close out loose ends, and it was all some time ago.'

'Well, that's kind of why I'm here,' as I fish the DVD out of my pocket and place it on the table. 'I was reviewing the old evidence I have, the disclosed information as part of my trial and appeal, and I came across this DVD.' DC Bovary picks up the DVD and reads the sleeve note as I continue. 'Well, as you can see, it indicates fast-forwarding to the time of the event that night'.

'Yes, and?'

'Well, I have always done that, fast forwarded to that time slot, and I suspect others have too.'

'And?'

'It's what is recorded earlier in the day that is of interest. I ran this from the beginning and noted that the external rear camera was working fine in the morning, but then a person walks into the bar, orders a drink, disappears out back, and when they return to the bar area, the camera is no longer working.'

'And what? Do you think this person damaged the camera? He could simply be visiting the toilet, couldn't he? Or going outside for a smoke?'

'Well, yes, I suppose so.'

'OK, I see where you are going with this. But it is a bit tenuous, don't you think? I'm sure this will have all been looked at during the original investigation and now, in this re-opened investigation.'

'Well, that's just it. At the original trial, I was the sole suspect, slam dunk. I doubt anyone looked further than me at the time of the event.'

'But that has changed now, sir, we are re-investigating this matter, so *everything* is being revisited, everything.'

'I'm sure it is, especially after the appeal when the judge voiced his displeasure with the extent of the original investigation and the conduct of the police.'

DC Bovery indicated displeasure in my comment. 'Sir, rest assured this is one of our top priorities'.

'One of?'

'Yes. Crimes continue to be committed, and there is a violent gangland feud going on at the moment; well, if you listen to the press, there is.'

'Yes, of course, I just want to make sure this aspect had been looked into previously, that's all.'

'I'm sure it has. If you leave this DVD with me, I'll make sure my DS looks it over, and we'll check our investigation records regarding this recording. I'm confident we'll find this has already been reviewed, and it didn't lead us anywhere. You know, the camera breaking hours before your incident could be nothing more than a coincidence, highly likely a dead end.'

'I'm sorry, but I think it could be more than that.'

'Well, as I say, leave it with us, and we'll look into it. We'll get back in touch with you, sir.' DC Bovary pushes her chair backwards and stands, outstretching her right hand, a clear signal this meeting is over. I stand, and we shake hands briefly.

'I'll show you back to the reception area. Please follow me,' and DC Bovary opens the door.

It dawns on me then that Bovary has my only copy of that recording. 'Er, detective, will I get that DVD back? It's the only copy I have.'

'Yes, of course, sir. I'll keep a hold of it for the time being, and we'll make a copy of it and let you know when you can collect it.'

'But you have got the original, I take it?'

'Yes, sir, we'll have it; it's just that this will be a quicker way of getting it in front of the DS. Otherwise, I'll have to trawl the archive boxes to find the right disk.'

'Oh, OK. I'll wait for your call.'

We leave the interview room, and I'm back outside the police station within a minute. Walking down the road, I do not feel that confident that this is actually new information, but I suppose I have to trust that the police have done and will do their job and that they'll be in touch shortly.

40

Samantha – London

I go into my office, sit at my desk and buzz Daryl. 'Daryl, no calls or interruptions for the next fifteen minutes please.'

'Yes, Samantha. Would you like me to push your 4 o'clock back?'

'Ah yes, please, Daryl, can we move it to 4.30 just in case?'

'Yes, not a problem, leave it with me.'

Picking up my mobile phone, I call the private investigator I've hired to update me on David's whereabouts and actions. 'Mark, it's Samantha, sorry I couldn't answer earlier, I was in a meeting. Have you got something for me?'

'Hi Samantha, yes. I'll email you the usual update log, but I thought you might want to hear about this sooner. David visited a police station earlier today with a copy of a DVD containing CCTV footage from the Tempest Arms pub on the night of the fight with Roberts. He thinks there is something on the footage that others may have missed, and he wanted to bring it to the attention of the police.'

'And is there something new? What did the police say?'

'It's in relation to footage from earlier in the day. David seems to think the rear CCTV camera had been intentionally damaged that day and that it may have been by the person who paid Roberts to start the fight. The current police position is that it's nothing new; it had been looked at previously, and it's simply a coincidence.'

'Do they believe that, or are they just saying that?'

'I'm not sure.'

'What do you think?'

'I've not got a copy of the CCTV footage in question. I'll try to get my hands on one and let you know.

It could simply be coincidence or, as David seems to be intimating, it's all part of the wider conspiracy and was planned, although I'm not sure how that plays into the fight that night.'

'OK, thank you, Mark. Can you leave this bit out of your regular update email? I don't want a trail indicating we have a route into the police and active cases?'

'Sure, no problem. Do you want me to look into that CCTV footage and let you know what it contains?'

'No, it's alright. I'll have a copy of it somewhere, or at least my lawyers will from the original trial. Can you just keep tabs on David and let me know of anything unusual, who he talks with, what he does and so on?'

'Yes, will do. Well, it'll be in my update, but he did bump into your old friend Christine, Chrissy, briefly on Wednesday evening in a small local pub near his father's apartment. It looked accidental; they briefly chatted, and then she left. David then escorted the barmaid back to his father's apartment that night, and they stayed there until late the following morning.'

'Um. That sounds like the old David to me. If he goes back to the police station or meets up with Chrissy again, please let me know straight away.'

'Will do.'

I hang up the call. Chrissy and David, I wonder what they said to each other. The police station thing is more interesting though, at the moment. Is David on to something? I touch the comm button, 'Daryl, please get a hold of Richard and ask him to call me on my mobile?'

'Yes, Samantha, straight away.'

I stand, walk towards the large window, and look out over the Thames. It looks just like another ordinary day, the hustle and bustle of a capital city, people busy with work or sightseeing. I see that road traffic has been stopped, and Tower Bridge is being raised as a Royal Navy ship slips its moorings beside HMS Belfast, ready to depart downriver and out to sea. The scene is broken when my mobile rings.

'Hi Richard, thank you for calling back so quickly. Do we still have copies of all the prosecution disclosure materials from David's trial?'

'Yes, we do; that is what we obtained and copied. David's legal advisors received all the disclosure information; we retained what we could at the time, what with you and David still married then. What we have will be in our archives. Do you mind if I ask as to your interest in it?'

'I may want to check something. I know you know I met up privately and quietly with David, and something he said I thought might be clarified if I looked at the disclosure information.'

'Would you like me to put one of our young associates on this? They can sift through the information and find what it is that you're interested in?'

'No, that's fine, Richard. I'd rather do it myself, keep this fairly low-key for the time being.'

'I can certainly have the information sent over by courier, although to be honest, I thought the outcome of your meeting was a clearing of the air and a final parting on reasonable terms. Do you really want to risk opening up matters again now that you have David put squarely behind you?'

Sternly, I answer, 'I think that is my decision and not your concern, Richard. Please have the information sent to my apartment in Kensington as soon as possible,' hanging up the call before Richard had a chance to respond.

I sigh deeply. Richard is no fool; I shouldn't be short with him like that. He is a loyal member of my team, a friend even. I type a quick text message to Richard and apologise for being curt. He replies instantly, indicating he knows no offence intended and none received, and he will have the materials forwarded to my apartment.

There is nothing further I can do now, and my mind turns to what my private investigator said about Chrissy and David bumping into each other. Could that really have been an accident? Chrissy in that part of town?

My desk phone beeps, 'Yes, Daryl?'

'Your four-thirty is about to start in the main board room. I have the briefing papers here with me, the new marketing campaign for South America.'

'Thank you, Daryl. Please bring the papers in and let the meeting know I'll be along shortly.'

Daryl is at my office door in seconds, very professional, briefing papers in hand, coloured tabs indicating the key points requiring decisions.

As Daryl leaves, I take a deep breath, open the folio and look at the content: another meeting, more decisions. Sometimes, I crave a simple day when I'm not in demand and have no decisions to make. I've forgotten what those simple days were like, and it wasn't all that long ago.

41

DC Bovary – Morton Road Police Station, Bolton

DC Bovary places the DVD on DS Jones' desk with a note saying, *"DVD from David Alexander – DA says possible evidence on this disk, watch all from beginning"*.

Bovary then returns to her desk and continues reviewing street CCTV files of the night of one of the latest gang killings, hoping to find a person, a car or a motorbike of interest around the crime scene between 23:00 and 01:45 hours. There are a dozen or so street and traffic cameras to work through, tedious work at best but a chance to shine if a critical bit of footage helps with the case.

DS Jones returns to the station late in the afternoon, grabs a coffee, and sits at his desk. Picking up the note and DVD, he calls across to Bovary, 'What is this about then? What new evidence?' waving the DVD in the air.

Bovary rose and walked over to Jones' desk.

'Yes, Boss, well that's what Alexander says anyhow. He came in earlier. Looks to me like old pub CCTV footage of the night of the fight. Can't see there being anything new on there, old stuff. The original investigation team will have reviewed it, and the re-investigation team looking into the case will have also. It'll just be a waste of our time, I think.'

'We are the re-investigation team, aren't we, or have you forgotten that?'

'Yes boss, I mean no boss, I've not forgotten, it's just that there are hours of footage to wade through on this bloody gang feud, current and real now, and the SIO has made it a priority over everything else, straight from the top apparently.'

'I hear you. I know we haven't the resources or budget to have someone sit down and watch the best part of some 8 to 10 hours of pub CCTV from an event from 5 years ago, when the victim, who is now the perpetrator, is dead, the perpetrator who has now become the victim is freed from prison, and he's looking at some hefty settlement for wrongful arrest and imprisonment. The case is cold, for fuck's sake, it's like we haven't got enough on our plate as it is. Have you logged the visit and inserted meeting notes on the system?'

'Yes, Boss,' I reply.

'Good, you also included this DVD disk reference number in the notes?'

'Er, yes, Boss'.

'OK, no further action for the time being. When we get some free time, we'll pick it back up. God knows when that'll be though. Now, how are you getting on with those street cameras? Have you found anything useful yet?

'No boss, nothing of interest, but still some way to go.'

'OK, keep at it; you never know when something ordinary looking is picked up on camera that can lead to a break in the case.'

'Yes, Boss.' I turn and head back to my desk, first checking that I logged the DVD reference number in the notes; happy, I then come out of that enquiry and return to the real problem in hand today: the recent

CCTV recordings that will provide something tangible and valuable.

42

Acting DI Jo Hansen – Bolton

The two bodies at the old Carrington Lane Brickworks are clearly suspicious deaths. I'm determined to follow the book, make sure every procedural step is ticked off, and that every lead is followed down to a definitive conclusion, everything logged on the system. Doing this is hard work. It's not that I need to prove I can do this; it's more like I want to prove I can do this to myself and others, but I'm thinking of myself first in this lineup. I want to prove that I have what it takes and that I'm not simply talking the talk.

It's hard enough being a female officer in the police force, let alone being SIO on a nearly all-male team. There are still some relics around that think I'm here to make the tea, to fill in the reports. And there will always be someone who takes shortcuts because their instincts said something different to them only to find out they didn't log or file information correctly; that's why I need to check and double-check everything.

This is why I'm tired. I'm reading everything that gets logged, reviewing all statements taken and making sure all alibi checks are run down, attending both post mortems and analysing the forensic reports, holding briefings up to senior management, daily actions meetings and reviews with the team around, being the front spokesperson at press briefings. My responsibilities have grown to include timesheets and cost reviews, sign-offs, forecasting resource needs for the coming weeks and balancing standard time working costs against overtime. I'm taking proactive budget control before the bean counters at Division start hitting me with emails as I'm fully aware my boss and the Commissioner will begin to complain about the time and costs involved if this runs on.

I know all this stuff goes with the SIO role, but sometimes I wonder whether it is too much of a distraction from my valuable experience and time. I know I am good at catching the bad guys; my boss kept referring to small but crucial cogs in a machine, and I now understand what he meant.

Looking around the floor, there is only one other person here, working. The lights are low, energy efficiency measures, with local lighting over me and my colleague across the room. I'm unsure who it is; I can only see the back of their head over the low work screens between workstations. I look at my watch and note it's 9.48 p.m.; I should think of getting home and crashing some sleep before the 8.00 a.m. team briefing in the morning.

I start to close down some of the tabs and packages open on my laptop when I note the little red flag icon in the bottom right-hand corner of the screen. Shall I?

Clicking on the flag opens to show there has been some activity on the Alexander re-investigation case, which gets my attention. Clicking into the update message, I note the record log from a DC Bovary regarding David Alexander's contact with the review team. Clicking into this further will show I have accessed the file, and to be honest, I have enough on my plate at the moment, including the need to get some food and, importantly, some decent sleep. I note the DVD file reference number in the message header, close everything down, and log off.

Heading home at this time of night is no problem, and I'm back in my apartment in less than twenty-five minutes of leaving my desk, complete with a healthy option quick meal from the local late store. Opening the fridge, I pull out a bottle of chilled beer, and sitting at my breakfast bar, I peel off the covering to the chicken, avocado and pomegranate salad and tuck in. I know I shouldn't really have the beer, but it feels like I need it, like I've earned it. Eating the food slowly, I think about tomorrow morning's briefing and actions and scribble some notes in my notebook. That yellow note sticky tag of the Alexander file number and DVD reference is looking back at me on the open page, and as much as I want to look into it, I'm tired, and it's late. I pull out the tag note and stick it to the top of the archive box of files I have; something for another day, I say to myself, and I return to my salad.

No, I have to be one better than the rest. It could be new information. It could be something that needs a follow-up. I need to look at it now.

I lift the archive box and put it on the chair beside me. Rummaging around the contents, I pull out the bundles of DVDs and find the one with the same filing reference I'd scribbled on the yellow sticky note. As I open the outer case, I see the message about watching this from time stamp 20:23hrs, and I know I've already looked at this. There was nothing not already addressed through the investigation or trial.

I'll need to access the central PolConnect system to find out what Alexander's information is, so I log in via the secure VPN route and access PolConnect remotely. Within a few clicks, I have the file report of Alexander's meeting with DC Bovary. Alexander says the CCTV recording during the day of the incident needs to be reviewed again as he thinks there's a link to the time the rear CCTV camera went unserviceable to a man in the pub at the same time; he's indicated the time slot to look at. I note the advice provided by Bovary to Alexander that these CCTV recordings had been previously reviewed and that there was nothing of interest. I must admit, it would have gone through the mill at the time, with the police, CPS, and defence viewing the recordings, so I think this is just some wild grasp at something, or more likely, probably making sure his case is being kept high up the list and being looked into.

I load the DVD onto my laptop, press play and fast forward to the time indicated by Alexander. As it plays, I take another large swallow of beer from the bottle, watching the screen for this mysterious person. I see the man in the bar area at lunchtime, and I can see when the rear camera goes offline. Not long after, the man returns to the bar to finish his drink and then leaves. It could be a coincidence, so I look into the file notes relating to the disk. A DC first reviewed the CCTV footage at the time of the original investigation, and the DC added a note about the time stamp and where to view from. The CCTV footage was considered, shown to Alexander during his interviews under caution, and passed to the CPS as substantiation to support the allegation against

Alexander. There is a note when it was disclosed in a bundle to the defence team during pre-trial disclosure.

There is no mention of anything untoward between the rear CCTV camera and this man. In fact, if anything, I note the time lag between the camera going off and this man returning to his table to finish his beer. This difference in time indicates the man didn't rush back to his chair after damaging the camera if indeed he did damage the camera.

I make a few notes on the pad I keep within the archive box, "*Nothing unusual here - considered previously*". It's already gone midnight. Yawning and stretching, the pull of my bed is getting intense, so I log out of the system, close my VPN access and return my laptop to my backpack, ready for the morning.

Finishing my beer, I walk into my bedroom, drop onto the bed with a deep sigh, and put my arm across my eyes to block out the light temporarily.

'WAKE UP! WAKE UP!' is spinning around in my head, 'WAKE UP! WAKE UP!'. My early morning wake-up alarm is sounding. As my head starts to become clearer, it dawns on me, 'Shit!' and I sit bolt upright, I'd fallen asleep still fully dressed. Luckily, my alarm call is set for 6.30 a.m. each morning, so I have time to get ready. What I'm not pleased about is falling asleep like that, but then who else cares? There's only me here these days, and I did sleep and recharge myself somewhat.

In the kitchen area, I flick the switch on the coffee machine and realise I've not cleaned it out since yesterday morning. 'Sod it,' turn it off again, and put some water in the kettle, instant coffee will have to do this morning. As the kettle boils, I strip quickly and jump in the shower; the temperature turned down low wakes me instantly and by 6.44 a.m. I'm sipping coffee between a bowl of muesli and scribbling in my notebook.

We've got to get a break in this double murder case soon. The trail is getting colder by the day, and the Commissioner is looking for arrests to assuage public opinion and concern. I'm still convinced hard, diligent work will crack this, and I need to get a result here for the victims, their families and, naturally, for me. I lock the apartment door behind me at 7.13 a.m. and return to the station. As I walk through the busy streets, my head is saying inside that I've got to make some time for me today for exercise, *a healthy body and a healthy mind work toward healthy outcomes.* It's just too damn full on though, and I need to stay focused on directing my team and keeping on top of the information flow.

I enter the station through the front doors at 7.29 a.m. and swipe my access card at the first secure door. Walking through the back corridors, phones are already ringing, and I hear voices talking in various side rooms and break-out areas, no doubt shift handovers and updates of the various events through the night. I swipe my card again and enter the Serious Crime team office, my team's home turf.

'Morning Boss,' from my left, 'Morning,' my reply. I'm not big on pleasantries first thing, especially after not much sleep and the knowledge of another full-on day.

I enter my office; well, I like to think it's an office, a corner work area bounded on three sides, two of brick and painted plaster, one of tinted glass. I remove my coat and hang it on the hook behind my desk, open my bag, pull out and switch on my laptop, and drop into my chair. I nod to myself as I purse my lips; today *is the day we'll get that important break.*

43

David – HMP Witchull

My visitor pass arrived from HMP Witchull, allowing me to meet up with Blade again and thank him properly.

Getting through Visitor Reception seems harder than escaping from the place. The checks, the searches, the emptying of pockets, the depositing of keys and phones. Opening and closing of doors. All understandable, I suppose.

We meet up again in the Visitor suite, and as I walk up to Blade, I can see he's been in some altercation from the faint bruising on his face and the two steri-strips above his left eye.

'In the wars again, I see Blade.'

'This, nah, just a minor disagreement. He came round to my way of thinking in the end. What about you? Out there in that big wide world again.'

'OK, I suppose. Weirdly, it feels like I'm starting afresh,' I say with some conviction.

'Good, then you'll know not to end up in here again. Let's keep it like that.'

'I wanted to thank you, Blade. I'm not sure I would have survived in here without you having my back.'

'It was pretty clear to me you aren't like the others in here; you're not the type. So how is the hunt going for the guy that paid Roberts to hit you?'

'Well, some interesting developments,' and I proceeded to tell Blade about the CCTV video, my discussing it with the police and then their, what felt like a polite but clear brush off.

'Don't leave it to the police, Dave, that's how I ended up in here. All they want is a conviction, to wipe the board clean, then start again on the next case. The re-investigation, whilst the right thing to do, will only embarrass them further, especially if looking elsewhere at the time would have prevented your conviction and actually got the person behind it. Are you any closer to finding out a motive for his actions?'

'No, not really; no one can identify him, so it's almost impossible to get to the motive. Maybe he was just the aggrieved partner of one of the women I slept with and just wanted to teach me a lesson; I don't know. I can't think of any other reason: nothing from business, prior threats, bad rugby tackles, nothing.'

'Well, as I say, don't leave it to the police. If you think there is something in that footage and that this guy was involved, keep at it, keep digging, something will turn up.'

'I will. Anyway, what about you Blade, any word on a release date?'

'Nothing further yet. I have a review coming up in a few weeks, and hopefully, the good conduct I had in the bag before this latest disagreement will be considered.'

'Do you need anything?

Can I do anything for you on the outside?'

'Nah, nothing doing outside for me, no one waiting. Been on my own for a long time now, nothing new. Tell you what, do me a favour, get out there and make something of yourself, then you can give me a decent job when I get out,' smiling as he said it.

'No worries, Blade, when you get your release date, let me know, and I'll meet you at the gates. You have me now for the outside.'

'You going all soft on me, Dave? I'm welling up here. You miss sharing a bunk with me, do you?' and we both laugh, which got the attention of the supervising prison officers.

'Look, I'm grateful you've come to see me; honestly, I am, but don't come back visiting. You've got to go and do your thing. Stepping back in time in this place isn't going to help anyone.'

'Blade, it's no bother. You're a mate, and mates should support each other. It didn't take long for me to find out what my mates were really like. I'll visit again.'

'No, the next time you come back here will be to give me a lift when I get out. I won't accept the visitor request if you send another; you know I won't if I say it.'

'Fair enough. Look, you've got my dad's address; I'm crashing there until the compensation comes through. Then I'll get a place, and when I do, I'll let you know the new address. If you need anything, anything at all, write to my dad's address and in my next letter I'll include my mobile phone number so you can reach me anytime. No worries, the call charges are on me. Deal?'

'Yep, deal.' And we both eyeball each other and nod gently.

'Now then, what about this ex of yours? You speak with her yet?'

'Ah, yes, we met up, all a bit cloak and dagger really, more your past than mine. Our meeting was kept secret; I was impressed by her personal security detail and choice of meeting place though. Nothing really to report. We both said our thing, made peace with each other, and left it at that.'

'Did you talk money with her?'

'No, I'm not interested in her money. Genuinely, I don't want any of it. I have my compensation, which will help me rebuild my life.'

'Well, they do say money doesn't buy happiness.'

'True enough. I thought I had happiness, a good living, a decent income, a great looking and talented wife, and all I did was ruin it by searching out what I thought I needed to make me happy. The years in here helped bring all that into focus.'

'Well then, Dave, it seems your time in here is done, and it wasn't wasted on you. Remember, if you want something, the best person to get it is you. Just think carefully about what you wish for before you start going after it.'

'Six years in here, Blade, and you've become a philosopher?'

'Nah, same as you, you get plenty of time to think in here.'

The bell rang, indicating the end of visiting time, and some of the visitors started to move. We look at each other, nod gently, and we shake hands.

'See you on the outside Blade.'

'See you there soon, Dave. Now remember, don't waste your time; make me proud.'

'Will do,' and with that, I stand to leave. 'I'll write soon Blade; watch your back and stay safe.'

'Don't you worry about me, I'll be fine. See ya later mate.'

I join the funnelling of visitors at the exit door, and as I look back, I see Blade watching me leave. He raises his right hand, and then I'm through the exit.

Heading back to Manchester, I think about what Blade said: don't leave it to the police whilst balancing it with being careful what you wish for. Do I really need to know who paid Roberts? What difference will it make now? Simple, he's still out there and what if he's not done with me yet? I've been all over the news recently, and I won't be that hard to find at my dad's place. Finding him is the last bit of the jigsaw, and I need to get the whole picture so I can move on. What if he's doing this to others? I do need to see this through.

I'll keep looking into this myself. There are more documents, statements and video files I can wade through, making sure not to skip anything, and to be thorough and diligent. I don't trust the police to solve this. Besides, at the moment, I have all the time in the world with enough incentive to remain focused. Who else has that?

That night haunts me to this day. Everything changed after my path crossed with Roberts. Someone unknown to me started this ball rolling, and now I need to trap it, pick it up and turn this game around.

44

Samantha – Knightsbridge, London

The doorman to my apartment had taken receipt of the boxes of documents couriered over by Richard, and after checking with Daryl, they had been placed in my study in the apartment.

Comprising seven boxes of documents to search through, it felt like a daunting task ahead of me to search out the DVD that David was interested in. However, as always, Richard and his team had meticulously documented and tabulated all the contents, and within a few minutes, I had a copy of the DVD in hand that David had discussed with the police.

Inserting it into the DVD reader, I played the CCTV recording from the beginning to see what it was that had caught David's attention. The four screens take a little getting used to, but as there's not a great deal happening, they're easy to follow. There were some people in the bar area, a barmaid serving, nothing surprising. Then one of the camera screens, camera 4, shows a grey kind of interference, no picture at all.

'Ah, this must be what Mark was referring to,' I tell myself quietly.

I stop the play and go back into rewind. Stop. Play. As it plays again, I pick up my second glass of chilled Sancerre and take a sip when I see a man enter the bar, order a drink and sit at one of the tables. After some time, he stands, goes to the bar, and then walks to the rear of the pub, in the direction of the toilets and rear door to the beer garden, if I recall correctly.

Then, after a few minutes, the camera goes offline, and not long afterwards, the man returns to his table. So, David thinks that this man has something to do with Roberts. Where does he get that connection from? Roberts is nowhere to be seen. But then again, there is something familiar about this man: the way he holds himself, his posture, the way he walks.

I hit the pause button, freezing a blurred image of the man. The picture quality is poor, and the image is flickering slightly. There's no way of making out his face; it's mostly obscured by the hat he is wearing anyway. But there is something ... something about him.

I rewind and replay it several times but glean nothing new. I'm not sure anyone will be able to determine the man's identity now, not from this recording, after so much time has passed. I take out the DVD, return it to its cover and file it away again. As I close the box, I can see why David is showing an interest in this and why he wants to know what was done to consider this man and the broken camera. I wonder what the police will make of this.

45

David – Bolton

It's a bright morning, and I'm up and ready for action early. I have a mission now, and I intend to take it as far as I can, hopefully, all the way to finding out who paid Roberts.

I take out all the information in the archive boxes, methodically check each file, folder, disc, flash drive, and document against the respective contents lists, and cross-check the disclosure lists from the CPS. All appears to be here.

Next, I consider chronology and roughly put dated documents into date order to follow events as they occurred or were recorded. This timeline should formulate the narrative demonstrating how things unfolded and then can be construed as argued. This takes me most of the morning, and to be honest, whilst interesting and important, it does tire me a little, what with all the scanning of documents for dates, re-ordering documents into correct date order, and constantly thinking of cross-referencing, memorising what I've seen for context and links.

Just before midday, I need a break. The weather is good, and I decide to take a short walk down along the river up to the weir and come back in thirty minutes or so. I step out of the apartment and walk along the hall, and as I open the door to the stairs, Mike is coming at me through the same door, and we surprise each other a little.

'Morning Mike, how are you doing today? Caught any more ne'er-do-wells about the place lately?'

'Afternoon now, Mr Alexander, no, nothing untoward happening. And it's Mikey to friends, remember?'

'Sorry, yes, Mikey.'

'Nah, it's all quiet on the western front, just doing some maintenance work about the place. You off out?'

'Yeh, a bit of fresh air. I need to clear my head a little; I've done a lot of reading this morning.'

'Oh, those archive boxes, is it? Did you find what you were looking for?'

'Early days, but I'm sure there is something in there of interest.'

'Good'o, don't let me keep you. Enjoy your walk.'

'Cheers, will do. I'll be back in about half an hour unless I get distracted,' I say with a wink and smile, and we pass each other. I leave the building, head out of the ground floor door, across the gardens at the rear, through the secure resident's entry gate and onto the river path.

It is pleasant and refreshing to get out. The river has the odd rowboat lapping along, and a canoeist easily slices the water, hardly making an impression on the slow-moving surface.

As I approach the weir, a dog walker throws a stick into the water and his black Labrador bounds in to retrieve it. I never really wanted a dog, but they do seem to make good companions; that is, until I reach the dog walker and the Labrador pads out of the water, shakes vigorously and showers me with cold spray.

'Bounder!! Sorry about that,' shouts the owner, holding his hand up.

'No bother,' my reply, 'he's enjoying himself,' as Bounder drops the stick at my feet. Picking up the stick, I indicate throwing it back in the river, and the owner nods with a smile, so I make it a decent throw to mid-river, and Bounder is off again. It does make me smile a little as I wave to the owner and turn around for the return journey.

Just as I climb the stairs to the first floor of the apartment building, my mobile rings, and I take it out of my pocket. "Number withheld" shows on the screen. I reach for the landing door whilst looking at the phone, and as I do, I look up and catch Mikey walking away down the hall, just further along than Dad's apartment door. I go to answer the call, and it rings off suddenly after only three rings. Wrong number, I suppose? I'll never know.

Entering the apartment, I head for the kettle to make a cup of tea and get a weird sixth sense feeling that someone is or has just been here. I look around and check the rooms, all empty; everything seems to be in order, nothing untoward, so I return to making my cuppa.

Sipping my tea, I look at my morning's clerical work, pondering my next step. Logically, it is to start reading from the earliest date forward. Picking up the first stack of papers, I begin to read and realise that the top document is not the earliest; it's a transcript of my last police interview before I was formally charged. There are documents before this date. Shrugging my shoulders and accepting it must have been a senior moment when I placed that document in the wrong place, I re-file it in the appropriate date order. Now, let's try again, picking up what should be the earliest dated document and off I go. Round two.

46

David – Bolton

After a few days of background reading, organising, filing, and looking for snippets of leads within the archive information, I start to realise this is going nowhere. Dad will return from Turkey soon, and his living area looks more like an office. I decide I may as well start to bundle packets of information together and re-box it, all the time adding notes to my pad.

I drop back onto the settee, close my eyes, take a deep breath and slowly release it. I need to think of a new angle, a new approach. Then it crossed my mind that none of Samantha's friends appear to have given any statements to the police at the time, but then again, why would they? They had nothing to do with the incident, were nowhere near and didn't know Roberts. However, no one had considered if they knew anything or could hold that morsel of a lead that could open this up now.

I've not spoken to any of them since being arrested, and it seems Samantha has lost touch with them too.

Chrissy! At the pub, she gave me her mobile number.

I pull her card from my wallet and start to dial the number, then stop. No. This will blow up on me if I'm not careful. She always was a flirt, especially with me, and we have had our moments together in the past. But that's what it is, in the past, so I start to dial again.

Chrissy answers, 'Hello, who's this?'

'Chrissy, it's me, David.'

'I *knew* you'd call me, and now I've got your number,' so the flirting begins.

'Hi, I was just wondering if you are free this evening and fancied a bite to eat? You know, a chance to catch up and all that?'

'Well, I did have something on this evening, but that can wait. Spending time with you, David, would be far more fun. Where are you thinking of taking me?'

'Oh, er, I don't know really, you probably have a better knowledge of good places to eat and chat.'

'I do. How about Benedict's on Bridgwater Street? Do you know it?'

'Nope, but I'm sure I'll be able to find it. Shall we say seven thirty?'

'Definitely. I'm looking forward to it, David. See you there,' and Chrissy hangs up.

I sigh even before the screen light fades away; what am I letting myself into here? I know what she's like, and Chrissy gets what Chrissy wants. Maybe this was a bad idea. I look back at my phone, thinking of cancelling it already. No, I need to think outside the box, I need to chat with Chrissy. Samantha told me about the blackmail attempt that happened way back, and Chrissy had seen the proof; maybe she could recall something.

I look up Benedict's on the laptop, and it looks like one of those trendy places that Chrissy would frequent. I phone the number and make a reservation for two, asking for a quiet table, if possible, then put my mobile down and carry on with the packing up.

47

David – Manchester

Arriving at Benedict's at twenty past seven, I want to make sure we have a quiet table to one side or a corner, as I don't want us to be disturbed if possible. I'm shown to a table within a brick alcove, low lights, very nice, cosy, and no sooner had I sat down, Chrissy was standing in front of me, arms outstretched.

'Hiya David. No hello hug for an old friend?'

I stand, and we hug, Chrissy kissing my cheek, 'It's been a long time since we last kissed.'

'Er, I think you just kissed me, not *we kissed*'.

'Oh, playing hard to get, I see, I like it,' Chrissy replied with a smile, 'Have you ordered drinks?'

'No, not yet, I couldn't remember what your drink was'.

'Well, I think I'll start with a Porn Star Martini.'

'Ah yeh, I remember. You haven't changed much.'

'I haven't changed at all; I'm still the same old Chrissy.'

'And that's what scares me,' and now it's my turn to smile back.

'You wouldn't want me any other way now, would you?'

'Probably not. It's actually quite nice to find something that hasn't changed since I went inside.'

'Hey, less of the something. How did your date go the other night, you know, the barmaid?'

'Oh Nicole, yeh, fine, no commitments there, just two grown-ups together enjoying themselves'.

'A bit like us then? It was fun, wasn't it?'

'That's not why I'm here Chrissy. I wanted to talk through some stuff with you, see if you can recall anything that might help me?'

'Spoilsport. We can leave that for later if you like?' with a wink and smile, 'Now let's get some drinks', and as if by magic, a waiter appears, and we order drinks.

'Chrissy. I want to ask you about Monica, the woman I was having a fling with. I think she tried blackmailing Samantha with some photos of her and me together.'

'Oh, we are dragging up some old events tonight, aren't we? Do you want to see the photos or the video?'

'No, no, thank you.' I sighed, 'No one can find Monica. Did you have any meetings with her? Is there an email address, phone number, or anything I could follow up on? I need to make contact with her.'

'Why?'

'You do know that someone paid Roberts to hit me, right?'

'Yes, and?'

'Well, the only thing I can think of is that her partner or husband or whatever he was was the one that paid Roberts.'

'I never met her, but Sammy did; she paid her off to keep the photos and videos going public. Just as well really, given where she is today and all.'

'Oh, right. So, you have nothing that can help me?'

'No, sorry. But we are here tonight and can still enjoy ourselves, can't we?'

My deep sigh was probably impolite, but I was only frustrated by this lead closing down in front of me and realising I would need to speak with Samantha again to take this any further.

'Charming,' reacted Chrissy.

'I'm sorry Chrissy, I didn't mean it like that. It's just that every time I seem to be getting somewhere, it's a dead end.'

'Let it go, David, what good will come of it now? Life is too short; enjoy it while you can.'

'People keep saying that to me, but I can't get this out of my head until I know who and why all this happened.'

'Well then, just accept it was Monica's other half because you were sleeping with her and then let it go.

Simple.'

'Nothing is ever that simple'.

'It is, believe me. Shit happens all the time, you've just got to keep your head above it and swim on.'

'I don't know if I can.'

'Look, we had fun together at Uni; we were young. How do you think Samantha would be if she found out we were having sex when the two of you were married? It would be shit, wouldn't it? But she would have to keep on swimming, wouldn't she?'

'She must never find out about us.'

'Oh, come on, do you think I'm that cold? Samantha is, was, and hopefully still is, my best friend. I don't want her ever to find out.'

'But you still led me on, still wanted me even though I was married to your best friend.'

'I don't recall you resisting very much at all. In fact, if I recall correctly, it may even have been you indicating some green lights back then.'

'I nearly didn't come here tonight; I was about to phone you back to cancel.'

'But then you remembered how good we were together.'

Chrissy's smile was warm and cheeky, but I won't let myself be taken in by it.

'No. I remembered you had some involvement around the time of the blackmail attempt and might be able to help me, but it doesn't look like you can.'

Chrissy picked up her glass and downed the cocktail. 'OK. I'm sorry. I got the wrong impression when you called me, forget what I said. Look, if you want any info on Monica, the only place you've any chance of getting it is from Samantha.'

'Right, I'm sorry too. I should have said why we needed to speak.'

'Do you still want dinner, share a table with one of your oldest friends?'

'Actually, if there are no strings attached, I'd love that.'

'Then no strings. I can do that.' Chrissy smiled at me, 'Honestly, just friends.'

'OK. Thank you. Would you like another drink?'

'Yes, please, and then you can tell me all about being a con banged up in prison.'

And then there was that Chrissy smile again.

48

David – Bolton

'How was the golf, Dad, worth the trip out to Turkey?

'Definitely, fabulous resort and some of the golf courses out there are championship quality.

Absolutely making that trip again. I may stay longer next time.'

'And why not? There's nothing to hold you back here, Dad, enjoy it.'

'Oh, I don't know, spending time with my son may be,' smiling as he says it.

'I know, but really, don't be around here just because I am. Enjoy yourself, Dad; I may even come out with you next time.'

'You? And Golf? I somehow don't see that happening.'

'I don't have to play golf. If the resorts are that good, I can just chill during the day, sightsee a little, sunbathe on the beach or by the pool, and we can catch up in the evenings.'

'OK, it's a deal. I'll let you know when I'm thinking of going out there again. Now tell me, how is your detective work going? Any new leads?'

'Well, yes and no. Nothing new from the archive boxes. I went through everything closely. There are no new leads as such, but I did meet up with Chrissy a few days ago. You remember Chrissy, Samanatha's best friend?'

'Oh, I remember Chrissy. She was always a flirty one, that one; I think she fancied you at one time.'

'Give over, Dad. Just because we chatted and laughed doesn't mean anything happened.'

'If you say so. So, was she of any help?'

'Not really. I was quizzing her about the woman I was having a fling with, Monica, but she couldn't remember much; she didn't have any contact details for her.'

'Monica, the woman named in the divorce papers?'

'Yep.'

'And why would Chrissy know anything about her?'

Ah, I need to be careful here; I'm not sure Dad knows about the blackmail attempt, 'Best friends with Samantha, you know, girl talk, thought Samantha may have said something to Chrissy.'

'Are you thinking Monica's partner was the one that paid Roberts?'

'Maybe. Possibly. Reasonable motive. Monica did tell me he was a bit shady, connections with some villains or something, hence why we were extra secretive.'

'You do like playing with fire, don't you?'

'I did Dad, did. Not anymore, I've changed.'

'So, Chrissy had nothing new?'

'Well, she did say that Samantha may know more. After all, Sam hired an investigator to get the dirt on me,' I thought this would test out what Dad knows.

'Ah, now that makes sense, I suppose. The investigator would have followed her and logged details and addresses.'

'Yes, exactly,' nice sidestep there, I thought to myself.

'OK, so what next? Reach out to Samantha again?'

'Yep'.

'Don't you think this is all best left alone, especially if he is some kind of villain?'

'I need to know; I just need to know if it was him. If not him, then it's obviously someone else, someone I may have known.'

'Just be careful Davey, be careful'.

'I will Dad, don't worry.'

I leave the apartment and walk along the river. I pull out my mobile and call Samantha's office in London, and on getting through, ask for Daryl.

'Daryl, please can you put me through to Samantha? I need to speak with her on a personal matter?'

'Mr Alexander, Samantha is busy all day today. I can pass a message to her if you like?'

'Yes, please. Please ask her to call me on my mobile. We need to meet up to discuss a sensitive matter, which I think is best face to face, private.'

'No problem, I'll pass that message to Samantha. Have a good day, Mr Alexander,' and Daryl hung up.

Later in the evening my mobile starts to ring, showing 'withheld number' and I answer it.

'David, it's Samantha. I have a message you want to speak with me about something personal. Is everything alright, is Henry OK?'

'Hi Samantha, yes everything's fine. I was wondering if you had time this week for us to meet up in person. I met with Chrissy a few days ago, and I have something I'd like to discuss with you face-to-face. I know how busy you are so I'm more than happy to travel to wherever suits you.'

'Gosh, David, even the Prime Minster is struggling to get some of my diary this week.'

Samantha really is moving in higher circles now.

'Err, OK, sorry, I just thought ... what about next week?'

'Wait a second David ....' and the phone went quiet. 'Can you be at Belfont Hall outside Macclesfield on Thursday morning at, say, 7.30 a.m.? We could have breakfast together.'

'Ah, yes, I can do that.'

'I'll get Daryl to make sure my diary is free for an hour. We can have breakfast in my suite, just the two of us.'

'That'll be great, thank you.'

'I'll see you on Thursday morning, just ask at reception, and you'll be shown up.'

'Thanks, Samantha, I'll be there. Bye.'

'Bye, David.'

49

David – Belfont Hall

Borrowing Dad's car, I set off early and arrive at 7.15 a.m. I can't afford to miss this time with Samantha. A beautiful morning, blue skies with a light breeze. The sweeping drive through perfect lawns up to the former stately home didn't leave any doubt this is a seriously expensive hotel. At the front of the hotel, Dad's car stands out from all the rest, it being the only car present that isn't a pedigree Italian or German supercar.

As I park, an immaculately dressed staff member approaches and opens the driver's door.

'Good morning, Mr Alexander, welcome to Belfont Hall. My name is Andrew. Do you have any luggage I can assist you with?'

I step out of the car and look at him smiling, 'No, thank you, Andrew, it's just me as I am.'

'Excellent, sir, please follow me, Miss Walsh is expecting you.'

And by just this very act, I'm blown away; how did he know it was me? I suppose Samantha advised the hotel to expect a regular car at about this time.

We walk through the open doors of the hotel, and the sheer opulence of the place takes away any lingering doubt; this is palatial. The entrance hall, complete with opposing twin cantilever twin staircases wrapped around walls adorned with large oil paintings of aristocracy and racehorses, overlooks marble sculptures and other works of art.

At the top of the staircase, Andrew approached a pair of large doors, knocked gently and, opened both simultaneously and stepped to one side, "Mr Alexander Miss Walsh,' he announced.

Samantha was stood by a large bay window looking out over the rear of the hotel, across colourful gardens and trimmed bushes. 'Thank you, Andrew. Please serve breakfast in the drawing room. Come in David.'

'Good morning, this is a rather special place.'

'It's all for work, David. We have a meeting with a Japanese medical conglomerate later this morning, and this setting goes down well with their executive board. Shall we go through?' as Samantha turns towards another pair of doors.

We sit at a formally laid table. A maid places a plate of salmon and scrambled eggs in front of Samantha and Eggs Florentine in front of me, 'Thank you,' I say, and I look to Samantha, 'You remembered?'

'Yes, and I will venture these will probably be the best you've ever tasted. The Chefs here are Michelin-trained. Perfection'. Sam looks up and speaks out to Andrew, 'Thank you. Can we have a little privacy, please?'

'Yes, certainly, Miss Walsh,' replies Andrew. The room empties, and the doors close behind them.

'Now, David, what is this mysterious private matter we need to discuss?'

'One moment, I must try these eggs.' I break the yolk with my knife, and the yolk oozes onto the spinach and English muffin. I take a cut of egg, spinach and muffin lightly coated with hollandaise sauce and place it in my mouth. 'Ummm', chewing slowly, 'Yes, you're right ... Wow'.

'So, you met up with Chrissy. How is she?' asked Samantha as she delicately sliced through the salmon.

'She's good. Still the same old Chrissy, life and soul of the party.'

'And what brought you two together?'

'Well, we know the police have re-opened the enquiry and are looking into the events surrounding the fight, but they do seem to be taking their time about it. So I thought, as I have time on my hands, I would look into it also, maybe from a slightly different angle.'

'Oh, I see. And what have you uncovered so far?'

'Well, not a lot from the original records of the investigation and the trial, but the one bit that seems to elude everyone is what happened to Monica; where is she?'

'And you thought Chrissy would have some knowledge not shared with us?'

'Well, yes.'

'But why is Monica important? Her involvement, as we both know, was in the adultery.'

'Uh, er, yes. Well, for me, I'm stuck on the motive. Roberts was paid; we don't know by whom or why.

The trail is cold.'

'And finding this out will achieve what?'

'Well, there could be charges to consider, but if nothing can stick, it'll at least put my mind at rest as to why someone would do this to me. We know now there was some other driver behind it all; it's just we have nothing further. So I thought Chrissy may have some information about Monica from the blackmail attempt.'

'And did she?'

'No. Chrissy said she never met Monica or had any dealings with her, but you did, and that's why I need to chat with you.'

'I did, but it was all handled through text messages on a couple of burner phones that Monica provided. I met her only once, at the pay-off for the photos and videos. Monica took both phones back when the deal was done.'

'Oh, so you have no contact details for her either?'

'No, sorry. Anyway, I couldn't wait to get away from that woman; she was not a very nice person at all. God knows what you saw in her unless it was just the sex?'

'Yes, it was really. I know it's a classic line, but it was just sex; she meant nothing to me.'

'David, you can see now why I do so much charity work with abused women; you were only one step away from treating her like a mere object; in fact, that is what you were doing. The next step is abuse.'

I place my knife and fork down and continue looking at my plate, 'Look, I know I deserve this and probably more, but I think I've paid my price for my indiscretions. I only wanted to know if you had any information that could help, and I didn't want any of this escaping and harming your reputation.'

'Well, that is probably the first real consideration you've given me in a long time.'

'I know, I'm sorry.' We continue to eat our breakfast in silence.

After clearing my plate, I look at Samantha, 'I'm sorry, Samantha, I should leave you alone and not interfere in your life anymore. If it was all related to Monica, I will find out and take it to the police, and they can handle it from there.' I place my napkin on the table, push my chair back and stand, 'Thank you for making time for me this morning, and I hope your deal goes well today.'

Samantha looks up at me. She still has a beautiful, radiant face that melts me and makes me angry with myself. 'David, I have access to some very discreet private investigators. Let me see what they can uncover. They really are good, you know. If they obtain any information, I'll pass it on to you. I can see this is eating away at you, and I don't want this ruining your chance at rebuilding your life.'

'Thank you. If you are comfortable that they will remain discreet, that will be a great help. If they can't find Monica, the trail will have gone cold, and I'll have to explore other options. I'll not rest until I resolve this.'

'I'll give them instructions today. Hopefully, they find Monica, and I'll be in touch soon.'

'I don't deserve this. You have suffered just as much as me, if not more, because of my actions.'

'David, I am happy now with my life, and I have the means to help you find happiness too.'

'Thank you. You really are a good person, Samantha, and deserve to be happy doing what you enjoy.'

I turn and walk to the door. As I open it, I look back at Samantha and see she is already typing a message into her mobile phone. I slip out of the room quietly and leave.

50

Samantha – Belfont Hall

'Apologies for the text message earlier, Richard, but I want to do something, something personal to me that I want to keep private. However, I'll need your help, and I know you'll have some reservations about this.'

'That all sounds a little sinister, Samantha. Is it illegal?'

'Oh, no, nothing like that. You're my most trusted advisor and confidant; I'm sure you'll be able to conclude this for me.'

'Whatever you need, Samantha, you know you can always rely upon me.'

'Thank you. I want to 'gift' a sum of money to David, my ex-husband. I know, and before you say anything, I have decided, and there is no going back on this.'

'Forgive me for asking, has he asked you for money? Is he putting you under some kind of pressure?'

'No, not all. You may think I'm weak, but we were a *team* in the early days, and my success was borne out of those early times together and, ironically, out of the events that followed. He hasn't asked me for money, and he's definitely not blackmailing me or coercing me for a payment.'

'But ...'

'No, Richard, please, my mind is made up. I met David again this morning here at Belfont Hall, and we talked some more. I know the affair was bad and hit me hard at the time, but we may have worked through it. I don't know, but going to prison did split us up for sure, and actually, that was for something he didn't do. I don't know ... I simply want to set David up in a comfortable lifestyle so he can overcome the issues he still carries, and lord knows I can afford it.'

'You really are one of the most generous, forgiving individuals I think I have ever met. If this is what you want to do, Samantha, then I am behind it all the way.'

'Thank you.'

'What are you thinking of? A bank transfer of a sum of money or a stipend of some kind?'

'Probably the former, a one-off transaction I think would be best.'

'Umm, I agree. Just confirm the sum, and I'll pull the necessary levers to make it happen.'

'Thank you, Richard. I'll give it some thought and let you know.'

'If you don't mind me asking, does David know you want to do this?'

'No, he doesn't, not yet.'

'I presume he'll be accepting of your "charity"?'

'Yes, I think so. He has a life to rebuild and a future to look for.'

51

Samantha – Edinburgh

Well, Richard has confirmed the finances are all sorted, and he is ready to transfer the sum to David when I indicate.

My private investigator, Mark, has completed his preliminary searches and investigation. I'm sure David will be surprised with the outcome. I think it best this is all kept below the radar again, a private meeting well away from the press and the Board. As I'll be travelling halfway around the world to New Zealand next week, I have decided I'll invite David out to my villa in Queensland, he can see where it all began and where I grew up, and I'm sure the news I have for him will change his life forever.

'Hello, David. Sorry to call you late in the evening. It's my first free opportunity over the last few days.'

'Hi, no problem, Samantha. I'm just chilling, watching some TV. Have your private investigators managed to locate Monica?'

'Yes and no. I have their report with some additional information I want to share with you, but not over the telephone, and my diary is absolutely full. I'm travelling to Christchurch, New Zealand, next week to host a conference and meet some government dignitaries and so on, and I've managed to work a couple of days free into my diary. I'll be calling in at my villa in Queensland and wondered if you would like to come out to my little retreat, my place, and we can talk quietly there, talk through this new information, and have a bit of *us* time to catch up. What do you think? Don't worry about travel costs, I'll arrange all that.'

I don't think David was expecting any of this. To be truthful, I don't think he thought I would be back in touch so soon or at all.

'That's fantastic, Samantha. I've never been to Australia and obviously can't wait to hear what you have for me. I'm still a free agent, so anytime next week is fine with me.'

'Great. I'll have Daryl contact you and make all the arrangements. It'll be warm out there this time of year, bring summer clothes. You still have a passport, I presume?'

'Oh ah, well, no. It was surrendered early on when I was arrested. To be honest, I think it would have expired by now anyway.'

'Not to worry, I have some good contacts. We'll rush a new one through, ready for next week. Daryl will arrange it all with you.'

'Well, er, thank you. I'm looking forward to it.'

'Yes, me too. I'll meet you out there as I'll stop off in Singapore on my way out, some business to attend to. I'll see you at the villa, David. Bye for now,' and I cancel the call.

I call Daryl and give him my instructions, and once again, it doesn't faze Daryl at all.

52

David – Bolton

'Really?' Henry questioned, 'Queensland?'

'Yes, I know. All paid for. But more importantly, Sam has some information for me: her private investigators have been looking for Monica. This could be the lead I've been waiting for.'

'Are you still going on about that? I thought you let it go?'

'No, Dad, I need to know, and Samantha offered to help.'

'When?'

'The other day, when I borrowed your car, we met at a hotel.'

'A hotel? Are you two back together?'

'No, no, Dad, that boat sailed a long time ago. We just had breakfast and a chat. Anyway, Samantha offered to help, and it seems she has come up trumps.'

'Oh, I see. And what is this *new information*?'

'That's why I'm going out to Queensland.'

'What, she can't tell you here?'

'No, you know what the media is like. Sam can't risk any bad press, and with all that phone hacking going on some time ago, I can see why she is being cautious. Her diary is chocker, but she has managed to wangle a couple of days free next week out in Queensland before going on to New Zealand.'

'Busy lady. Well, I hope it all works out for you. Be careful.'

'It will Dad, and I will, don't worry about me,' and with a wry smile, 'any chance of a lift to the airport on Tuesday?'

'Cheeky sod, no change there. Alright then, why not.'

53

David – Cape Tribulation, Queensland

The flight out to Australia was long, with a couple of hours on the ground in Dubai, changing flights to Sydney, and then another flight to Cairns. Travelling in Business Class does make a difference.

However, the helicopter flight from Cairns airport was not expected. I've never been in a helicopter before; quite a number of firsts for me on this journey. Daryl had said I would be met at the airport, and I just thought it would be a taxi or private car. The pilot introduced himself as Ben, a bloody big bloke I wouldn't like to ruck up against on the field. He's not an overly chatty type, but he seems OK.

As we took off and cut across towards the coastline, I was feeling pretty impressed; what a way to travel, first-class style all the way. We banked to the left and paralleled the coastline a hundred metres or so out to sea. Now and then, Ben would comment on local features, flying over Port Douglas, Mossman off to the left, the Daintree River with the Mount Lewis and Daintree National Parks in the distance. Green forests meet the ocean, interspersed with long stretches of sandy beach between the headlands. Beautiful. Beautiful but dangerous, Dad's words still ringing in my ears from when he drove me to Manchester Airport.

After about forty minutes of flying, we banked again to the left and slowed down, coming in squarely across the coastline to what looked like an elevated former colonial-type house surrounded by tall trees.

Ben hovered gently over a large lawn and placed the helicopter down without so much as a bump, then started the shutdown sequence of the helicopter.

As the rotors slowed, I noted they were dropping slightly, and I waited for Ben to tell me what to do, not being sure when it was safe to step out. Ben removed his headset, clambered out of the cockpit, moved to the rear door, and opened it for me. My cue to step out. I carefully removed my headset and stepped out of the cabin into the warm air. I looked up towards the house and saw Sam walking down the steps heading our way, looking very relaxed in a loose-fitting white cotton dress and broad-rim hat.

'Hello David, how was the journey?'

'Hi. It was fantastic, and I didn't expect this,' putting my hand out in an arc that took in the house, gardens and the helicopter.

Ben was already carrying my case up the steps as I approached Samantha. We hug, and Samantha kisses me on my cheek, 'I'm glad you're here, David. We have so much to talk about and can do without prying eyes and pricked ears. Come, I'll show you where I escape to.' Samantha took hold of my left hand, and with her left arm coming across her, she held the top of my arm and came in close. She led me up the steps, past a beautifully tranquil infinity swimming pool, towards the main house.

'I have a guest house here that you can use,' as she points to a small but very neat-looking detached building.' At least until we get to know each other a little better,' she said as she squeezed my hand tighter in an affectionate, mildly cheeky way.

As we reached the patio area, a housemaid was about to pour champagne into one of the two waiting glasses on the table. 'Thank you, Fiona, don't worry, I'll take care of that. Can you bring us some of your fabulous little treats, please?'

'Yes, miss, one moment,' placing the champagne bottle back in the chiller before turning for the house.

As Samantha poured, I looked around and then directly at her, 'I'm seriously impressed, Sammy.'

'You've not called me Sammy for so long,' smiling and offering me a glass of bubbles.

'Oh, sorry, I didn't mean to ...'

'No, it's fine; I quite like it. No one uses that name with me anymore; it's quite endearing.'

I raise my glass, 'To your success, Sammy.'

'And to you and yours also,' replied Samantha, our glasses chinking gently. We both sip. Samantha puts out her arm and wipes it across the horizon, 'Welcome to my home, David, my birthplace, the place I grew up before we moved to the UK. I do love it here. This is heaven on earth to me.'

'I can see why; it is stunning. Did your parents own this house? You lived here?'

'No, silly, we lived further down the coast, in Port Douglas. I saw this come up on the market about a year ago, and I just had to buy it. Spent some time renovating and remodelling, but all finished now.'

Fiona returned with platters of delicacies, hors-d'oeuvres of local seafood and fruits and placed them on the table. 'Thank you, Fiona. Please ask Ben to place Mr Alexander's luggage in the Guest House.'

'Certainly Miss Walsh.'

'Thank you, Fiona.'

Samantha turned to me, 'Now, you must be peckish. Try some of these; they are absolutely delightful.'

Placing some of the delicious-looking creations on our plates, we sit on a pair of comfortable chairs near the pool.

As I placed the first gem into my mouth, Samantha said quietly, 'Now, no shop talk, no bad news stories, let's just catch up with each other and enjoy the rest of the afternoon. We can talk about Roberts and what you have discovered over dinner, and I can let you know what the private investigators have uncovered.'

'Sounds good to me, Sammy. Umm, these are stunning little bites.'

'I know, Fiona is a miracle worker in the kitchen. I do miss her food when I'm away.'

We talked for a few hours, swapping family and friends updates. Samantha spoke about OxyRuco, the good work she is doing around the world, and how her success has allowed her to fund her charities. It was good to catch up, be put at ease by Samantha's graciousness and calm, and just take in the overall atmosphere.

At about four-thirty, Samantha guided me to the Guest House with a quick introduction to the amenities.

This little house was better equipped than many main houses I've experienced before, with lots of mod cons, interactive controls and systems, very tastefully decorated, minimalist but stylish. Samantha then left to prepare and dress for dinner. I shaved and showered, using some of the local environmentally friendly products laid out in the bathroom. Walking around in a white linen robe, I thought of calling Dad back in the UK, then remembered the time difference. It wasn't too early, but I thought better of it; I'd been caught out before with my international phone calling to Dad.

As six o'clock approached, I had dressed in smart casual clothes, decided to leave my mobile phone on charge on the side table and was walking out of the Guest House, heading across the grass and patio to enter the large house via the open French style patio doors.

Gentle music is playing in the background, and I can hear light singing from the room adjacent to the dining area, which I presume is the kitchen. As I walk through the door, Samantha is by the central island preparing food, a glass of champagne beside her. She looked absolutely radiant and happy, and a passing thought ran through my head of what a fool I'd been to jeopardise our marriage, providing Samantha the reason to divorce me.

Samantha turned slightly and, looking up, saw me looking at her, 'Now there you are,' she said softly, 'a glass or two of bubbles before dinner?' as she raised her glass and tilted her head slightly to her right.

'Yes, please, that'll be nice.' Samantha placed her glass on the worktop, picked up an empty glass, gracefully tipped the bottle contents gently into a flute for me, let the bubbles settle slightly and tipped a little more in whilst slowly walking towards me with my glass outstretched in front of her. 'Thank you.'

Samantha returns to the worktop, places the bottle back in the silver bucket and picks up her glass, looks at me and says, 'Here's to an enjoyable evening,' as we chink glasses and sip the cool champagne.

'And what delicacy has Fiona prepared for this evening?'

'Ah ha! Not so fast. Fiona merely prepared the ingredients, *je suis la chef cuisinier* ce soir, monsieur.

Take this,' passing me the three-quarter bottle of champagne in the bucket, 'and sit outside while the sun goes down. I promise you it's worth it.'

'Can I help? I'm pretty good at burning things.'

Samantha laughed, 'No thank you, I have it all in hand, now go on, shoo, enjoy the sunset,' as she brushes me off with butterfly hands.

'OK, but only if you're sure?'

'Yes, go, shoo, shoo,' blowing me a light kiss.

I retrace my steps back out of the house, place the champagne bucket beside the shade of the table on the patio, and sit in one of the comfortable chairs, looking out towards the coast and sea. It was magical, a gentle, warm breeze, not overly humid and with the blend of an ochre setting sun behind me and the champagne, I felt myself relax even further as if I could chill any more than I already was.

As the sun was just about to dip below the forest behind me, Samantha came onto the patio and silently crept up to me. From behind, she places her hands over my eyes and whispers, 'Dinner is served.'

Startled a little, pleasantly so, I stand and turn to look at Samantha. She smiles and turns towards the house, where I notice the dining table now gently lit with candles and low room lighting.

Samantha pulls out a chair for me, and I playfully bow slightly and sit down. 'Merci, madam.' She walks around the table and sits opposite me, 'I hope you don't mind,' as she indicates a bottle of wine in a chiller, 'I'm still a softy for a crisp Sancerre?'

'No, not at all, that's an excellent choice,' as I reach for the bottle and pour Samantha a glass and one for myself. Raising our glasses whilst looking at each other, Samantha asks, 'What shall our toast be?'

'How's about your success, Sammy and my freedom? May the best of our past be the worst of our future.'

Samantha nods slightly, smiling, 'I like that, cheers,' we raise our glasses and sip in unison.

Fiona appears and places a plated appetiser in front of Samantha, 'Thank you, Fiona,' and then in front of me, 'Thank you, it looks delicious.'

Samantha looks at me, 'Red snapper crudo with watercress pesto.'

'Impressive. You prepared this?'

'Of course. I do love to cook when I get the opportunity; it helps me relax, focus and clear my mind of business decisions and everyday pressures. Bon appetite.'

The sun had lost the fight with the horizon, and skies darkened quickly as we ate and talked our way through a further three courses of absolutely sublime cuisine with carefully selected wines to complement each dish. We talked about the good times when we met, our time at university, the parties, our friends, my marriage proposal in Crete and how the hotel staff danced with us that night on the news of our engagement. Our setting up the business and working together. Neither of us dared to touch on anything considered unsafe ground. We were too focused on enjoying the evening together. It had been so long since I had laughed like this and been with a woman who I really, really wanted to be with.

As Fiona returned to serve dessert, Samantha looks up at her, 'Thank you, Fiona, that will be all this evening. We'll look after ourselves from here.'

'Thank you, Miss, I'll return in the morning.'

'No rush, Fiona, midday tomorrow will be fine.'

'Ah, thank you, Miss. Have a good evening, ma'am, sir,' and Fiona retires to the kitchen.

Looking at me, Samantha said quietly, 'Fiona is an absolute godsend. I'd be lost out here without her.'

'Does she live nearby?'

'Not too far away, I have a couple of small houses on the edge of the grounds; Fiona lives in one.

She returns to family near Port Douglas when I'm away.'

'That's nice. Now, what do we have here? What is this delight?'

'Vanilla panna cotta, rhubarb and ginger.'

'Stunning Sammy. You live very well.'

'Thank you, hard work pays off.'

'So true.'

We quietly enjoy dessert, and I am secretly wishing for another serving; it is gorgeous.

Samantha then breaks the moment, 'Now that we are alone, David, shall we discuss Roberts? I'm intrigued to discover what new evidence you have uncovered about that night.'

Placing my cutlery across my plate, I look to Samantha, 'Well, as I mentioned previously, I have been doing some digging of my own. The police are supposedly looking into this again, but they seem awfully slow and sometimes unhelpful to the point of almost seemingly being obstructive.'

'Really? I thought the police would want to get to the bottom of this sooner rather than later?'

'My thoughts entirely, but a friend of mine said not to trust the police to resolve this as the whole episode will always reflect badly on them, and he expects the police will just hope it withers and dies away.'

'Who is this friend?'

'A cellmate from when I was in prison.'

'Well then, he would be anti-police, I would suggest, already being a convicted criminal.'

'No, he's not like that. He's an honest bloke caught up in something he couldn't control and was left to carry the can for his former business colleague. You seem to have forgotten I was also officially once a convicted criminal. Anyway, carefully pushing that to one side, I've been looking into this myself, and I've got a strong feeling that Roberts was paid by Bonning-Wallace, the man who stalked and attacked you.'

'Wow, seriously? How have you come to that opinion?'

'I must admit, Sammy, Roberts really did piss me off that night. I was out with my mates on a pretty cool, relaxed evening, and this moron wanted to mix it up with me. I wasn't interested, but he kept pushing and then went for me, and I thought, 'OK, here you go then, have some,' and it ended up killing him. To be honest, that part of it didn't bother me. He was just a wannabe, someone who thought he ruled the roost, and I was just some convenient bloke to pick a fight with. I'm kind of glad he died; he didn't deserve to occupy the same space as normal, honest people. And he's not missed, you know, his family only wanted their 15 minutes of fame, milk the tabloids for a few quid and some free sympathy cider down the local. It's clear now he was willing to take a few pounds to punch out some guy he'd never even met before, a great example of honour and chivalry; he probably thought honour and chivalry was a local hooker and a brand of whisky.'

'Yeh, but he is dead, and you killed him.'

'But someone else set it all up. He wasn't meant to die...or was he?'

'What do you mean?'

'Well, as you know now, I've had a few brawls in my time, and I've laid down a few men. I certainly didn't expect that knockdown would turn out like that.'

'There's a lot about you, David, I didn't know,' as Samantha placed her glass on the table. 'Anyway, that's all behind us now. We're no longer an item. We've gone our different ways and, to be clear, not likely to get back together.'

Now, that surprised me a little, given how the day and evening had gone so far and how we had started a reconnection process. I was beginning to wonder whether there was a reconciliation in play here, but now Samantha has been clear, I'd better maintain composure.

'I know, time has alas moved on. I'm not suggesting we hook back up far from it. I just want to get to the bottom of what happened ... and why. Somebody paid Roberts. We all know that now. I had no enemies, no rivals in business or sport, nothing that would warrant someone to pay another person to attack me. The most obvious candidate to me *has to* be Bonning-Wallace.'

'I don't get it, why Bonning-Wallace?'

'Let's assume he was already stalking you back then, before the night of the fight. He would have known about me, that you were married and that I was, shall we say, physically fit and could look after myself; he would know this from seeing us together. He had to get me off the scene somehow or catch you when he knew I wouldn't be around. That last part was more difficult as we worked together and spent much of our spare time together, and when I played rugby, you were with friends or shopping.'

'This all sounds a little implausible to me, David.'

'No, not really. Think about it: he did manage to get me off the scene and then track you to a place he knew you would be alone, at your farmhouse.'

'I suppose you have a point, but why wait so long after your arrest to come after me?'

'That I don't know, that's the bit that has been puzzling me. Maybe it's not him, but if I can work out why the delay in attacking you, then maybe I'll have the answer.'

'Well, I suppose if it was Bonning-Wallace, then he could have been working away, overseas or something, or being followed himself by the police as he had, at that time, recently been acquitted at court for other sexual assault allegations.'

'Had he? How do you know that?'

'It all came out in the inquest, I think, or Richard told me, or maybe one of the detectives. Anyway, there could be a reasonable explanation for the delay, that is, if it was him, of course.'

'My instincts are telling me there is something more to this that I have yet to uncover. What about your resources? What did your private investigators turn up?'

'Nothing really substantial. Why don't we just let it lie at Roberts being paid by Bonning-Wallace? Both are now no longer with us.'

'It's just that it all seems too neatly tidied up, and life isn't like that, not for me anyway.'

'I think you have just become a little cynical in your old age,' Samantha said with a smile.

'Hey, less of the old age. But I have become more aware of wider matters, people with agendas, people protecting their own interests, and selfishly harming others along the way. Prison can do this to a person, I suppose, make them look critically at their life and the people around them, and a whole lot more, believe me.'

'I do, but sometimes people see ghosts and shadows where there are none. Your prison mate seems to have fuelled a paranoia in you.'

'No, no, he hasn't,' pausing to think of what to say next. 'I think he just got me to open my eyes to a more realistic world, one uglier than most see or want to see.'

'I know it's ugly. That's why my work is aimed at helping so many people around the world, both medically and psychologically. I want to help people rebuild their lives and realise their inner potential, the potential that is often oppressed or subdued by others.'

'I think you're talking more about your charity work now than the cancer treatments?'

'I suppose I am,' Samantha admitted, gently nodding acceptance.

'If someone had told me ten years ago that you would become a leading light for women's rights, I would have laughed.'

'Why?' putting the wine glass down hard on the table, 'why would you have laughed?'

'Oh, I don't know, I just would have. All you wanted to do was enjoy life and, of course, discover a medical treatment from your beloved flat fish.'

'It's not a flat fish, and you know that!' Her tone obvious that my poor attempt at humour was not well received.

'I do, I know, I'm just playing with you.'

'Is that because you think you can? Because you can belittle the work of a woman?'

'Whooaaa! No. It's not that at all. Please don't get all uptight here, Sammy; I thought we were cool with each other. I'm sorry if I've offended you, and I'll take my words back.'

'Hard to do that now when they're already in the wind.'

'OK, OK. I'll play nice, I'm sorry. Now, if you don't mind, I must pay my respects to a call of nature.' As I stand to go to the bathroom, I go lightheaded and slightly lose my balance, grabbing the table and chair arm for support rattling the table contents.

'Opps, a little too much Barolo or Sancerre or Burgundy, me thinks', I quip as I steady myself.

'Not forgetting the Champagne David, oh and the Tokaji,' she said, teasing me with a little smile, now seemingly calming slightly after I offended her.

'I go now, but I shall return,' I say. 'Well, I would if I knew where I was going and where to return from,' as I hold out my hands, gesturing as though I were looking to catch an invisible object. Samantha stood and walked around the table, took me by the arm and guided me to the hall, to the washroom tucked beneath the stairs to the upper floor. 'Are you OK, shall I wait for you?' she asked quietly.

'No, no, I'll be fine, thank you. It's probably the flying, jet lag, and I may be a bit dehydrated,' I say quietly as I cautiously and carefully make my way into the washroom.

54

David – Cape Tribulation, Queensland

A few minutes later, suitably relieved, I wash, and as I turn to reach for the hand towel, my legs just give way, and in tumbling, I reach out and grab the sink, helping to arrest my fall. 'What the fuck?' I mumble to myself, 'Come on, Dave, you've had heavier drinking sessions than this.' I try to stand again, but my legs don't want to respond to my brain signals.

Samantha knocks on the door, 'Are you OK in there, David? Do you need anything?'

'Yes, er, no, I mean, I'm fine, but it seems my legs aren't.'

'I'll come in if that's OK with you?'

'Yes, please, although I am embarrassed by this.'

The door opens slowly, and Samantha is standing, looking at me quizzically.

'Not used to mixing your drinks, David? That's not like you.'

'I know. I can't explain this. Can you help me stand, please?'

As Samantha walks into the washroom, I notice Ben, the helicopter pilot, standing behind her. 'What's he doing here, Sammy?'

'He's here to carry you.'

'That was a quick response; I only just asked for your help.'

Samantha instructs quite crisply, 'Ben, can you pick him up please and bring him to the living room?'

Ben just nods. As Samantha stands aside, the behemoth that Ben seems to have become effortlessly picks me up, throws my right arm over his shoulder and unceremoniously assists me to the living room, dropping me on the settee. He turned to Samantha, 'How long will this take?'

Samantha looks at him and replies quietly, 'Not long now, it's already taking effect. Can you give us a few minutes alone, please, darling? I just need to talk to David about what will come next.'

'Sure, just call me. I'll be in the dining room; there'll be some wine left for me, I hope?'

'Yes, of course, help yourself.'

'What's going on Sammy?'

'David, listen carefully. This is your very last evening. Please stay calm; we don't want this to get ugly.'

'What do you mean *'my last evening'*? Don't want *what* to get ugly?'

'I had to take some positive action, David. You were obviously getting a little too close to the truth for me not to take some steps to control the situation.'

Wondering what the hell is going on, I try to sit up, but my legs are immobile, and pulling myself up straight is hard. 'What do you mean take *some steps*? I'm confused.'

'I thought you might be. I wasn't sure how much you had pieced together, so I needed to find out. I knew it wouldn't be long if I left you unchecked, that you would see the whole picture and as you know, I don't like leaving things to chance; I prefer to be in control all the time.'

'What do you mean? Have you poisoned me?'

'Kind of, it's a natural toxin found in this part of the world. When you are found in the next day or so, it will all look like an unfortunate but explainable accident. Naturally, questions will be asked, but all directions will lead to the simple conclusion that you went for a late-night walk along the water line and unfortunately stepped on a stonefish, quite prevalent around these areas, you know, *my favourite flat fish*. The toxin seems to have reacted quicker than I expected, though, possibly the level of alcohol you've taken in or some of the prescription drugs I found in your hand luggage, who knows, maybe both? If not treated quickly, this toxin can be fatal, as it will be in your case.'

'What? What are you talking about? Are you trying to kill me?'

'No, not trying, David, succeeding. You're nearly there, David; you've nearly solved the puzzle. You're only a few steps away from realising it was me all along, and I can't have that. I can't waste everything I've done and have yet to do. Come on, David, you were never really an angel, were you? All those women, before and after we were married. I don't like being taken for a fool. I knew what was going on, well, after we were married anyway. I was deeply in love with you, and you really hurt me, and that hurt changed me, brought other deeply buried issues to the front again and then sex with Chrissy, my best friend; that was too much too far, and that was it. It certainly made me stronger and instilled a drive in me to be independent of any man; men just cannot be trusted.'

'Sammy, stop this now, get me the antidote or to a hospital before it's too late. I have loved you all along. I've learned my lesson; I am a changed person now.'

'No, David, trust has to be earned, and you are so far from the start line now that there is no further reason to keep you around to risk ruining my life any further.'

'But Sammm,' pausing as my words were beginning to slur a little, and I notice my breathing is shorter and a little faster, 'No.... sttoppp, I can't... let you...'

'David, my mind is made up. Everything is planned, your unfortunate accident, ironically with the same toxin that is curing people of cancer; how the world will wonder at this. The story is already scripted and will play out according to how I planned it, just like events have up to today. I knew you wouldn't let it go when you found out about Roberts being paid to hit you. Your inner soul would want an answer as to who did this and why ... it was me. I planned it all. Chrissy was the last straw. I had to plan everything carefully, especially as I had already discovered the protein mix that would become OxyRuco, and my future was assured. I just needed to delay the news of the discovery until I'd got you well and truly off the scene. Yes, all discovered before that night, David. I needed to get you out of my life and be sure you couldn't benefit from my discovery. I couldn't use Chrissy for the divorce; I hoped to remain friends with her. We were, after all, best friends long before you even arrived on the scene. No, I needed something different, so I hired Monica to set the stage and let it play out.'

'Monica? *You ... hired ... Monica*?'

'Yes. Well, actually, she is called Julieta. I found her online, and willing to play this role for me. For money, admittedly, quite a bit, and she was happy to travel from Argentina on her own passport. And when Julieta, role-playing as Monica, had all the photos and videos I needed, she returned to Argentina again as herself ... thus, to all looking for her, Monica had simply disappeared. In fact, she is one of my trusted employees down there now, running my operations in Buenos Aires. Trust, trust and loyalty, David. Just words wasted on you, but they mean so much more to women.'

'But her partner? How? What?'

'Fiction David, all a creation. Why do you think no one could find her or this brute of a partner that you think paid Roberts to attack you? I needed a narrative in case that fight didn't quite pan out, in case someone started to ask why Roberts had been paid. I still needed the grounds for divorce to be solid. You should have just let it go, David, been happy with your compensation and got on with your life. But no, you couldn't, and as you were getting too close, I had to modify my plan slightly.'

'But ... But.'

'Now I just have to inject these spines into your foot to make it more credible to the coroner. Ordinarily, I'd say sit still and don't move, that you'll only feel a little scratch, but as you're immobile now and your nerves are dying, you won't feel a thing.'

Samantha puts on a pair of surgical gloves and unzips a little black leather case, removes a couple of plastic tubes, unscrews the lids, and pulls out thin spines removed from a stonefish. She moves to my left foot, and I can see her apply some pressure when injecting the spines, but I can't feel a thing.

'I'll just leave some small traces of these spines in one of the wounds; it'll help with the narrative; I think the coroner will appreciate that. Fiona and Ben will attest to everything being convivial between us; even your stomach contents will show an exceptional meal enjoyed by us both. Nothing will indicate anything other than an unfortunate accident occurred here tonight.'

'Buutt ...'

'Goodbye, David,' She says coldly.

At this point, my eyes are moving in and out of focus. I can't move much of anything. 'Saaaaa....' My vision is becoming more distorted. 'Saaam.' My eyelids are heavy, I can feel a darkness creeping in, and my breathing is more challenging.

'No, not so fast, David, we need you in the water breathing in some ocean.' Samantha slaps my face and shouts out, 'Ben, it's time.'

Ben comes out of the dining room, 'Ready now?' he asks.

'Yes, but we need to move quickly. His breathing is shallow, and we need to be sure he has seawater in his lungs. You'll have to hold him under, face up, and make sure you see air bubbles coming from his mouth, he'll need to gag on seawater for a few minutes.'

'OK, I've got this,' Ben says, bending down and picking me up, raising me in a fireman's lift like a rag doll. I hear him say, 'Leave this to me. You tidy the place up. I'll be back soon.'

I can't do anything; nothing moves to my command.

55

Samantha – Cape Tribulation, Queensland

Ben walks out of the house carrying David without much effort. I watch them fade away into the darkness, heading towards the beach.

Some twenty minutes or so later, Ben returns to the house, walks straight past me without looking at me or saying anything. He walks into the bathroom off the main bedroom, strips and steps into the shower.

I lock the front door, tidy the last of the glasses and plates to the kitchen and head to the main bedroom. Undressing, I slip into the shower beside Ben. Without saying anything to each other, we kiss passionately and enjoy each other's company until falling into an exhausted sleep.

The following morning, there is a loud knock at the door. I look over to Ben; he is sleeping soundly. Another knock, this time louder and with intent. I look at the clock beside my bed; it's 8.06 a.m., and Fiona is not due back until midday. I roll towards Ben and shake his solid shoulder, 'Ben. Ben. There's someone at the front door. I'm not expecting anyone, are you?'

Ben stirred out of a deep sleep, 'What?'

'There is someone at the front door, and I'm not expecting anyone.'

'What time is it?' rubbing sleep from his eyes.

'It's early, just turned eight. I'll have to go the door, Fiona's not due back here until noon. You stay in here out of sight, stay quiet.' Ben grunted a low acknowledgement as his head dropped back down on the pillow.

I dress quickly in shorts and a T-shirt and pull on a pair of light pumps. The knocking is now louder and has real purpose. The knock occurs again just as I unlock and open the door. I see a police car and a small saloon car behind the three people standing at my door.

In a deep Australian accent, 'Good morning, Miss Walsh. I apologise for the early call.'

'Yes, well, I was sleeping, and you've disturbed me, Chief.'

'Again, my apologies. I'm here with a Detective from the UK,' as he turned slightly, indicating the person stood just off his left shoulder. 'This is Detective Inspector Jo Hansen, and this officer is my colleague, Constable Bryant.'

Before I could speak, the woman spoke, 'Yes, good morning, Miss Walsh, I am Detective Inspector Jo Hanson, North Manchester Police, CID.' May we come in to discuss a sensitive matter?'

'Ah yes, we've met before Detective Inspector Hansen, but then you were a Detective Sergeant taking my statement at the local police station. Well, normally, all my meetings are by prior arrangement these days. Do I need a lawyer present for this conversation?' I say, unsure why a British police officer is here at my villa, never mind this early and unannounced.

'You have a good memory, Miss Walsh. I'm not sure why you would think you would need a lawyer,' the Detective replies, 'I just need to ask you a few questions regarding your former husband, David Alexander.'

'Oh my, really? You've travelled all this way to ask a few questions about my former husband; we could have done this by email or video conference and saved you the journey.'

'Well, as we're here now, please, may we come inside?' she replies confidently.

'I suppose so, although Chief,' looking back at Munro with an air of authority and displeasure, 'A bit of prior notice would have been welcome.'

Superintendent John Munro, known to all locally as "Chief", responds a little subdued, 'As I've said, I apologise for this unannounced visit, but DI Hansen here only arrived late yesterday and is returning to the UK as soon as possible, so time is not a luxury we have currently.'

'Alright, I don't want to be seen as unhelpful, and you have travelled a long way, Detective Inspector; please come in.'

I take a step back to allow all three law officers to walk into my house, my home, and they all walk through to the living area. I sit on one of the three large settees and raise my arm, indicating to the officers to take a seat. DI Hansen and Chief sit, but Constable Bryant remains standing to one side, his hands crossed in front of his utility belt.

'Now, what is it that I can help with, Detective Inspector?'

56

DI Jo Hansen - Cape Tribulation, Queensland

I unzip my folio, pull out a pen and flip open a black notebook, 'We understand that your former husband, David Alexander, travelled out here arriving yesterday to meet up with you; is that correct?'

'Yes, that's correct. Is it David you wish to speak with? I can ...'

'Yes, we do want to speak with him, but not just yet, thank you,' I interrupt; I want to control this conversation. 'We will speak with Mr Alexander shortly. In the meantime, we have some questions for you first, if you don't mind?'

'Oh, not at all, fire away.'

'Firstly, could I ask why you have invited your ex-husband all the way out here?'

'I don't see how that is any of your business Detective.'

Is Samantha Walsh resentful at the intrusion or being defensive? I can't quite say yet. I continue.

'Well, it seems to me that you had both agreed to go your separate ways. However, you are very wealthy, and your ex-husband is not. He lost out on the success of er...' looking down at my notebook for effect, even though I do know all the details, and then look back up at Samantha, 'OxyRuco, did he not?'

'Well, I think the facts speak for themselves, Detective. He was convicted, wrongfully, we all now know, and because of his extra-marital affairs, we divorced well before my discovery, leading to OxyRuco. So yes, David *lost out*, as you say.'

'Is he trying to coerce you in any way, Miss Walsh? Extort or leverage cash from you?'

'No! Absolutely not.'

'Then why is he here?' I ask again, looking straight at her confidently, maintaining a blank expression, awaiting the answer.

'David has been looking back into the fight that night, The one he was arrested for. He's doing what the police should have done all those years ago, you know, investigate to find the real perpetrator. It seems to me he is doing your job for you.'

Her tone is smug, trying to manoeuvre a little, steer my questioning her way. Stay calm; I've got this, I say to myself.

'Erm,' I sniff, looking back down at my pad, 'It seems he is showing some interest in a certain CCTV recording, footage recorded that day and night at the Tempest Arms.'

'And?'

'Well, it seems you are interested in the same CCTV also.'

'I'm only trying to assist David with his wish,' she says calmly, 'Why shouldn't I?'

'Assisting to the extent that you have appointed a private investigator?' Again, briefly looking down at my pad and turning a couple of pages, 'A one ... Mark Broome. I've spoken with Mr Broome, and he has been quite helpful with my enquiries.'

I can see the realisation dawning on her that there is a little more to this visit and my questions.

'Your enquiries? I didn't know you were a part of the re-investigation team, DI Hansen. And how has Mr Broome been helpful to you?'

'Broome couldn't comment on the CCTV recordings as he didn't have them to review. However, he did try to obtain copies from archives at the home of Mr Henry Alexander, David's father.'

'What do you mean he tried to obtain copies? What, from Henry? Why would Henry have copies?'

I ignore her questions and look at her again with growing confidence; this conversation is leaning my way again. 'Mr Broome has been most helpful, especially after realising that he would be obstructing a police officer in the course of their duty, potentially perverting the course of justice. His unlawful entry into private property coupled with his use of a false identity to gain trust would be enough for him to lose his licence, face fines and possibly some prison time depending on what unfolds from this whole affair.'

'I don't know anything about that. Mr Broome's actions were not known to me, and certainly, I don't condone that kind of behaviour. I simply asked if he could help David in his quest.'

'Broome informed me of your interest in a certain CCTV recording. He provided the reference ID for it. I know David is also interested in this recording; he had previously been into the police station, and it was logged for further review,' crossing my hands, lowering my pad to my lap. 'I have reviewed it. And, I have since spoken with Richard Stanley, your lawyer.'

Samantha cut in quickly, 'My dealings with my lawyer are protected by client-attorney privilege; they are private. Richard is not permitted to divulge any information or the matter of our conversations.'

'Not a problem; I am aware of your protected privilege; Richard was the consummate legal professional, confidentiality respected and maintained. You are quick to jump to client/solicitor privilege, though, Miss Walsh. Have you something to protect, something to hide?'

'Of course not. I'm just indicating the relationship we have and the legal privilege that exists.'

'Noted, thank you. I am well versed in privilege and legal ethics. Well, I realised I wasn't going to get very far with Richard, so I carried on looking. A discussion with your doorman at your apartment block was interesting. He mentioned how a courier had delivered several boxes to your apartment not long ago from a big law firm in town. The courier company details were noted in the doorman's logbook, so I then spoke with the courier service. They gave me the courier's name and provided the collection business address, which coincidentally was the same name as Richard's legal practice, "Fothergill Stanley and Jones LLP".

'Yes, well, they were just a collection of business documents, I recall, nothing strange there.'

Samantha has not yet realised I'm leading the dialogue and setting triggers for her impromptu responses.

'True, if they really were just business papers. However, the courier mentioned that each box contained a large "R v David Alexander" label and dates aligning with the court case. *David Alexander* was all over the news at the time with his release from prison, so it meant something to him. Are you digging back into the past, Miss Walsh?

What kind of business in these boxes got your interest?'

'I'm not so sure I can say. It's all privileged information, and you shouldn't have been informed of any of it anyway. I'll certainly have words with the building management company when I return to the UK.'

'Alas, these boxes are not a privileged communication between you and your lawyer; what I have is information regarding a delivery from one place to another, all signed for, all seven boxes.' I'm moving pieces across the board now, feeling more confident of the direction this questioning is going. 'Granted, what is inside the boxes may or may not fall under legal privilege. Were you looking for something, Samantha?'

'No, not particularly, just my interest was pricked when I'd heard David was looking back into the night of the fight. And it's *'Miss Walsh'* to you if you don't mind.'

Now I know I'm touching some raw nerves.

'A busy woman like you, *"with not two minutes spare in her hectic diary"* and you want to spend time trawling through information that is years old, for events passed relating to your former husband who doesn't concern you anymore? You have assistants for things like that, don't you?'

'For all you know, Detective, David and I may be discussing our relationship further. After all, our marriage was knocked off track by events that night and the events that followed. If that fight had not happened, we would still be together.'

'Really? Even after the extra-marital affairs and the blackmail attempt by one of his former lovers? .... *Monica*, I think she's called.'

'Blackmail attempt. How did you find out about the blackmail attempt?'

'Your old friend Chrissy, a very obliging individual, was more than happy to help the police find out who was behind David being falsely imprisoned. After all, she is also a good friend to David; you do realise that? That reminds me, Miss Walsh, where is David at the moment? We know he's here. Flight records show him landing in Cairns. Private charter and CCTV at Cairn airports put him on a helicopter here. The private charter helicopter is outside on the lawn; it didn't return, so he must still be here. The ground crew know all about your affair with the pilot; he's been bragging a little when drunk, *a sexy, rich little English girl* and all that, his words, not mine. I hope David turning up expecting to rekindle the relationship hasn't led to any friction with Ben?'

Before Samantha can respond, an incoming mobile phone call starts to ring out, and Chief Munro pulls his phone from his pocket and looks at the screen. He stands. 'Excuse me, I need to take this outside,' and Chief steps out of the front door, leaving it slightly ajar.

I use the opportunity to stand also, to move about a little. Samantha remains seated. I continue, 'Let's go back to the CCTV recording. David has a point: there may be a link between the man in the pub and the damaged rear CCTV camera. You'll have watched it by now, what do you think?

'Seems like a coincidence to me,' followed by a small sniff.

I've unnerved her now. Her response is short and dismissive.

'There's that word again, *coincidence*. Two things get me about that word coincidence. One, I don't believe in coincidence, especially when serious crime is involved, and two, smack bang in the middle of coincidence is C I D. Ironic, isn't it, that officers in the Criminal Investigation Department are often told something simply happened by *coincidence*. So, David thinks there is something familiar about that man in the pub, but he couldn't put his finger on it. He raised it with us, and I looked at it again. I wondered whether or not we could enhance the quality of the image, but no, too poor to start with. Then I wondered if we could define certain characteristics for the man, you know, height, weight, gait, mannerisms, that kind of thing. The FBI at Quantico have some great software that can assist with this, but you know, it takes time, it costs a lot, we get nothing for free from our American cousins, and it's not foolproof, although it can help. But no, I didn't go down that route.'

Samantha responds, now a little more alert, 'I'm not sure why you're telling me all this?'

Ignoring the question again, I continue, 'We used good old coppering. So, I checked out how this man paid in the pub. It had to be cash; no card was used at exactly that time, nothing doing there. Then I checked with other customers in the pub that day, including the barmaid. Nothing, no one can even recall him being there. *A grey man*. So, I cast the net a little wider, beyond the pub. I pulled in all local traffic camera info, CCTV from local shops, and even cash machine videos, as, after all, he paid with cash. And guess what? After many hours of viewing boring recordings, I got a hit, well more than one, actually. Any ideas Samantha?'

'No, I haven't, but I hope you're going to tell me that this is the man who paid Roberts and that the broken camera ties him in somehow. David and I can then move on from this whole nightmare.'

'Well, yes and no. Well, to be more accurate, I have identified the man. It wasn't hard in the end as he used his own bank account to draw cash ten minutes before going into the pub, so then I looked for his car, and it was picked up driving into and out of the local area, and he was wearing the same jacket and hat. Some would say circumstantial, *coincidence* even.'

'And? Well, who is he then?' Samantha questioned.

'Before I could give an identity to him, as a person of interest, that is, I had to do some more solid police work, revisit what had gone before. So, if David is right and this is the man who paid Roberts, why would this man, with forethought, actually break the camera at the rear of the pub? This had me mulling things over a bit. There is still no link to Roberts. We all know Roberts was paid in cash; that's accepted as fact now, in part, it's what got David released from prison. But I still didn't have a viable link.'

I pause for effect and turn back towards Samantha, still sitting on the settee. Officer Bryant listening intently, seemingly interested in how this was developing.

'David couldn't think of anyone who would want to put Roberts up to this, save for a jealous partner of one of his affairs. Possible. Tenuous may be, but worth looking into. But no, to me, there was a more glaring link that didn't happen that night because it happened sometime later, months later, in fact. The man in the pub that day, who may have disabled the CCTV camera, turned out to be someone well known to you, Samantha.'

'Me? Months later, what are you talking about? Who is it?'

57

DI Jo Hansen - Cape Tribulation, Queensland

I pause for a few moments and reply, 'Who was it, not who is it? He is no longer with us.' I remain focussing on Samantha to read any tells in her body language, 'It was Hugo Bonning-Wallace. Remember him?'

'Yes, of course, I do, Bonning-Wallace, my stalker? You're saying he was the man in the pub CCTV? Was he the man who paid Roberts to attack David? Why would he do that?'

'Good questions. Well, at first, I thought he was just that, a jealous or jilted lover, and he wanted to teach David a lesson. He set the whole thing up that night. What he hadn't bargained on was David hitting Roberts, with the end result of Roberts dying from injuries after the fight. *Or did he*?' pausing for effect, '... I will come back to that.'

'So, you're saying Bonning-Wallace, the stalker that broke into my farmhouse and attacked me, paid and set up Roberts to attack David? Why, for god's sake? What could he possibly gain from that?'

I continue to pace again, gently but consistently keeping an eye on Samantha. 'Getting into the mind of a stalker for their motives can be a deep and dark journey, or a relatively simple one of infatuation with the person stalked. Whichever twisted motive Bonning-Wallace had, one thing is clear: having David locked up in prison and off the scene would give Bonning-Wallace a better opportunity at being *with you*.'

'Hold on, I'm lost here. What do you mean by a better opportunity at *being with me*? He was a sexual predator.'

'Without doubt, he was, but there is more to this.'

Without announcement, the front door opens wide, and Chief walks back into the room with a solemn expression. He walks up to me and whispers behind a shielding hand. I lean back slightly and look at Chief, 'Are you sure?'

'I'd say as sure as we can be at his time. Seems to be no doubt from my officers.'

I look back towards Samantha and bluntly ask her, 'Where is David Alexander right now?'

'I'm not sure. We had a couple of late drinks last night, well quite a few, actually, possibly a couple too many. Anyway, I went to bed at about twelve-thirty, 'ish, but David said his head was still on UK time, and he was wide awake, jet lag and all, so he went for a walk. I expect he'll still be in the Guest Lodge by the pool, sleeping now.'

Turning to Chief, I ask, well kind of order really, 'Can you send Constable Bryant down to wake him and bring him here, please?'

'Really?' he queried.

'Yes, now, please, Chief. David needs to hear this at the same time as Samantha.'

'Er, OK.' Turning to the young constable standing quietly at the end of one of the settees, Chief instructed, 'Bryant, go down to the Guest House and bring Alexander up here, please, pronto. Wake him if he's still sleeping.'

'Yes sir,' the young constable turned and walked out of the patio doors, heading towards the pool area.

Samantha watched him leave and turned back to Chief and I, 'This is mind-blowing information. I can't believe Bonning-Wallace was the man who orchestrated the chain of events that night. All congratulations to you, Detective. Excellent detective work and policing, from the sounds of it. David will be surprised, no doubt saying he'll wish that you would have been the investigating officer of the events of that night, saving him from his wrongful arrest and time in prison. How things would have turned out differently.'

'Yes, well, my colleagues at the time were probably under significant pressure, pressures from policy initiatives and targets, etcetera, but it doesn't justify poor attention to detail. Detail is the foundation and building blocks for what makes a solid and proper case leading to a sound guilty conviction. I'm passionate about details, you see.'

'I can see that, Detective. Well done.'

Chief chipped in, 'If the helicopter is still here, where is the pilot?'

'Oh, we have some staff quarters at the rear of the plot, a couple of small bungalows. He often stays over when he ferries me out late at night or when there is bad weather closing in.'

'Umm, but none of those happened yesterday or last night, did they?' I say, looking at Samantha first, then at Chief.

Chief shook his head slightly. 'Nope.'

'Ah no, he just asked if he could stay over this time, and I thought yes, why not? After all, I wasn't sure how David would be with me or how long he would stay.'

'Why not? I thought you had cleared the air between you both when you met up at Greenwich?'

That visibly stunned Samantha.

'That was a private meeting. How did *you* know we met up in Greenwich?'

'It's my job to know.'

This discussion is not going Samantha's way, and it's becoming clear I have been more thorough than she expected of a regular copper. 'Henry, your former father-in-law ... I told you it's all about the detail. Nice venue for a *clandestine meeting*, The Octagon Room at the Royal Observatory, not many could arrange that. Like David, the first time I'd been there also.'

'I wouldn't exactly call it clandestine, a very private meeting, yes.'

'OK, different ways of looking at the same thing, I suppose. It's what makes us all that little bit different, I guess.'

Samantha shrugged slightly, but I'd already noticed the little chink in her armour.

In an attempt to change the direction of the conversation, Samantha chipped in, 'My apologies, forgive my lack of manners, you've travelled a long way, please can I offer you some refreshment, iced water, lemon tea?'

'No, thank you, we're fine,' I respond, not allowing time for Chief to voice his opinion. I want to keep an eye on Samantha, not allow her the opportunity to break from my questioning and regroup.

The young officer reappears through the patio doors, 'Sorry, Sir, he doesn't seem to be there. There is an open suitcase in the room and a small flight bag by the bed, but the bed hasn't been slept in.'

Chief and I look to Samantha, and she tips her hands open, 'Well, maybe he got up early, went for another walk, and the maid has already visited his room whilst he was out.'

'Are you telling us or asking us?' Chief asks.

And Samantha just looked at him squarely. I interject, 'OK, let's stop this dance, shall we? Samantha, where is David?'

'Well, I thought he was in the Guest House, obviously he's not, so I don't know. I'm not his keeper; he can do what he likes.'

Then I'm on the offensive again, 'I'm pretty sure he would like to breathe at this point.'

'And what's that supposed to mean, Detective?' Samantha queries but with a slightly flushed complexion now.

'The body of a white male has been found in the water down near your private jetty. Chief's officers strongly believe it is David Alexander.'

Raising both hands to her mouth, Samantha muttered through her fingers, 'Oh my god, no, it can't be. Are you sure? He was fine last night; everything was good between us. In the water? Did he drown? Suicide? I don't believe it.'

'Suicide?' I flip back, 'that's a funny position to take. Why would you think that?'

'Well, I don't know, I just presumed as David was a great swimmer, that's how he kept in shape; he swam three times a week at the local pool when we were married.'

I postulate, 'It could have been an accident or ... he could have been murdered.'

'What? No, there's no crime around here; this is not London or Manchester. The worst that happens out here is a drunken yachtsman or a family domestic dispute. Isn't that right Chief? Who would possibly want to kill him, Detective?'

'Well, now, that is a good question. Where is that pilot of yours? It seems to me he may have a strong motive if you and David were planning on getting back together again. He is here, isn't he ... Ben?'

58

'Chief' Munro

The double doors at the end of the living room burst open, and the pilot storms in, partly dressed, and briskly walks across the floor to Samantha. Samantha jumps up and stands rigid, facing him.

'What the fuck is all this about, Sam? People dead in the UK? I don't remember you telling me about them. A stalker, prison, what else have you not told me about? You said your ex was blackmailing you over some sex video and photos he had of you, had been for years and that the only way to free yourself from him, for us, was that he had to be stopped. I'm not going down for this, Sam. I'm not going back inside because of rich people's games. I'm not going to be your scapegoat.'

Samantha shouts at him, 'Shut up, Ben, keep quiet!'

'You don't give the orders anymore,' Ben shouted, putting his left arm around Samantha's neck, and as he leaned backwards slightly, pulled his right arm from behind his back and pointed a Colt .45 at me. Out of the corner of his eye, Ben could see the young officer fumbling with his side holster and averting his aim from me to Bryant ...

'Stop it! Don't. I'm quicker than you, copper. You too Chief! Hands off the guns and up in the air. NOW!

DO IT!'

I slowly raise my hands to shoulder level, 'Now calm down, Ben, calm down, let's all be sensible here. No need for anyone to get hurt. Come on, you know me. I'm a family man, overweight and no hero, and this young constable here is still as green as the grass out there. You know Brit cops don't carry guns, so we'll all be sensible, won't we?'

Ben looks at the young officer, slowly shaking his head from side to side, then at Jo.

Jo raises her hands as she looks at me, then back to Ben.

Ben squeezed Samantha's neck tighter by contracting his left forearm around her neck. Samantha gasped a little as her air supply was cut off briefly.

'It might look old, but this Colt 1911 still works pretty damn fine, and it's fully loaded. My Grandpa's from the war, and he used it, a notch on the holster for each soldier he took, nine of 'em. I'm not afraid to use it either. He taught me good he did. Always said I'd need it one day.'

Jo and I look at the Colt, the hammer cocked, ready to fire.

Jo said in a quiet, steady voice, 'Ben. Look at me. We're calm, Ben. We don't want anyone getting hurt today. We know it's not you, Ben; you're an unfortunate pawn caught up in this game. Samantha is behind this whole thing; she masterminded everything from the beginning to get what she wanted. Isn't that right, Samantha?'

Ben kept his Colt on me and squeezed Samantha a little more, but Samantha couldn't answer; she was clearly struggling to breathe, her eyes were wide, and she was scrabbling her feet on the wooden flooring.

Jo continued, 'Ben, let her breathe a bit, no mistakes, we all want to see the day through. Ben?'

Ben relaxed his forearm lock slightly, allowing Samantha to gulp in oxygen while she could, her chest rising and falling quickly.

Jo looks directly at her, 'We know about your past with Bonning-Wallace Samantha, how you exacted your revenge on him and very nearly got away with everything. Multiple perfect crimes with you, the poor unfortunate repeat victim with everyone on your side, the world's saviour in the fight against cancer, the endless charity works with oppressed and battered women. Commendable work, Samantha, but still, the crimes exacted against you didn't warrant murder. No one gets away with murder. Or was it all for the money? The fame? For revenge? All three? What was it? Why did all three of them have to die?'

Ben squeezes Samantha in a snatching move, and she yelps. 'What do you mean all three of them? Answer the detective, Sam, or I'll break your fucking neck right now.'

'I... I ... I don't know what you're talking about,' Samantha manages to squeak out.

'You do, Samantha, yes you do,' as Jo nodded her head. 'Men don't know what it's like to be a woman. To be pawed at, used, pitied in business, ridiculed when you aim at a dream or have ambition. We do, we both do, we've both been there.'

Samantha swallowed hard and coughed. Ben snatched at her again.

'Ben, let her speak, will you please? Samantha needs to get it off her chest; she needs to confess to relieve her burden. Her past has caught up with her; she's just realising it but has not accepted it yet.'

In a menacing voice, Ben spoke, 'No funny business, or I'll start shooting. I will. Don't test me. Speak up bitch, what have you got me involved in? Three murders? What's she talking about?' and he released his tight grip around her throat, but not fully; she was useful as a shield and a hostage at the same time.

Ben looked at Bryant, 'Copper, move around here next to Chief so I can see all three of you together,' waving the Colt with flicks of his wrist, 'Keep your hands up, no sudden moves.'

Bryant slowly sidestepped towards me, hands up, shaking slightly, his skin pale now with beads of sweat forming on his forehead.

Quietly, looking at Bryant, I try to keep things under control, 'It's OK, son. Ben's not a bad lad; I've known him since he was a nipper. That right Ben? We go back aways, don't we, Ben?'

'We do, Chief, and I don't want this, but I'm not going back inside; you know what it's like in there for us mixed-race boys. I'd rather die first.'

'No, Ben, we don't want anyone to get hurt,' Jo said quietly. 'Samantha doesn't want you to get hurt either; you've not wronged her. She's not planned anything for you. Isn't that right, Samantha?'

Samantha looked puzzled at Jo.

'Isn't that right, Samantha?' Jo said, slightly widening her eyes, trying to convey a message to her.

'Yes, yes, that's right. I love you, Ben. It wasn't meant to turn out like this.'

The confusion on Ben's face was clear to see; he was involved in something he had no idea of. 'Fuck me, woman, you a serial killer or something?'

'No, no, it's all a mistake; they've got everything mixed up. I haven't killed anyone,' Samantha pleaded.

59

DI Jo Hansen

I'm starting to think this is probably an excellent opportunity to get, and hear, the truth from Samantha Walsh.

This could lead to a confession before witnesses, although this is turning into a situation I didn't expect. My training tells me I must remain calm, work to gain trust and manipulate the situation to my advantage.

I need to own the narrative again and take control.

Looking at Samantha, 'We know Bonner-Wallace was stalking you; we all saw the evidence, the photos, the restaurant reservations, the GPS tracking reports. But that's what you wanted everyone to believe. I looked closer at all this evidence, I mean *really* close. The first thing that dawned on me was that the photos on his phone weren't really of you; they were selfies or scene shots where you were in the background. They weren't close-ups; you weren't the subject of the photos; they weren't focused on you. I believe you put yourself in his background shots by careful planning, photobombing the kids call it these days, I think.'

Still held by Ben, Samantha responded, 'Rubbish, that's nonsense. Those photos were all part of the evidence that he was stalking me.'

'OK, but when looked at without any other consideration, they would be circumstantial at best. You're bright; you knew more would be needed, so I needed to dig deeper. I looked at the restaurant bookings. You were both at the same restaurants on numerous occasions at the same time, again part of a stalker's trait, their MO, his modus operandi. I checked the restaurant and hotel reservations, and it was all there in black and white, irrefutable. However, when I checked closer at the details, all those reservations made on digital systems showed that your booking reservations were all timed after his, either within a few minutes or a couple of hours. So then aligning these against your diary movements with the ever-professional and meticulous Daryl showed that the reservations you or Daryl made hours later were all down to you being either tied up in meetings or in different time zones. It presented quite a telling picture once I lined all this up.'

I pause, keeping my hands raised, alternating eye contact between Ben, Samantha and the pistol.

'And then there are the GPS tracking records. How could you possibly manipulate GPS tracking to make it look like he was following you? Now, this is my favourite, this was genius, it really was. You had your private and very shady private detective hack into his diary and list out all his movements. This hacking helped with restaurant bookings and other venues, but it also helped with GPS. You knew where he was, where he was going to be and, fair play to Bonner-Wallace's secretary, you could also see what mode of transport he was taking, whether driving, a train, a plane. All you had to do was ensure your GPS was active on your phone and then get in front of him. To any overworked forensic systems analyst, it looks like he is following you, whereas he didn't actually know you were in front of him at all. Genius.'

I have them all listening. Samantha slows her resistance, and Ben looks at me with his raised gun.

'But the best were the trains and planes. You knew where he was going, saw his seat reservations online and then bought tickets in front of him; you taking a seat in first class. Again, the booking time receipts for your tickets show this; they were all made after his.'

Samantha's questions started, 'So what you're saying, Detective, is that you think I planned the whole stalking episode? That actually, it's the other way around, I was the one stalking him?'

'Yes, in effect, that is what I'm saying.'

'Ludicrous! Why would I possibly go to all that trouble? He was the one that broke into my farmhouse and attacked me, remember.'

'Samantha. From what I've said, you must now know I do the detail and leave no stone unturned. Let's see; you studied at Warwick University. Whilst you were at Warwick, Bonning-Wallace visited Warwick with some of his pals as part of a drawn-out stag party that seemed to have lasted two to three weeks. Again, we can put you both in the same area at the same time. Coincidence again, one might say.'

'Clearly a coincidence. That was nearly 15 years ago. We never met,' Samantha pled as Ben kept his vice-like grip on her.

'The two of you did meet, probably on a party night somewhere after which, Bonning-Wallace raped you. He wouldn't have used his real name, and knowing how cunning Bonning-Wallace had been over the years, he knew to avoid cameras. Street and door CCTV wasn't as prolific then as it is now, so not that hard to avoid them. You knew it was him just as soon as you saw his face plastered all over the TV and press in the UK after that rape case against him at the Old Bailey collapsed. You reported the rape during your second year at university, but no one believed you. There was no evidence, no semen samples, no defensive marks, nothing. Local police dismissed it as a party night with a stranger, both drunk and the day after you regretted having sex. However, you know you were raped, and I believe you, it was Bonning-Wallace. He was an animal, steadily getting worse as the years progressed. You're a seriously bright and intelligent woman, and seeing him in the news, you knew nothing would come of speaking to the police now after all these years, and of course, you have your pristine image to protect. But he couldn't get away with it, you couldn't let him get away with it, you wouldn't let it go. You knew what he was like, what he had become, all those women over the years since. *All those victims of unsolved sexual abuse.* You had to stop him. And I get that, I really do, but not murder Samantha, never murder.'

Adopting a defensive position, Samantha replies quietly, 'Everyone knows I killed him; it was self-defence, not murder. He broke into my farmhouse and attacked me. It was self-defence. He would have raped me and probably killed me if I hadn't fought back. The police and court confirmed he was a sexual delinquent, a predator.'

'Yes, that is what you wanted them to believe. That was the outcome you intended. You planned the whole thing; you planned it to make it look like you were the victim.'

'What, because he raped me? I murdered him because he raped me?'

'Yes and no. He had to go, didn't he? Not just for the rape, although that was a bonus for you, he was the man you enticed to initiate the pub fight with David. And why would you do that? We know David was having affairs behind your back, all that came out during the divorce. But you knew about them at the time and said nothing. You were in business together, on the brink of creating some new miracle drug, and a divorce under those circumstances would have still left David in your life, in the business. He owned a large slice of the company; you would still see him every day, and if you made your breakthrough, he would profit from it just as much as you. You found out about David's past, a 14-year-old teenager with anger issues, quick to fight when pushed. You could still see that flicker in him at times. For David, rugby brought control and a way to channel his frustrations; he directed and used his energy on the field, possibly making him such a good player. But if you could just get him to crack at the right moment, he would get a police record, which was not good for him, as the shareholder agreement was tight, and you knew this. Any criminal record would initiate his removal from the company, leaving you open then to action the divorce without residual issues.'

Holding everyone's attention and the peace, I continue, 'I think you had already made this miraculous medical discovery whilst still married to David. All you had to do was wait a reasonable amount of time following the divorce before announcing OxyRuco to the world. Some of your staff have already indicated you were working nights and weekends, the results being kept to yourself, and following the divorce and the attack, you retracted even more and became more isolated, a self-protection reaction following all the events that had happened to you. But no, I suggest you had found the solution and were testing it, refining it, all the time keeping quiet, sending your research team down paths that wouldn't end up with the same success. Bonning-Wallace just had to bide his time until you gave him the green light, wait for you to contact him, and then you invited him to your farmhouse.'

I could see Samantha needed to debunk this, 'This is all circumstantial, coincidence, it's delusional, it's almost as if you have manipulated a myriad of loose threads to weave a magic carpet. I think you have lost the plot, Detective. You're looking to create a grand conspiracy to mask over the police's earlier mistakes with David and trying to pin it on someone who is in the limelight. The press frenzy and conspiracy theorists would have a field day, deflect their attention from the police.'

Bryant's hands were slowly lowering, and Ben noticed, 'Hands up, copper! Keep them up!' as he flicked the Colt in an upward motion.

'Bryant, do as he says,' instructed Chief. 'No heroics, son, steady.'

Samantha levelled back at me, 'This is all fiction, Detective. Anyway, Roberts was the one who started the fight'.

'Oh. It was Roberts who started the fight, was it? The witnesses said it was David,' picking her up on her choice of words.

'No, that's not what I meant. See, now you're twisting my words. It was Roberts, not Bonning-Wallace, in the fight. How does that work out then in your version of events?'

'Again, simple but a little twisted. You initiated a brief contact with Bonning-Wallace, probably something innocent like bumping into each other on a train or in a restaurant. You needed to know if he remembered you. He didn't, so you started leading Bonning-Wallace along a little, brave, considering you knew what he could be like. I'd suggest you were getting a little closer but then put a stop to it, saying you were married to a man that was a brute, and if only he could be out of your life, you'd be free to be with Bonning-Wallace, and you'd both be wealthy. If it were all done in a certain way, David would get a criminal record, and you could blame David for the divorce and get David out of the business, freeing you up to be with him. Bonning-Wallace was only too willing to help, probably lapping it all up, given what future he was promised with you.'

'Now that is all supposition, Detective, and you know it is.'

'Yes ... true. It'll have been something like that. Anyway, Bonning-Wallace then saw how physically fit David was and didn't fancy his chances in a fight. Plus, he didn't want any undue police attention on himself, given what pastimes he enjoyed. So, he hired a thug, a street brawler. Enter Roberts. Now, it all went well on the night, to plan, but Bonning-Wallace wanted to make sure David not only got a police record but that he went away to prison for a good long stretch. So Bonning-Wallace hatched his own little plan, unbeknown to you, in which he would have Roberts take a punch or two from your husband, then he arranged to meet Roberts in the rear beer garden afterwards to pay up the balance in cash.'

The room was still, and all were listening to me.

'What Roberts didn't know was what kind of person Bonning-Wallace was and what his real plan was all along. When Roberts left the pub by the rear door and went to the beer garden after the confrontation in the pub to get the balance of his payment, Bonning-Wallace, having earlier in the day disabled the rear CCTV camera, then surprised Roberts by jumping from the shadows and either hit him with the coping stone off the garden wall or pushed Roberts down and smacking his head against the coping stone, with sufficient force to fracture his skull and ultimately kill him. This would put David away for a long time as it would look like David started the fight that led to Roberts succumbing to delayed injury, falling, striking his head and dying not long after.'

Samantha, Ben, Chief and Bryant were all taking this in, absorbing my narrative.

'Bonning-Wallace, to boot, had eliminated his link to David and you, or so he thought. You had both agreed to lay low for the time being to let all the other actions take their course: the investigation, the court appearance, sentencing, divorce. However, you hadn't factored in the death of Roberts, which turned out to be a bonus for you regarding David's conviction.'

Samantha interjects, 'I'm still hearing lots of conjecture here, Detective. I'm still unsure how I murdered Bonning-Wallace when he attacked me.'

'Now, this is the clever bit. You play the role of a damaged person, a victim yourself, using work as a distraction, wanting solitude in your own time, retreating to the farmhouse to be alone when possible. At an appropriate time, you then invite your accomplice in crime, Bonning-Wallace, to the farmhouse one evening to get rid of him. But you needed it to look like he broke in and attacked you. There needed to be a reason for this, hence all the stalking, photos, GPS crumbs, and ingredients that make a perfect cake when put together. You set the scene for any investigator to see him as a sexual predator, planning his next victim by stalking her to a remote location. After all, he had recently managed to sidestep a criminal case for serious sexual assault not long before.'

Samantha's look could turn me to stone; I am on the right path now.

'But it had to look good. You invite him to the farmhouse, a good private location where no one would see you together. Now, to stage the scene perfectly, you inform Bonning-Wallace that the cattle grid on the approach to the farmhouse had recently been repaired and not to drive over it as the concrete was still curing. He'll need to park his car on the verge near the cattle grid and then walk up to the house. To add to this illusion, you had left your Range Rover parked by the verge, put three traffic cones in front of the cattle grid and strung out some warning tape between the gate posts for added effect. Very convincing.'

Samantha had heard enough, 'Oh come on, this is just ridiculous. Chief, even this must be sounding far-fetched to you?'

'Admittedly, yes, it does, Miss Walsh,' replied Chief, 'but it is interesting. Continue, Detective Inspector, please.'

60

DI Jo Hansen

'I went to your farmhouse, had a good look around and found something a little unusual for a moorland farmhouse. Why would you keep three traffic cones and a roll of construction warning tape in the barn at the rear? That made me think a little further. Your Range Rover tyre tracks were noted in the mud on the verge, 300 yards from the farmhouse; why would they be there? On any normal day, you would drive along the road to the farmhouse straight over the cattle grid. Scene of Crime Officers took casts; they are meticulous like that, you know, especially when a fatality is involved. Plaster casts and photos of tyre markings are needed to identify and exclude vehicles from those of interest. As it turns out, there was a perfect tyre set matched to your Range Rover, the one you sold not long afterwards, but we had the make and tread details in the evidence files for exclusion purposes, and these tread markings were excluded because they fit your car. But why were they there?'

'So, all you needed to do now was kill him, stage it to look like a break-in, call the police in a distressed state and job done. You couldn't let Bonning-Wallace walk around free in the knowledge that he had caused the death of Roberts and set up David for prison; he could use that knowledge to incriminate you or, worse, blackmail you at any time for money or other perverted acts. He had done your dirty work for you, and more than ever, you wanted justice for him raping you years earlier and inflicting harm on other women since.'

Ben squeezes Samantha tighter, 'Is this true, Sam? Did you do this?'

Samantha tries to wriggle free, but Ben's grip is solid.

I continue, 'And now David is dead. Why would that be Samantha? What line were you spinning to poor Ben here? That David was a blackmailer, going to tarnish your perfect image with sordid sex tapes?'

Samantha responded, 'If it is David that's dead, it wasn't me; he drowned. We were seriously drunk last night, and he went out walking. I should probably have stopped him. If not an accident, then he committed suicide.'

Ben is having none of it. 'What have you got me mixed up in? Three men dead Sam!'

He looks at me, 'I had nothing to do with the dead in England, OK, you see that, don't you?'

'Of course, Ben, I do. It was all before your time. You're not involved, as far as I can tell. But it seems you are involved in David's death now. Help yourself here Ben. What happened last night?'

'Fuck!' Ben lowers his head and then looks up. 'Sam told me about being blackmailed and how her status and role in charities had to be protected. She said her ex was squeezing her for increasing demands for cash, or he would sell these videos and pictures to the newspapers. She couldn't have that; it would rub out all the good she had done. So she invited him here and ...'

'Shut the fuck up, Ben!' Samantha shouts.

Ben grimaces and reacts by tightening his arm around her neck again, and Samantha is clearly struggling.

Ben looks back at me, 'So why was he here, Detective? You have a theory for that?'

'Yes, I do.' Looking at Ben, I continue, 'Henry, David's father, told me that David had started digging deeper into the events of the pub fight that night. He had a hunch of a link between his mistress Monica and Roberts, and he had discussed it further with you, Samantha.' I move my gaze to her and control my breathing. 'He wanted to ask Samantha if she knew anything that would help. David thought Samantha would have some way of contacting Monica so he could find out who was behind all this. Before travelling here, David told Henry that Samantha had appointed a private investigator to assist in looking for Monica and that he had found out some information that would interest David. The next thing, Samantha, indicating she wanted to keep this information close and confidential, invited David out here to Queensland, paid for his long-haul flight and arranged for you, Ben, to fly him up here yesterday.'

'Hang on. Who's this Monica, and what about all this blackmailing that David was doing?' Ben said with a confused look.

'David wasn't blackmailing anyone, Ben. That's the line that Samantha fed you to get you to help her.

Monica was the other woman David had an affair with, leading to them getting a divorce, and it was Monica who was said to be blackmailing Samantha. It is David down by the jetty, then I take it?

You know it's him, don't you, Ben?'

When I ask that question, I immediately think I might have gone too far and risk losing control of the situation; it's not good procedure to annoy the person holding the gun.

Ben moves the Colt and presses it hard into Samantha's temple just behind her right eye, and she closes her eyes in fear. 'Is that true? He wasn't blackmailing you at all. You killed him because he was getting closer to the truth? Talk to me, Sam, or so help me God, I'll finish this right here, right now.'

'It's not true, Ben, he was blackmailing me, I promise.'

'So, it is David's body down there,' I chip in. Keeping a clear position of authority, I start my well-rehearsed line, 'Samantha Walsh, I am arresting you for the murder of Hugo Bonning-Wallace, the murder of David Alexander, conspiracy to murder, perverting the course of justice, obstructing a police officer in the course of their duty, and anything else I can think of. Anything you say may ...'

Ben shouts out, drowning my words, 'WHOA! Hold on a second, English! It's me that's holding all the cards here, remember? I'm getting out of here now, and she's coming with me as security,' as he yanks at Samantha again, and she yelps. 'Now stay here and don't move you three. I've nothing against any of you, but I ain't going back to prison. This bitch is going to get what's coming to her, trust me.' Looking at Bryant, 'Copper! Very slowly, take out your handcuffs and put them on Sam here. NOW!'

Bryant looks at Chief, who nods, 'It's OK, son, do as the man asks.'

Slowly, Bryant reaches around his utility belt, unclips his handcuffs, and slowly moves towards them, holding them up to show Ben.

Ben jerks Samantha, 'Put your hands out front now.'

'No!' Samantha replies, which gets an instant reaction from Ben, who pushes her head hard with the muzzle of the Colt.

'Do it now or else.'

Samantha brings her arms down from gripping Ben's forearm and pushes them out horizontally towards Bryant. The young constable looks at Ben and reacts to the instruction, 'Just put them on real tight, no funny business, OK copper?' Ben is definitely the one giving the orders now. Bryant closes the cuffs around Samantha's wrists.

'Now back up copper,' Ben says, pointing the Colt in his direction, 'No sudden moves, OK.'

Bryant retraces his steps to stand beside me.

'Now we're leaving. I'm flying us out of here. Don't do anything stupid or brave; just let us go. You'll find Samantha handcuffed to the helicopter when I'm done. You can do with her what you want then. I don't give a shit about this lying scheming bitch. Always thought this was too good to be true; I'm just the hired help, always have been, always will be.'

I raise my voice slightly but firmly, 'Ben, don't do this. We can attest to you being an unwitting participant in events here, and we can even forget about you pulling a gun on police officers. Think about it. You'll always be running, law enforcement around the world will be wired your description, and you'll be looking over your shoulder constantly. You'll get maybe less than ten years at the moment, but running will definitely make it worse.'

'I told you I'm not going back inside.' With that, he yanks hard on Samantha's neck, and she struggles to find her feet with his mass moving backwards. 'C'mon bitch move it.' Ben slowly steps back, pulling Samantha with him. He reaches the patio doors and steps out, lifting Samantha by simply leaning backwards, his sheer strength and body mass no match for Samantha's frame.

61

The Gardens

They keep moving backwards, slowly around the pool, down the three steps to the large lawn towards the helicopter. Jo, Chief and Bryant walk up to and through the patio doors and stand with the pool between them and the helicopter.

'How far can he get in that thing?' Jo asks Chief quietly.

'Not sure. It all depends on how much fuel he has left. But my guess is a couple of hundred miles fairly quickly. And knowing Ben he won't go to an airport, he knows they'll all be on alert within minutes. No, he'll have a place or two dotted about with fuel drums to help him keep running. He's a former Australian Defence Force trained pilot; he'll know about keeping below radar, escaping and evading, and staying away from built-up areas. No, if he takes off, he's gone.'

'Then we've got to stop him taking off,' replies Jo, looking around.

On reaching the helicopter, Ben bundles Samantha into the second pilot seat with his pistol pointing at her constantly. He rounds the front of the helicopter, opens the pilot's door, and climbs into the pilot seat. Without delay, Ben commences the start-up sequence. The four main blades start to turn slowly to the increasing whine of the twin turboshaft engines, the shrouded tail rotor already at speed and getting faster.

'We have to stop them,' Jo shouts over the increasing noise as grass and other vegetation fan out from the increasing downwash.

Looking around, Jo spots a long pole with a cleaning net used for the pool; without a second thought, she runs over and picks it up. Maintaining momentum, she approaches the helicopter and launches it javelin-style at the rear rotor. As the end of the pole hits the small blades, they mash together; blades buckle and shear as the pole breaks up, and a third of the pole flicks upwards and hits the main rotors. Bits of aluminium shrapnel fly out in all directions as Jo hits the floor hard to avoid being hit.

Alarms start to ring out in the cockpit. Ben looks out towards Jo, lying on the grass and realises what's happened, 'Shit! Fucking English.'

All his training and experience kick in. He knows he can't risk taking off and starts to shut down the engines. Anger gets the better of him now, and he looks straight into Samantha's terrified eyes, 'You fucking bitch! I hope you rot in hell for this.' He reaches for his door handle, and as he opens the door, he turns his upper body to step out. A single shot rings out.

Ben is hit in his top left shoulder, the .4 calibre round fracturing, smashing bone on its passage through his upper arm into his chest. Ben lets out a long, low moan, and with the momentum of the impact, he slumps back into the helicopter and slightly forward over the central control area. Samantha screams out as blood spatters over the inside of the windshield and instruments.

Jo raises her head, looking back over her shoulder towards Chief. He was about ten metres away from her, stood prone, two hands aiming his Glock 22 at the helicopter.

As the rotors continue to slow down and the whine reduces, Chief shouts a firm order to Jo, 'Don't move. Let's make sure he's down. Bryant! Cover me.'

Constable Bryant pulls out his pistol and points it in the general direction of the helicopter. Chief moves forward, approaching the helicopter in a stooped position, trying to make a smaller target of himself, his Glock never wavering from the pilot's door. As he passes Jo, without looking at her, he speaks up loudly, 'You OK, Jo? Stay put for a minute, he's still armed.'

Bryant is moving in slowly, vectored on a slightly different approach to not put Chief in his line of fire.

Looking through the sights of his pistol, Chief reaches the helicopter and quickly opens the door, stepping to one side to avoid any shot coming his way. From inside and over the now almost quiet engines, he hears a mix of deep guttural groaning sounds and hysterical screaming. Chief is scanning the scene, looking for the Colt. He can't see it. Has Ben still got it? Ben is slumped over the central panel, groaning. He lifts the Glock and places the muzzle into the middle of Ben's back between his shoulder blades. 'Now don't you move, Ben, for god's sake, don't you move.'

Chief leans into the cabin, and with his left hand reaching across Ben, he tucks his hand beneath him and feels for the Colt. He finds it in Ben's right hand, down the nearside of the central control panel, Ben's grasp still around the handgrip but loose. A warm sticky substance coats the gun as Chief frees Ben's fingers from the grip, 'Now Ben, I'll be taking that gun. Don't you move now.'

Ben groans and coughs out, aspirating blood over Samantha's legs. She screams out loud. Chief didn't wait; he grabbed the Colt and threw his weight backwards so that his momentum would free him from Ben.

Chief steps back and stumbles for his footing but recovers. 'Bryant! Get over here!'

Jo stands up and walks towards Chief. 'Get her out of there, will you, Jo?' Chief asks.

Jo sprints around the front of the helicopter and opens the other door. Samantha is hysterical. Jo reaches in and grabs hold of Samantha's top, attempting to pull her out, but She is rigid with fright. 'Samantha! Come on! Let's get you out of here.'

Samantha turned to Jo, her face ashen, eyes streaming, 'I can't move,' she replied in a trembling low voice.

Jo convincingly replies, 'Come on. It's all over.'

62

Samantha

Jo helps me out of the helicopter. I can hardly walk, Jo supporting me as we come around the helicopter stumbling towards Chief.

I see Constable Bryant stepping down from the patio area and walking towards us, lowering his pistol.

Now. I punch Jo hard in the side of her ribs, a full right uppercut and break free, stand upright and take a couple of steps to one side. Jo, folding over and gripping her side, lets out a yelp and looks up at me, confused.

I shout across to Chief curtly, 'They know too much! You know what to do, Chief.'

Chief, looking directly at me, 'Yes, I know,' he turns about-face, raises Ben's Colt, aims directly at Bryant and coldly says, 'I'm sorry, son,' as he fires a shot straight into Bryant's chest.

Bryant falls backwards, dropping his Glock, quarter spins and hits the grass. He doesn't move. Jo screams and looks at Chief, who is already turning back towards her with the Colt raised. With the wind knocked out of her, Jo can hardly move.

'What ... what are you doing?' Jo gasps.

'Wait!' I shout.

Jo looks across at me, 'What the fuck do you think you are doing?'

'Acting Detective Inspector Joanna Hansen, North Manchester CID. Aged 33 years, the only child of divorced parents. Single, committed to the job.

Promising officer for senior promotion. SIO and arresting officer on the recent gangland shootings in and around the Manchester, Bolton and Bury areas, no partner, no pets ...' I deliver calmly, 'You see, I've been doing my homework too.'

'What the ...?'

'Connections in the right places Joanna, serious money and position generate influence. Influence leads to knowledge, and knowledge is real power.'

Jo looks up at Chief Munro, 'You? You're a police officer ...'

'Sorry Jo,' he replies, 'Me and the wife owe so much to Miss Walsh, and well, I, we could never repay her for what she has done for our daughter.'

'What are you talking about?' as Jo tries to stand up straight.

Chief slowly walks around Jo, heading towards the helicopter door, keeping the Colt pointed at her, and speaks calmly.

'Our Emily went backpacking, you see, against my advice. She got loved up with some lad in the Philippines, but he got her hooked on the white stuff and then started pimping her out on the sex tourist market. By the time I found them, she was in a really bad state. Em needed a lot of help. She refused to return to Queensland, ashamed, damaged, dirtied, and couldn't face her mum or anyone. Bastard. Well, rest assured, he'll never be found; I made sure of that.' Chief kept moving around slowly using small side steps.

'We couldn't afford much. Got her to a local safe house just outside Manila. When Samantha heard about this young girl from Queensland battered and damaged in one of the safe houses, Samantha sent people over and took her into one of her charities, cleaned our Em up good, got all the help she needed, and she needed a lot, believe me. Em's still out there, safe now, working with one of Samantha's charities, working to help other women caught up in this awful fucking world we live in.'

I look at Jo, 'You just wouldn't let it go either, would you? In a different place, a different time, we could have been terrific friends, Jo, you and me. I know how hard you have worked to get those successes, more than any man on the force. I also know your seniors have told you they don't believe any of what you have pitched here today. You're out here on your own crusade, chancing your arm trying to elicit a confession in front of another senior officer, one you thought was impartial and had no axe to grind. However, alas, my reach is far higher than you can imagine. Yes, I killed Bonning-Wallace and David last night; they both had it coming. David was getting too close to the truth of what happened, but my, you were a lot closer than any of them. You had it all, all but Monica. I'm sorry too, Jo, but it has to be this way.'

I could see Jo was struggling to process the extent of what was going on, but her professional head seemed stayed clear. 'Why kill that young Constable? Why? And what about me? How can you possibly get away with this?'

'I'm doing good work, Jo, outstanding work, too good to be left unfinished and be de-railed by one person. I'm sure you can see and appreciate the logic of this. Yes, this will all take some explaining, and I have it covered; unfortunate timing, *coincidence*, shall we say? The story will go along the lines that Ben was becoming increasingly paranoid, convinced he was being hunted for something he hadn't done. Chief and Officer Bryant arrived at my villa to tell me about finding David's body, but Ben loses it with me, thinking I've called the police on him and he'll be blamed for David's death, takes me hostage, and ... Well, you can see where this is going. Such terrible luck I have around people ...'

'Your logic has lost all sense of morality, you fucking monster!' Jo screams back at me.

I look away, 'John, we don't have much time. Your fellow officers may have heard the gunshots. I've squared this away in the UK; both Jo's DCI and the Chief Constable of Manchester have the messages to cascade through their team, the Commissioner in London is in the loop, Jo was overworked, stressed, a little paranoid, etcetera, and decided at short notice to take some leave, came out here on her own time, ambitious and all that, we spoke, we spoke briefly, that's it, and she left in her little hire car, this all kicked off afterwards with Ben when Jo wasn't around. We don't know where she is, remember? She left. She simply has to disappear. These mangrove swamps around here are full of crocs; for heaven's sake, they even swim in the sea.'

'I know.' He sighs, looking down at the floor, slightly shaking his head from side to side, then gently up and down. He slowly raises his head, looks straight at Jo and says in a low voice, 'I'm very sorry, Jo', aims and squeezes the trigger.

63

Epilogue

Benjamin Kamarre, a former ADF Pilot, died of his wounds before paramedics arrived on the scene. The actions of Ben Kamarre over those two days were explained in testimony and statements from both Superintendent Munro and Miss Samantha Walsh. It was accepted that Ben, possibly originating from his earlier war service and PTSD condition, had suffered some form of mental breakdown or episode triggered by the police visit to Samantha Walsh's house that morning. It seems he was under the false impression that he was to be arrested for something he did not do, and, coupled with the bad experience of former prison time, he attempted to escape, taking Miss Walsh as a hostage when Superintendent Munro and Officer Bryant called.

Superintendent John Munro of the Queensland Police Service, known to all as 'Chief', endured a formal internal investigation into the use of his firearm. He maintained that after disabling the helicopter, he saw Benjamin Kamarre open the helicopter door, raise the Colt M1911 pistol, and aware of his exposed position near the helicopter, he adopted a low firing position, but in those few seconds, Ben Kamarre fired first hitting and fatally wounding Officer Bryant. John Munro returned fire and fatally injured Ben Kamarre. Superintendent Munro was cleared to return to full active service after the internal investigation. However, after many years of exemplary service, he submitted his retirement papers. It was the first time he had killed a person in the line of duty, and knowing Benjamin Kamarre since he was a boy weighed heavily on him. He was also devastated at the loss of a young Police Officer in his charge, although there was nothing more he could have done in that situation.

David Alexander's autopsy indicated high levels of verruca toxin from the genus Synanceia, the Stonefish, and his lungs contained seawater. The Coroner concluded accidental death after David Alexander stepped on a Stonefish whilst walking in seawater near the Villa, and that coupled with high levels of alcohol and prescription medication in his system, the effects of the toxin were accelerated, and David drowned after collapsing into the sea.

After hearing of David's death, Henry Alexander, David's father, was bereft with guilt and regret. Although it was a terrible accident, he blamed himself for not stopping David from travelling to Australia. He locked himself away from the world and his friends, becoming reclusive and remorseful. David's mother remained detached, showing no interest in any of the events, even though her son was innocent of the original crime and her ex-husband was now in need of support. She refuses to discuss anything related to David and Henry. Still, she is content to mention her former daughter-in-law, Samantha Walsh, in conversation and of her successes and global recognition.

The Chief Constable of North Manchester Constabulary and her fellow Bolton officers mourn the loss of their highly respected colleague, DI Joanna Hansen, whilst on holiday in Queensland. Joanna

Hansen's hire car was found parked near the Daintree River, along with a small tent and some belongings, found alongside the riverbank. After extensive searches, Queensland Police Force, along with Rangers from the Parks and Wildlife Commission, concluded it highly likely that a large crocodile had taken Joanna Hansen. Following a Coroner's Inquest, Joanna Hansen's disappearance was formally recorded as a death caused by a crocodile attack. The Coroner instructed the Parks and Wildlife Commission to install additional signage along all crocodile-inhabited rivers, creeks and beaches and maintain a constant public awareness campaign in the region.

A separate police team from New South Wales investigated the death of three persons in a relatively close timeframe and location. No link was found between the disappearance of Joanna Hansen and the two deaths at the Villa; it was considered and eventually ruled purely coincidental.

OxyRuco© continues to be a significant success. After further research and trials, other benefits came to light, helping ease or cure other critical medical conditions.

The charities established by Samantha Walsh in numerous cities worldwide to support abused women remain operational, funded by the Trusts set up by Samantha Walsh. Further regional charities, "Homes", are planned in other countries across the globe. Samantha Walsh's good work continues.

Following investiture at Buckingham Palace, Dame Samantha Walsh continued in her role as Chief Executive with a number of the businesses she founded. Dame Walsh maintained her personal ambition to help develop further medicines and treatments for the benefit of all and support women who have suffered badly at the hands of male abusers.

Hard work really does pay off.

Seven months after the search for Jo's body was officially called off in Queensland, Blade was released from HMP Witchull. He exited the prison gates wearing the clothes he wore when he entered; there was no one outside the gates to greet him. He had two personal things to do. The first was clear, to see through a promise he made to himself years earlier with a visit to an old friend in Thailand. The second, he wanted to know more about what had happened to his mate David. Only then would he let it go.

A note from the author

Thank you for reading my book, I hope you found it entertaining. If you would like to pass a comment to me, please do so via email to mark@markhurstauthor.com and I will reply.

You may have already downloaded my FREE shorter story "The Last Woman", but if not, it is still available, please visit my web site at www.woodedhillbooks.com and click on the download link.

About the author

Born and raised in Bolton, UK, a true Lancastrian and a child of the sixties, Mark finally decided to pursue his passion for storytelling after a long and eventful career in a completely different industry, that sometimes involved more fiction than fact!

He entered construction at the age of 18 and has been involved with hundreds of large civil engineering projects for the last 40 years as a Civil Engineer and Surveyor, Estimator and Commercial Director, working in various far-flung locations such as Hong Kong, Scandinavia and Wigan.

Mark has a passion for reading legal, crime and psychological thrillers and enjoys firsthand accounts of military and espionage events. When he's not reading and writing, he can be found watching the History Channel.

Married with two grown children and four grandchildren, his son Daniel convinced him it was time to start committing some of his own stories to print ... and there are a few. Drawing on his own life experiences, Mark weaves them into his stories but with a twist ... it all could have happened.

Why Wooded Hill Books?

The origin of the surname Hurst – ancient Anglo-Saxon topographic name for someone who lived near a wooded hill or thicket.

PLEASE KEEP IN TOUCH

Facebook.com/markhurstauthor

www.woodedhillbooks.com

Front cover design by 100Covers

Wooded Hill Books Limited

Printed in Great Britain
by Amazon

41099218R10182